S I D E S H O W

Also by Anne D. LeClaire

GRACE POINT
EVERY MOTHER'S SON
LAND'S END

SIDESHOW

ANNE D. LECLAIRE

VIKING

VIKING
Published by the Penguin Group
Penguin Books USA Inc., 375 Hudson Street, New York, New York 10014, U.S.A.
Penguin Books Ltd, 27 Wrights Lane, London W8 5TZ, England
Penguin Books Australia Ltd, Ringwood, Victoria, Australia
Penguin Books Canada Ltd, 10 Alcorn Avenue, Toronto, Ontario, Canada M4V 3B2
Penguin Books (N.Z.) Ltd, 182–190 Wairau Road, Auckland 10, New Zealand

Penguin Books Ltd, Registered Offices: Harmondsworth, Middlesex, England

First published in 1994 by Viking Penguin, a division of Penguin Books USA Inc.

1   3   5   7   9   10   8   6   4   2

Grateful acknowledgment is made for permission to reprint an excerpt from
"The Call," by Jules Supervielle, translated by Geoffrey Gardner. First
appeared in *The American Poetry Review.* By permission of Geoffrey Gardner.

LIBRARY OF CONGRESS CATALOGING IN PUBLICATION DATA
LeClaire, Anne D.
Sideshow/Anne D. LeClaire.
p. cm.
ISBN 0-670-84328-8
1. Women librarians—Massachusetts—Boston—Fiction.   2. Orphans—
United States—Fiction.   3. Girls—United States—Fiction.
4. Dreams—Fiction.   I. Title.
PS3562.E2778S53   1994
813'.54—dc20   94–12219

Printed in the United States of America
Set in Garamond No. Three   Designed by Brian Mulligan

For my mother,
Louise Eekhoff Dickinson

and

In memory of my father,
Edward Louis Dickinson

ACKNOWLEDGMENTS

First, my heartfelt gratitude to the Ragdale Foundation, Lake Forest, Illinois, and the Virginia Center for Creative Arts, Sweet Briar, Virginia, for providing me with the time and space in which to complete major segments of this book.

At Penguin USA, I am indebted to Pamela Dorman and Audrey LaFehr for their gifted and tireless editing, their patience and persistence, and their unwavering belief in the story of Shoe and Soleil.

During the writing of this novel, a number of people sustained me with their support and aid. I wish to thank my agent and friend Andrea Cirillo, and friends Margaret Moore, North Cairn, Elizabeth Jordan Moore, and Anne Farrow.

Special thanks also to Evelyn and David Doane for their research assistance and endless enthusiasm in ferreting out odd facts, and to the staff of the Harrison F. Lyman Library, Museum of Science, Boston, Massachusetts.

For their generous sharing of medical knowledge and insights, I am grateful to Dr. Lenny Mees, Joelle LeClair, R.N., and Barbara Clancy, R.N., Nurse Manager at the ICU, Cape Cod Hospital.

On the home front, I have been supported by a rich foundation. My love and appreciation to Hillary, Hope, and Chris.

If a man could pass thro' Paradise in a Dream
& have a flower presented to him as a pledge
that his soul had really been there, & found
that flower in his hand when he awoke—
Aye! and what then?
                                    —Samuel Taylor Coleridge
                                    The Notebooks, Vol. 3

And it was then that in the depths of sleep
Someone breathed to me: "You alone can do it,
    Come immediately."
                            —Jules Supervielle
                            from "The Call"
                            translated by Geoffrey Gardner

SIDESHOW

PROLOGUE

An oversized yellow banner hung in the corridor outside the exhibition hall: "DREAMSCAPE: An Artistic and Scientific Glimpse into the Mysterious World of the Sleeping Brain."

The exhibition team, comprised of a research scientist, a composer, and a photographer, had partitioned the exhibit into two sections. They intended Light Space, the sphere the public first entered, to be a narrative, explanatory complement to Dark Space, the area where the volunteer slept.

Slide projections of brain cell tissue formed abstract murals on one section of Light Space wall panels. Time-lapse photos, studies of a sleeping man taken at four-minute intervals during a single night's sleep, hung next to the slide projections. On the expanse opposite these, framed posters of a dozen different dream quotes were mounted. Two of them read:

> "All we see or seem is but a dream within a dream."
> —Edgar Allan Poe

and

> "Dreams are real while they last. Can we say more of
> life?"
>
> —Havelock Ellis

It took several minutes for the eyes to adjust to the shadows of Dark Space. In the center of this room, amid a show of laser lights and beside a bell jar holding a pale and waxy-looking human brain, was a glass booth.

The volunteer was visible through the glass walls. Visitors found Dark Space vaguely disquieting and were overcome by an uneasy sense of intruding, of trespassing in the most defenseless and private of worlds.

Inside the booth, watched by these strangers, Soleil Browne slept.

Her fingers curled on the cold glass knob.

Go back. Go back. Before it is too late.

Ignoring the warning, she turned the knob. The door opened.

CHAPTER 1

FORTUNE GROVES, OHIO
July 1932

After the accident, Shoe's sense of smell sharpened.

The doctors couldn't explain it. Perhaps the olfactory nerve was traumatized by the blow, said one, an oily man who resembled President Hoover. They all agreed her sensitivity to odors would fade as time went on, but it never did.

In the days following her return from the hospital, she lay in her bedroom, her head heavy with bandages, and discovered that solely by their smell, she knew who was walking past her closed door. Ma she recognized by the sour film of sickness. Thomas, by the smell of the bowling alley, a smoky haze that clung to his skin even after he washed. Pa was the odor of manure and sweat, underscored by the faint smell of rusty metal. Like a pitchfork left in the rain all spring. Or blood.

She had names for the smells of her family. Thomas's was Weakness. Her ma's was Fear. Her pa's she called Death. And when she recovered and could go outside, she discovered, beneath the scent of sweet clover and tilled earth, the smell of their farm. Its name was Poor.

Later, after her ma died, she discovered another smell, one so faint she was afraid she'd only made it up. Each night she lay in bed and, as another child might summon a guardian angel, she squeezed her eyes shut and waited for this gentle smell. It held a trace of fall apples and a hint of pastures newly mown.

Sometimes this fragrance could even lift the dangerous stench of Pa. Or ease the sound of his footsteps on the stairs, the snap of his leather belt as he whipped Thomas.

She never named this delicate scent.

Now, hiding under the dining-room table, she tried to call up its apple-tinged sweetness.

"Shoe?"

"I ain't comin' out," she whispered from her refuge.

"Shooooe?"

"They can be hollerin' my name all they want to, but I ain't answerin'."

Miss Rogers hated it when she said "ain't." Ladies don't use that word, her teacher said. Shoe didn't care. She didn't want to be a lady. She hated ladies. She folded her arms and legs against herself and rolled into a tight, still ball.

A long cloth that hung to the floor covered the table. It was the cloth her ma used on Thanksgiving and Christmas. She could see the discoloration of bleached-out stains and twice-darned holes. Her ma always did her mending in the rocking chair. Shoe shut her eyes against the memories, but still she could hear her ma's cough and the mocking sound of the chair as it arced back and forth on the worn linoleum. *Not enough money. Not enough money,* it sighed.

When she heard this chant, she thought of Thomas. Maybe it wasn't so bad to be deaf.

The weight of her pa pressed down through the table. Down on her. It was dark beneath the table, like underwater. This was how dark it must be in the deepest part of the Stonelick, in spring when the ice was nearly gone and the river so swollen the lower pasture flooded.

"Shoe? Shoe, dear, where are you?"

Fat Mrs. Simms was calling, but Shoe didn't answer. They thought she was hiding because she was afraid or scared, but she wasn't. She hid because she didn't want them to see that she was glad. Glad her pa was gone and the beatings were over.

"Shooooe?"

Shoe wasn't her real name. She had been baptized Reba Grace, after her pa's sister Reba and her ma's aunt Grace. Sometimes she thought about making everyone call her by her old name again, but it didn't seem to fit anymore. Now she was used to Shoe.

The kitchen door swung open. Cooking smells flooded in as the women soft-stepped into the room. She could see their feet in the space between the hem of the white cloth and the floor.

They spoke in hushed voices, same as in church.

"Well, she's not in the house. She must be outside."

"You don't think the child's gone to the barn, do you? She really shouldn't be there."

One pair of feet inched even closer to the table. The leather of these shoes was scuffed, and heavy stockings sagged around thin ankles.

"She hasn't shed one tear, you know," said Mrs. Sparks. "Why, even my Sarah wept, but not that child. Not one tear from her."

Shoe knew Mrs. Sparks. When Shoe won the seventh-grade spelling bee, Mrs. Sparks had come to the schoolhouse and demanded that Miss Rogers give the prize ribbon to Sarah because the word she'd misspelled was *intrigue*. She said there shouldn't be foreign words in an American spelling bee. Miss Rogers had stood up tall—right up in front by the pictures of George Washington and Abraham Lincoln and President

Hoover—and stared directly at Mrs. Sparks. Everyone knows Reba Grace Arnett is the best speller in the class and most certainly deserves the ribbon, she'd said. After that, Shoe didn't say "ain't" for a week.

She wondered if Miss Rogers would be coming to the farm like the other women. Her teacher, who smelled dry, like chalk dust and dead lavender, was the only person in all of Fortune Groves who still called her Reba Grace.

"The Devil's child, she is," Mrs. Sparks said now. "She's not a'tall like the boy."

"Lord, no. Not like the boy a'tall," Cora Simms said. "He's a sweet one, that Thomas, sweet as she is sassy. Shame about him being deaf, a dear boy like that."

The women's voices soaked up sugar when they talked about Thomas, like blackstrap was dripping from their mouths instead of words. Heat flooded her cheeks and she pressed her face against the carpet. She wished she had something cold to hold against her forehead. She longed for soft fingers to brush the hair back out of her eyes. Fingers that would not recoil from her cheek and jaw. Fingers that smelled of apples and new-mown hay. It made her stomach ache just to think of it.

"It's a real shame about Hod," Cora Simms continued, and Shoe's stomach hurt even more, like she'd eaten too many slices of Cora's sour berry pie. "There wasn't even a warning. Why, my Homer says—"

"Well, of course, it's no more than to be expected," interrupted Shelby Mathews. "Reverend Hill says nothin' good can ever come of sin."

Shoe unfolded from her tight ball and stretched her legs out. Her feet were inches from Mrs. Simms's fleshy ankles and Mrs. Sparks's puny ones and she fought the urge to kick out. What did they know anyway? She rolled away from the mean, scuffed toes, stopping just short of the far side of the table. She felt around in the pocket of her overalls until her fingers brushed the square of paper.

Carefully, so as not to make any noise, she drew it out of her pocket. In the dim light beneath the table, she could barely make out the thin, curling letters. She held it close to her lips, smelling it as if it still held all the magic of the carnival and could make the women disappear. She would rather give up the spelling bee ribbon than have this taken from her. She closed her eyes and remembered.

The frontman had arrived in Fortune last Wednesday. By noon, he'd nailed posters up on most every telephone pole and fence in Fortune as well as on a dozen barn doors. The store windows on Main Street had them taped to the glass. Even Mrs. Bellington's dress shop. WILLY WADE'S CARNIVAL, JULY 8–15, it proclaimed in fancy red and yellow letters with thick black borders.

Sunday, in the middle of the night, the carnival itself rolled in. It took most of the day to set up in Ames's pasture west of town.

Shoe dreamed about the carnival Monday night. He'd have to let her go. Wouldn't he?

"We got no money for foolishness like that," her pa said on Tuesday. "No sense you askin'. You hear me, girl?"

The threat silenced her and she knew better than to beg, but she kept thinking about it.

Three days before the carnival was to leave Fortune, she found the Mason jar on the top shelf in her pa's closet.

She sat on the edge of the bed, astonished by the weight of the jar against her thighs. It held at least a hundred quarters. Some dimes and nickels, as well, but mostly quarters.

She unscrewed the top and dipped her right hand in. Half

the time, Pa hadn't the money to pay for flour at the general store, and it'd been months since he'd settled up at the grain store. The silver felt cool and heavy in her palm. She held it until it grew warm. After a while, her left hand crept up and she let her fingers brush over her cheek and jaw. *We need more money. We need more money.*

She put the Mason jar back in the closet, just as she'd found it, but as she went to feed the hens, she couldn't forget the cool weight of the quarters in her hand.

It hadn't rained in weeks and as she crossed to the barn, the dust in the chicken yard puffed over her feet. *A whole jar of quarters.* She picked up the wooden scoop and carefully pushed aside the cover of the grain barrel. Once she'd seen a rat as big as a cat in the bin. Pa had cornered it right in the barrel and killed it with a pitchfork. She could still picture it impaled on the end of the fork, could hear its squeal as blood leaked out to taint the grain. *A whole Mason jar of quarters. How long had they been there?*

She skirted the ancient black stain in the center of the barn floor and crossed to the yard where a half dozen scrawny chickens pecked and scratched. She called out their names as she scattered the grain. Red Boy, Broken Beak, Mr. Big Toes. Once she and Thomas had asked their pa for a dog. "We got no money to be feedin' some fool dog," he'd said. She had opened her mouth to plead, but the look in her brother's eyes had warned her. *Not enough money.* But how much did a dog cost?

When the hens were fed, she hung the scoop back on the wall by the bin. She didn't bother to check the coop before she returned to the house. The hens hadn't laid in days, as if they were drying up right along side the farm.

That night, after the supper dishes were washed and dried, she spoke to her pa as he rolled a cigarette.

"The carnival is leavin' town on Saturday, Pa."

He concentrated on the rolling.

"Can I go?"

"No sense askin', girl. You got no money to spend."

"I thought . . ." The memory of the Mason jar gave her courage. "I thought maybe you'd give me a dime. Just this once."

"We got no money for foolishness like that. No money."

"Just a dime?"

"Stop askin' me, girl." His voice was hard, with the edge it got just before he used his fists.

All Friday morning, she daydreamed about the pictures she'd seen on the posters and the red and yellow letters shouting out WILLY WADE'S CARNIVAL. She'd die if she couldn't go.

The afternoon, after Thomas had left for the bowling alley and while Pa worked in the west pasture, she climbed the stairs. Her fingers tensed as she turned the doorknob. What if the money was gone? What if she had dreamed it?

She took a dime. Only one dime. Surely he owed her at least that.

Nothing good ever came out of sin.

The whispers of women and the smell of dying roses brought her back to the dining room.

"So what's to become of them?"

The silence stretched on so long and loud it hurt Shoe's ears. Finally Cora Simms spoke. "The Town Farm, I guess."

Shoe choked back a cry. This was the first time anyone had mentioned the Farm.

Once in the fall when she and Thomas had walked out to the Archibald place to gather windfalls, they'd passed the Farm and seen people sitting on the run-down porch. Dark, thin, hopeless-faced men too tired to be mean. Dirty-faced children who looked like they never got enough to eat. And women, dried out and used up. As bad as things got, Shoe always consoled herself with the thought that at least they didn't have to live at the Town Farm.

"I don't know," Shelby Mathews was saying. "Someone might take in the boy. He might be deaf as a post, but he's a hard worker. Gerney says the boy's the best pin setter he ever had at the alley."

"He's a hard worker for sure. Not like her."

"She's a queer child, all right. Always daydreamin'."

"Or readin' some book," Mrs. Simms said.

"That's true. Don't think I've ever seen the child without she's got her nose in a book."

" 'Course I blame the teacher for that," Mrs. Sparks said.

"Now, the boy, he's sweet-natured."

"Not hard to look at either," Mrs. Mathews continued. " 'Course I feel sorry for the girl. You all know that."

"Lord knows," Mrs. Simms said in a hushed voice, "it was a terrible thing happened to the child."

"Well, it was a tragedy, true enough," Mrs. Sparks said after a minute, "but truth be told, I wouldn't want to have that ruined face sittin' across the table from me while I was eating."

Words came from Shoe in a stream. "I hate you." She kicked back the cloth and rolled out from under the table. "I hate you. You're just a bunch of stupid old women and I hate you. I hate you all."

She dashed from the room, but her legs couldn't go fast enough. Not fast enough to shut out the glimpse of her pa's body stretched out on the dining room table. Not quick enough to cut off the soft, terrifying words of Reverend Hill's wife.

"The Lord reminds us we must be charitable. Right must be done by that child."

CHAPTER 2

A shaft of light cut through the gable window in the barn. A million hay particles danced in the light. Shoe rubbed her nose to cut off a sneeze; not that it mattered if she made a noise. Here in the top of the loft, hidden by mounds of hay, she was safe. The women wouldn't follow her here.

She exhaled heavily on the grimy glass, rubbed a spot clear with her shirttail, and looked down on the farmhouse. No one had come out yet. Hateful old women. They were probably still standing in the dining room with their mouths hanging open.

Even from this distance, she could see the splintered treads of the sagging farmhouse steps and the gray shingles where the paint had worn bare. Half the balusters on the porch railing were broken or missing.

Each fall, her ma used to vow that come spring they'd make repairs. And each year, every bit of money went into grain for the livestock and seed for the fields or was put aside to pay for

11

the crew that came in August to help with the haying. After her ma died, there was no more talk about fixing up the house.

Atop the roof, a lightning rod glinted in the sun. Every barn in Fortune had one attached to its ridgepole, but the Arnett farm was the only place with a rod on the house as well. Shoe used to think that this made them special, safer than those families who lived in unprotected homes. Then, as she grew older, she saw it differently. Maybe, she thought, their house needed extra protection. In the end, not even the rod had saved them.

Through the barn window, she heard the fitful sound of an engine cutting out. Below, Harley Mathews bent forward in the seat of her father's old John Deere and concentrated as he cultivated the field. She watched the soil part, a long, liquid wave curling back darkly from the worn and rusty discs of the harrow. The beat of the engine's labor rose up to her. *We need more mon-ey. We need more mon-ey,* it drummed.

She crouched down and cupped her hands over her ears. She hummed—a long, droning, tuneless song—but she could not shut out the words of the John Deere. *We need more mon-ey.* Humming even louder, she burrowed into the hay.

The prickle of tears stung her eyes. She turned onto her side and picked out a single loft board. The trick was to find something to look at or think about until you could get lost. She stared hard at the board, traced the whorls and patterns and details of the grain, like the fingerprints of the tree.

Miss Rogers had told her class that every person alive had a set of fingerprints and no two were ever alike. Like snowflakes, she had said. Every single snowflake was different. To prove this, she let them smudge their fingers on an ink pad and then press their prints on paper. The boys had whistled when they saw their prints and the girls had said, "Ohhh," which just showed Shoe how dumb they were. All you have to do is open your eyes and look, she thought, and you can see that *everything* is different. Every barn board, every spider's web. Even things that looked the same if you looked quick-like, things like cottonwood bark or snakeweed, were really different. Studying these differences was how you got to know a thing.

Her eyes were dry now. She rolled on her back and stared straight up at the rafters.

A faint rustling in a corner of the loft caught her attention. She strained to hear more, but there was only silence.

Once, when she was six, she and Thomas had found a nest of kittens not far from this spot. The mother, a stray, had birthed them just hours before she was run over by a car on River Road.

Thomas had picked up each tiny ball of fur—light as milkweed pods, they were, dried and busting with fluff—and he'd climbed down the ladder, cupping them tightly against his chest. Together, they carried the kittens to the abandoned tack room next to the milking shed.

She'd held them in her lap, warming them with her hands, while Thomas stole some milk. They were the only living things she'd ever held in the palm of her hand. And soft. They were so soft even their bones gave way beneath her fingers. She laughed at their flat, pink noses and long, serious whiskers. Their eyes were still puffed shut.

Patiently, drop by drop, Thomas had nursed the kittens with an eyedropper from their mother's medicine drawer. All the while, Shoe had hopped from foot to foot and tugged at his shirt until at last he'd given her one to feed. She nursed it, so it became hers. She named it Sandy, because its tiny tongue rubbed against her fingers like sandpaper.

She'd buried her face in its gray fur and breathed in its milk-scented sweetness. The kitten nuzzled against her. Its whole body vibrated with the sound of its purring.

"Oh, Thomas, Thomas," she cried as she thrust the kitten into her brother's hands. "Listen. You can feel it purr."

Before they left the tack room, they had concealed the bed of grain sacks they had made behind a row of dented milk cans.

On the third day, Sandy's eyes opened. They were green. Already, he'd begun to wander away from the other kittens, but Shoe always found him before he could investigate the world beyond the tack room. "You naughty boy," she would scold gently as she scooped him up. "Whatever am I going to do with you?" Then she'd nuzzle her mouth and cheeks against the fragile-boned body, wondering at the softness against her skin.

She wished her brother was with her now.

Once, a long time ago, this part of the loft had been a secret place where they could go to hide. She missed him. Thomas would know what to do. He would fix everything. She wished he would come home and throw those women out of their house, the mean women who walked around the kitchen as if it were their own, *tsk-tsk*ing about how dirty it was, and saying Lord, but wasn't it a shame the way Hod let the place go downhill since Lydia passed on, and Mercy, but wasn't it too bad the girl's face was ruined and that the boy was deaf and dumb. She hated it when people called Thomas dumb. They were wrong. Just because he was deaf, people treated him like he was stupid, but he was the smartest person Shoe knew.

She would just have to wait for him to come home. It wouldn't feel so lonely if she had seen him that morning, but when she woke up, he'd already left for the bowling alley. She hadn't seen him since late the night before. Thomas had been the one to find their pa. He'd found him crumpled in a heap on the barn floor, smack in the middle of the creeping, dark place beneath the metal hook.

She wouldn't think about Pa right now. She burrowed down

into the hay, stifling another sneeze. Thomas would make everything all right. They would take care of each other. He would find some way so they wouldn't have to go to the Town Farm.

But what was it that Mrs. Mathews had said? *"I don't know. Someone might take in the boy."* A bolt of fear cut through Shoe. *"Someone might take in the boy."* They wouldn't do that, would they? Separate them? The idea was so terrible she couldn't even think about it. Something else. Think about something else. Anything else.

It had been just about a week after she and Thomas had found the kittens when she saw their pa crossing the yard. He was whistling and heading for the road. Two potato sacks were slung over his shoulder and jostled against his back with each step he took.

"Where you goin', Pa?"

"Over to the preacher's."

Occasionally he'd let her go along when he delivered vegetables to Preacher Hill's, and before they left, Mrs. Hill would give her a sugar cookie. Once, she'd been given a piece of barley candy.

She ran across the yard. "Can I come? Can I, Pa? Please?"

"Got your chores all done?'

"Yep."

"Well, I guess there's no harm to it."

He did not slow his pace, so she had to take little running steps to keep up with him. As they walked down the road, she reached up and clasped his hand. After a slight hesitation, his work-thickened fingers swallowed hers, concealing her hand all the way up to her wrist. She looked up at him and wondered why it couldn't always be like this, but of course she didn't ask.

A pickup approached, but her pa didn't move off the road. The driver, swerving to avoid them, hit his horn for a long, angry howl before disappearing from view. Her pa did not stop his whistling. Shoe loved to hear him whistle. He was good at it. He could make it sound like two notes at once were coming from between his lips. She skipped in time to the tune.

As they drew near the bridge by the Stonelick, his steps slowed. He dropped her hand and, moving so fast she didn't have time for a thought, he shrugged one sack of potatoes off his shoulder. He approached the railing and, quick-like, just like he was pitching horseshoes, he swung the sack out and flung it off the bridge.

Shoe heard the splash as the bag hit water. She poked her head through the rails and watched as it sank below the surface. It lay for a moment on the riverbed and then the burlap began to twist and turn. Then she understood. The kittens were in the bag.

She watched the water carry the bag downstream, twisting and rolling.

Her pa never stopped his whistling.

Shoe stared up at the barn rafters and an idea took hold. With Pa gone, maybe she and Thomas could get a kitten. Except now that she was twelve, she'd rather have a dog.

She crawled out of the hay and crossed back to the window. The tractor still rolled across the field, cutting open the earth. The soil was dark brown. It should be red, she thought. The red of all our blood. Mine and ma's and pa's. And Thomas's. Red just like the place on the barn floor where the cow hung to drain after Barney Saunders slit its throat with one stroke of his knife. Year after year, as if they would never get enough, the splintered planks drank up the slaughter until the spot beneath the hook was permanently stained.

As the barn floor had absorbed the cow's blood, so too had the farm taken their family, taking until they had nothing left to give. One by one, the sacrifices had been made, but not one of them had been enough. Not the finger her pa had lost to the silo conveyor belt. Not her brother's hearing. Not her ma's life. Nor her pa's. Never enough. Not even her own face.

CHAPTER 3

The booth was no larger than a cell. Quarters for a monk, Soleil thought. Or a nun. Except, of course, for the glass walls and the wire cables that hung from the outlet above the bed. She turned away from the cables.

The museum staff had spent nearly three months planning and assembling *Dreamscape,* but cloistered in her office, she had heard very little about the exhibit. This was not unusual. The museum library was a separate domain on the third floor and although she tried, she couldn't always keep up with what was happening on the first two floors. Except for major shows like the Mayan exhibition, exhibits were often installed and open to the public before she even got to see them.

She surveyed the booth again. The bed was narrow, the linens white, with tight hospital corners, just like every bed she'd ever slept in as a child. The top sheet was turned back to form a perfect isosceles triangle.

The pajamas Connolly had sent an assistant rushing over to

the Galleria to buy were folded neatly at the foot of the bed. More than the wires, the glass wall, or even the bed, they made the whole thing seem utterly, terrifyingly real. I can't do this, she thought. She couldn't believe she'd allowed herself to be talked into sleeping in public.

Earlier, when Connolly had approached her at the emergency staff meeting, it had seemed simple. A favor that he and the museum would be—what were his exact words?—"ever so grateful for." She'd had no idea it would be like this. With the *cables* and the *pajamas*.

She stiffened at the thought of returning upstairs and facing the museum's director. There was no way she could back out now without looking like a fool. She reached for the pajamas. They were blue.

In the dressing room, she stripped to her underwear. She folded her skirt and blouse neatly and piled them on the plastic bench. She kept her bra and panties on beneath.

Her hair was a problem. Released from the clip that normally kept it off her face, it dipped over her cheeks and fell freely on her shoulders. She stared in the mirror and flushed. It looked too . . . too loose. Sensual.

I cannot, absolutely cannot do this. With chilly fingers, she groped through her tote until she found an elastic band. She braided her hair into a thick plait and wrapped the band tightly at the end. Then she returned to the glass room.

As soon as she stepped into the booth, a tremor ran through her body. She was overcome with apprehension, a disquieting premonition. But of what? A sense of being drawn into something. She needed to move, but the booth was too small for pacing. She gave a little shiver and crossed to the bed, averting her eyes from the mass of cables that hung above the headboard. Nervously, she smoothed the white triangle of sheet and as her fingers touched the muslin, a childhood memory flooded back.

She was seven—the year she and her mother had lived with the Henleys in Acton—and was kneeling by her bed, hands pressed together to say her prayers. (". . . and God bless Mrs. Henley and God bless Mr. Henley . . . and God bless Bingo . . ."—at his name the collie drummed his tail against the floor in a comforting tattoo—". . . and God bless Mamom and Gless bless me" . . . *and God bless my daddy, too.*) While she recited, her mother turned back the bedclothes to form a triangle, performing her part of this nightly ritual with meticulous devotion.

Even now, distanced by twenty-nine years, Soleil felt that devotion. The weight of it oppressed her. She sighed and turned toward the plate glass. She imagined people standing on the other side, peering in, watching her sleep. God, it was like being some kind of trained rat. Nearly naked, stripped of control. That's what it was like.

She felt a flash of anger at Connolly, and then at herself, for she really had no one to blame but herself. Why hadn't she lied when the director canvassed the staff, looking for someone who hadn't slept the night before? Why hadn't she said no? Or at least stalled until she had learned more about the exhibit and what would be expected of her? Well, that's what came of acting on impulse. It always ended up worse than you expected.

"Oh, come on, Soleil," Alison, the intern from Northeastern, had said. "You're not going to refuse Mr. 'Hunk-of-the-Month' Connolly, are you?"

"For God's sake, Alison, he'll hear you," she'd whispered, wishing the intern could be more circumspect when the director was within earshot.

Undaunted, Alison had continued. "It'll be fun. I'd do it if I didn't have classes. Just imagine. With all those people looking in at you, you'll be like Sleeping Beauty."

The very thought made her nearly ill.

"A Life Experience," Alison had said. "That's what it is.

With a capital E." The intern was nineteen and very big on Life Experiences.

What Soleil had learned about Life Experiences was that they were often easy to get into, but extricating oneself was something else. Generally she worked to avoid them, with or without capitals, and she was quite content to continue that way. Where did it get you anyway? Wired up like some kind of lab chimp so a bunch of strangers could gawk at you while you slept.

Behind her, the booth door opened and she turned.

"Soleil?"

She didn't know if she saw him first or heard him say her name. Impossible, she thought. Shock and disbelief merged with another emotion she wouldn't put a name to.

The booth shrunk. She remembered that about him. How he always filled the space he was in so that any room—any bed— felt automatically smaller. How the air in her apartment felt thinner somehow after he had gone.

Impossibleimpossibleimpossible, her brain sang. But a smaller voice in the back of her brain crowed peevishly, "I tried to warn you." A Rumpelstiltskin figure jumping up and down, beard imprisoned in a crack of stone, cried, "You should have known. You should have known." She understood then that this was what the premonition had been about. Andy.

He repeated her name, but she couldn't meet his eyes. Not yet. Not yet. She fastened her gaze on the clipboard he carried and then on the plastic name tag pinned to his lab coat. Dr. Andrew McKey. Andy. Not in California. Here.

How many times during the past six years had she fantasized about seeing him again? How often had she imagined their meeting, playing out the scenario in dramatic detail as if practicing for just this moment? Countless times, but nothing she could have done or imagined would have prepared her for this.

"Hello, Andy." She didn't trust her voice to say more. His light brown hair was a little longer than he used to wear it. The faintest of lines fanned out from his eyes.

"Soleil," he said again.

She felt the urge to move into his arms. There was an instant when, honest to God, she might actually have *thrown* herself against him, whispering his name again and again, but she fought the impulse and the moment passed.

His expression was wary, cautious, and stubborn, yes, stubborn even now, after all this time. When they again began to speak—they who had shared so much—it was with a forced civility, the detached manner of casual acquaintances.

"I was wondering if I'd run into you here. How long has it been? Five years? Five and a half?"

His tone was casual, but she listened with ears trained to hear every nuance of his voice and understood instantly that he'd known she was the staff member who'd agreed to participate. Unlike her, he'd had time to prepare.

"Six years," she corrected automatically. She looked at him, his light brown hair, his green eyes, his swimmer's body, all defined shoulders and slim hips. His wonderful height, which had always made her feel so protected. It could have been six days, not years.

"So you're the one Connolly talked into filling in," he said.

"Yes," she said, her tone as careful as his. How could she not have known? It was inconceivable that he had actually been in the building for days—weeks—and she had not known. Had not sensed his presence. She realized, too, that although he would have been in the museum dozens of times during the past weeks, he had not sought her out. Certainly he must have known she still worked here. This thought hurt more than she would have thought possible. So he still had the power to wound her.

"Who could believe it?" he said. "Opening day of our exhibit and the volunteer gets hit by a cab? That's something, huh?"

"Something," she echoed. The soles of her bare feet were icy on the floor. Her fingers plucked at the hem of the pajama shirt.

He smiled then, just a quick flash, and she saw the chip on his front tooth. Instantly she recalled the roughness of it against her tongue. The memory brought a fluttering deep in her belly. Jesus. She had to get control here.

"Connolly said you didn't get much sleep last night so they drafted you." He set the clipboard down on the foot of the bed and reached over for the cables. "What kept you awake?" They didn't meet each other's eyes.

"A neighbor's dog." *Worrying about my mother.* But she didn't mention her mother's stroke. She wouldn't—couldn't—let him into her life again.

"Good break for us," he said.

"It's a corgi." Her voice sounded like it belonged to another woman. Her fingers folded the pajama hem into little pleats.

He looked blank.

"My neighbor's dog. A Welsh corgi." But of course he knew Tootsie. Knew Mr. Tannazzo. His gaze followed her fingers as they fidgeted. She dropped her hands to her sides.

"Amazing coincidence," he said.

"Amazing coincidence," she repeated. They both knew she wasn't talking about her sleepless night. For an instant, their eyes locked. He turned away first but not before she saw the shadow in his, the flicker of pain, and she realized that this was hard for him too.

He looked at his watch. "We'd better get going," he said. "The exhibit opens in a little less than an hour." His voice had turned professional. But he'd always been able to do that. Compartmentalize. It was one of the several things they had argued about during that summer six years ago.

"What should I do?" She struggled to match his detachment.

"Just relax while I get you hitched up." He took a tube of ointment from the pocket of his lab coat. "I don't know how much Connolly told you, but I'll explain it as we go along. Okay?"

She couldn't do it. Couldn't sleep, not with him there in the next booth watching her. "Okay," she said.

"First thing we need is to get you in bed." She blushed at this and he coughed, an embarrassed little noise in the back of his throat. He stepped aside, but as she slid by, her arm brushed his and she drew back. She lay on the bed. The sheets were the institutional kind that always chafe the skin. She pulled the blanket up over her chest.

"Do you need to use the bathroom before we begin?" he asked.

I'm not a child, she wanted to say. But, in fact, in the blue pajamas, in the narrow bed with Andy bending over her, looking for all the world as if he were preparing to tuck her in, she felt horribly like a child. "No," she said. "I'm fine."

"Hey, just checking. We don't want to get you all hooked up and then undo it all again."

She twisted the thin silver band on her right ring finger. "Really. I'm fine," she said again.

He pulled a stool closer to the bed. She watched as he began to smear paste on the surface of each disc. Beneath the blanket, her feet were still icy. *I can't do this.* But she could not make herself say it.

"The ointment will ensure we get a good connection," he said. He attached the electrodes to her forehead with practiced movements. She held perfectly still, as if he were applying makeup. Once his fingers brushed against her skin and she felt their faint trembling and was glad to see he wasn't as calm as he seemed. He pulled away, made a pretense of checking his clipboard before resuming.

"These," he explained as he placed two more at each side of her jaw, "are to register muscle activity." He put a length of tape over each disc, then ran a thumb over the tape to smooth it. His hands were steady now.

Maybe he was right. Compartmentalizing was a way to get through things. She tried to concentrate on his explanations.

"What I'm doing now," he continued, "is attaching the electrooculogram cables. They'll record your eye movement." He bent so close she could see the pores of his cheeks. She closed her eyes while he taped the final two discs on her temples. She breathed, inhaling the remembered scent of him. She steadied herself with a deep breath. Her skin felt tight from the tape.

"The ones on your forehead are for the EEG—the electroencephalogram. It measures your brain signals." She checked his left hand, noted that he wasn't wearing a wedding band. But she would have known if he was married. Surely, somehow she would have known.

He plugged the cables attached to each disc into the sockets on the wall panel. "These wires run to a central line of the polysomnographic equipment," he said. "It's in a booth on the other side of the partition, and that's my station. I'll be in there monitoring it while you sleep. Do you know much about the exhibit?"

She started to shake her head but stopped, afraid the motion would dislodge the discs. "No."

"The polygraph, which prints out data obtained from these"—he paused and indicated the discs—"is hitched up to a synthesizer and computerized laser light system. They'll translate your sleep patterns into musical compositions and a light display that will play against the walls of the exhibit hall. It's really something."

Enthusiasm lit his face, his voice, and she understood then that Dr. Andrew McKey was one of the team who had invented *Dreamscape*.

He capped the tube of ointment and rechecked the cable connections. "Any questions before I leave you to get some sleep?" he asked.

Sleep? She looked up at the infrared camera that hung from one corner of the ceiling. The lens was focused on the bed. She'd never be able to sleep now.

"What happens if—if I can't fall asleep?"

He grinned. "Fake it."

"But really," she persisted. "What if I don't?"

"You were awake most of last night, right?"

She nodded.

"So don't worry. You'll sleep. And I promise that we won't open the exhibit till we have a nice set of waves to show the public."

She was conscious of the weight of the electrodes against her skin. The overhead light reflected darkly off the walls. The glass was one-way so that if she awoke, she would not see the faces of the exhibit-goers as they peered in at her. "What if I roll over in my sleep?"

"No problem," he said. "Normal movements won't dislodge the electrodes or interfere with their functioning. Don't worry. You'll be fine." He adjusted the rheostat until the room was in shadow. A low-wattage bulb shone gently on the bed. He tapped the intercom with a knuckle. "This thing's on, so if you need anything, just holler."

He paused at the door. "Soleil?"

"Yes?"

"It's good to see you again." He left the booth before she could respond. She felt a surge of resentment that he would drop that sentence so casually and then walk away with so much left unsaid. This was followed by a breathlessness in her throat, a fluttering in her stomach. A reaction born of anger, and beneath that, the stirring of desire.

She lay in the darkened room. It was silent. Acoustic tile covered the exhibit walls and the floor was carpeted with a thin layer of blue synthetic to muffle the sound of footsteps and voices. The stillness was unnerving. She was aware of her heartbeat, rapid, loud. Steady, she told herself. Breathe. She thought of him on the other side of the partition, following the printout of her pulse. She wondered if it gave her away.

She inhaled deeply to offset the quaver inside and, moving gingerly, rolled onto her side.

She thought back to the first time they met.

She had had an invitation to the opening of the Museum of Fine Art's new Asian Wing. When the friend she'd arranged to go with canceled at the last minute, she almost stayed home. She and Andy had joked about that later. About how they almost hadn't met.

She arrived late and immediately felt as if she had wandered onto a movie set where everyone else knew the script. Kimono-clad waitresses passed sake and rice wine and appetizers to women dressed in silk dresses and men in linen suits.

The thought of staying, of dredging up enough energy to talk with strangers, drained her. She was about to slip out when a voice at her side said, "Promise you'll never drag me to one of these again."

She turned and looked up into extraordinary green eyes. Clear, direct eyes that saw more of her than she wanted known. Her stomach gave a queer jump and her legs felt weak. It was as if she were being pulled into a magnetic field. What was that story of Goethe's? The one about an iron mountain, its field so powerful that it pulled the nails from ships passing by, leaving the ships to sink and the crews to drown? She felt like that, like she could drown in those deep green eyes. Swooning, she thought. An old-fashioned word that belonged to weak-kneed heroines in second-rate novels. But she was.

You don't even know this man, her brain had whispered, but her softened joints did not listen to reason. Her senses greedily sucked in details. His posture. His coloring. His faint New England accent.

This hunger astonished her. She'd had a college classmate, Joan Ross, whom she'd always thought particularly crude. "I'd like to jump his bones," Joan said about any man who attracted her. Now, looking into the greenest eyes she'd ever seen, she thought, *I'd like to jump his bones,* and grinned.

He smiled at her in a sleepy, knowing way, and she actually blushed.

"Well, what about it?" he said. "Is it a promise? No more museum openings?"

She was no good at this kind of banter. "As long as you don't make me go to any more faculty teas," she said, and immediately felt stupid.

He laughed. "A deal."

She was ridiculously grateful for his laughter.

He asked her name.

"Soleil Browne."

"Soleil? Interesting name."

"My mother chose it. It's French. 'The sun.'" She willed herself to stop babbling.

"I'm Andy. Andy McKey." He grinned. "My mother chose it. It's Scottish."

She wondered if he was making fun of her, but his eyes were kind. A waitress in a blue and black kimono passed by with little cups of warm sake. She took one, grateful for something to do with her hands. Another waitress, this one in a pink-flowered robe, held out a tray of skewered scallops. She shook her head. She couldn't even think about eating.

She was conscious, in a heightened way, of everything around her. The smell of the caterers' trays wafting ginger and garlic. The heat-heightened perfume of women. Adam McKey's silk tie, knotted loosely at his throat. He must hate wearing a tie, she thought.

He asked about her job. As she answered, she heard a foreign, flirtatious tone in her voice.

He deposited their empty sake cups on the caterers' table near the wall. As naturally as if they had planned it, they walked down the museum steps together.

"How about dinner?" he asked. She still couldn't think about eating but didn't want to leave him. He hailed a taxi. When he opened the door, he took her arm to help her, and her stomach gave that queer lurch again. In the cab, he pulled off his tie and stuffed it in his pocket. "Do you mind?" he asked. "I hate ties," and she felt a jolt of possessive pride.

He took her to a Thai restaurant. In between mouthfuls of shrimp in lemon grass sauce, he told her about himself. He was the oldest of four children. His parents lived in Portsmouth, New Hampshire, the same house they had lived in all their married life. She took that in, felt a vague longing.

They talked about movies, museums, books. She asked him to write down the title of a novel he'd just read. He tore a square off his place mat, jotted down the name and author, then added, "your admirer." She felt her face flush. Then he reclaimed the paper and added a caret between "your" and "admirer" and inserted "new." This open display of his attraction to her was disconcerting, exciting.

He took her home. As they climbed the three flights of stairs to her apartment, she felt light-headed and nervous. She debated whether or not to invite him in, afraid to do anything that might spoil the evening. Or make him run.

At her door, she turned to him, trying to read his face. He smiled. Then he reached out and cupped his hand against her neck. His thumb stroked her jaw. The pulse in her throat skipped a fast and reckless beat.

"Good night, Sunshine," he said. He kissed her lightly on the forehead.

She waited in the hall, listened to the sound of his footsteps descend the full three flights of stairs. Somewhere around the second-floor landing, he begin to hum, a tone so off-key it made her smile.

She couldn't sleep. She tossed in her bed, aware of the ache in her breasts, the dull heat in her hips and stomach.

In the morning before she had left for the museum, he called and they agreed to meet later for dinner at a neighborhood café. At work, she couldn't concentrate. For the first time since she had been hired, she left the museum early. She showered, shampooed her hair, shaved her legs.

They met at the café. Afterward, he walked her back to her apartment. Lyrics from old songs, tunes from the thirties and forties, songs she hadn't even realized she knew, swirled through her head. *Zing went the strings of my heart stood still the whole night through is dream of you.*

In her apartment, he took her in his arms and she grew so weak—that swooning sensation again—she thought she might faint. The old warnings, her mother's sharp, cautionary voice, edged in, delineating how decent girls behaved, how men wanted only one thing and once they got it were out the door, but these words were drowned out by the heat in her belly. The wetness below.

Always he could do that to her.

He undressed her slowly, his face serious. She was amazed

there was no awkwardness between them, no embarrassment. As his hands and lips touched her, she shivered. "Cold?" he asked. "No. Not cold," she whispered. And she wasn't. Not cold at all.

When she was fully naked, she undressed him, fumbling with the buttons of his shirt. As she unzipped his jeans, she heard his swift intake of breath. The hardness of him, freed, sprang against her hand. She pulled the jeans down over his hips, sank to her knees, and took him in her mouth. Never had she done that before with a man, had never wanted to, but the hunger she felt for him was new, fierce. It was like someone else—some eager, wanton stranger—had taken possession of her body.

He was not the first man she'd ever slept with. There had been others. Not out of desire—or what she knew of desire—but because she wanted to be normal. Usually these brief affairs ended up badly, in disappointment and shame. But with Andy it was utterly different.

Afterward, lying in his arms, she wanted to share all the emotions that tumbled through her: pleasure, delight, gratitude, greed. She was astonished by the greed. By how, even now as her body lay curled in his arms, relaxed and satisfied, there was already an edge of hunger creeping in, growing, wanting more.

But above all she felt happy, an immense, heart-pumping happiness, a happiness so huge it scared her.

"I wanted you last night, you know," he said. "I wanted to ask you to invite me in." He was stroking her lazily with a forefinger, running random patterns over her ribs and breasts and the hollow of her neck. Sweat was still drying on her skin.

"Why didn't you?"

He shifted slightly and stared up at the ceiling. After a minute he said, "I was afraid."

"Of what?"

"I don't know. I guess most of all of scaring you away. It seemed important to go slow."

"I see," she said. She propped herself on an elbow, surveyed the room, their clothes scattered carelessly on the floor, and grinned. "And you call this slow?"

It wasn't that funny, but they laughed for a long time, delighted in their laughter, their bodies, each other. That was new, too, for her.

"Soleil?" His voice drifted in through the intercom speaker.

She took several deep breaths, willed away the memory. Finally she trusted her voice. "Yes?"

"You want me to sing a lullaby?"

"I'll be fine," she said. "Just getting sleepy."

"Try counting sheep," he said. "I can guarantee it will be better than my singing."

The thought of his energetic, off-key renditions evoked another bittersweet wave of memory. Gradually her heart settled. She closed her eyes, conscious of all the wires connecting her to the sockets above the bed. It was like being in a hospital. Was this what it was like for her mother?

She thought about her mother, and about hospitals, and about Welsh corgis and airheaded interns who liked to Live. Then, thinking about a green-eyed, tone-deaf Scot who had once broken her heart, she finally fell asleep.

"Wake up, Sunshine."

Andy was at her side. She surfaced slowly, staring at him in disbelief, as if he were part of a lingering dream. Then she remembered.

"How did it go?" she asked. Was it really over? Had she slept through the entire afternoon?

"You were a star. Fantastic. Like you've been sleeping all your life."

He gave her a minute to shake off sleep, then began detaching the cables.

"Want to see your dreams?" he asked.

"See my dreams?"

"Yeah. The printout. I can also rerun the light and music tapes. You had some pretty groovy dreams. Quite a show."

It was over. Soleil felt giddy with relief. She hadn't made a fool of herself, hadn't let him know how completely shaken she'd been to see him again. "No one says groovy anymore."

"They haven't seen your dreams. So what do you say? Shall I run the tapes?"

She checked her watch. She'd have to grab a cab to the hospital to catch the end of the afternoon visiting hours.

"Tomorrow," she said. "Tomorrow you can show me my dreams."

She didn't tell him she had no intention of returning. She had done what Connolly had asked. By the morning, her boss would have enlisted one of the backup volunteers, and she would be back in her office on the third floor, safely away from Andy, and away from all the memories, all the desires and pain that he evoked.

CHAPTER 4

"It rained this morning. We really needed the rain."

Soleil searched her mother's face for a sign that she was listening, but there was no movement beneath the lowered lids. The stroke had been swift, surprising. A subarachnoid hemorrhage, the doctor had reported.

"Is there a family member you want to talk to before you make any decision?" he'd asked the first day.

"Decision?"

"About extreme measures. Given your mother's age and the extent of the shock, do you want us to stop short of such measures?"

"She's never been sick a day in her life," Soleil had said.

"What about her husband? Is she widowed?"

"Not one day. Never sick."

"Is there a relative who would want to be consulted? A brother or sister? An aunt, perhaps, or uncle?"

"No. There's no one else." Or no one that she knew of. Her mother never talked about her past, or her family. She had been born in Ohio, that much Soleil knew, that and nothing more. She had taken that fact and tucked it away, as if she understood that it was important to store each precious bit of information, like old ladies who saved string, adding it to a ball for future use. Once she'd asked Helen, "Can we go there someday? To Ohio? To visit."

"No sense," her mother had replied. "I have no reason to go back. My parents are both gone. There's nothing left there for me."

"So you are the only living relative," the doctor had responded. Then he asked her about putting a DNR on the chart and she'd looked at him blankly, not knowing what that meant. "Do Not Resuscitate," he'd told her. His eyes had not been unkind.

Soleil had felt panic tighten her throat. She'd needed to stop his talk of death. Whatever it took, he must help her mother recover. After the doctor left, she'd gone to the nurse's station and told the floor nurses that her mother was once a nurse too, thinking they might give her extra care if they knew.

Now she pulled the chair closer to her mother. The odors of the hospital room, of disinfectant and dentures, of flowers gone by and the faint smell of urine, overwhelmed her. The electronic pulse of the intravenous feed measured seconds off like a clock while the tube dripped fluid into her mother's wasted arm.

You aren't going to die. You hear me, Mamom? The childhood name came easily to her lips. *I know you aren't going to die.*

Her mother's body was flat and shrunken beneath the blanket. There didn't seem enough body left to house all the bones and muscles and organs necessary for life.

She cupped one of her mother's hands in her own. The skin was dry and the nails had grown ragged. They were the hands of an old woman. When had her mother grown old?

I've never seen your hands so still, Mamom. And Lord, but they're thin. No more than skin and bones. All the mysteries that those hands hold. Wake up, Mamom. Tell me all the things you've never shared.

She reached for her canvas tote bag, hoping she'd remembered to bring clippers. Holding one finger at a time between her own, she pared her mother's nails, taking care not to catch any flesh between the blades of the clipper, as if she were cutting the nails of an infant.

Her mother's nails were brittle, marred with raised ridges, and so colorless they were nearly translucent. Next to her own polished nails, they looked naked.

Once, when she was eight or nine and they'd been living in Acton, she had found a bottle of fingernail polish in the middle drawer of her mother's bureau, hidden beneath a pile of worn cotton underwear and mended slips. "Fire and Ice," by Revlon. She'd stared at the label and the exotic, private life it seemed to suggest. What did it mean? Why would her mother, who never even used lipstick or powder, have this bottle of enamel? If she understood about the polish, would she somehow understand her mother's life? She'd held the bottle tightly, as if it held every secret her mother knew, and let her mind wander to the biggest mystery of all.

"Where's my daddy?" she had asked over and over when she was five and six. They'd lived in Wellesley then while her mother did private duty nursing for a woman confined to a wheelchair. "When is he coming home?"

Later, at twelve and fourteen—Cos Cob, Connecticut, and Londonderry, New Hampshire—the question became an accusation. "What did you do to make him leave?" she would scream. "What did you do?"

"What does he look like?" she asked many times. In every new town, she stared at men's faces, trying to find the one who could be her father, always believing she'd know him if she saw him.

Why did he leave? When is he coming back? What does he look like?

One steamy night when she was ten—Beverly, Massachusetts—and it was too hot for sleep, her mother brought her from her bed to sit on the back porch. She curled up on the glider and stared at the stars while her mother stroked her back. After a while Helen began to point out the constellations overhead.

"There's Draco."

"Where?"

"There. See?" Helen showed her how to find it by first locating Polaris.

She squinted, trying to see the dragon in the field of silver sprinkles on blue. "I see it," she squealed finally. "I see it."

Patiently, her mother guided her around the sky, murmuring names that sounded like words in a magic spell. Cepheus. Hercules. She started to feel sleepy. Cygnus. Arcturus. She fought to keep her eyes open. Cassiopeia.

Cassiopeia, cassiopeia, cassiopeiacassiopeia. The word ran together in her head like a song, its intonation as lulling as the swaying of the glider. She could barely recognize her mother's voice. It had grown soft and distant, as if she were floating off toward the galaxy whose stars she named.

"Where did you learn their names?" she asked uneasily. She needed her mother to talk in her regular way.

There was a long, slow moment. A white moth flew into the circle cast by the porch lamp. "Mamom?" she said. When she looked over, her mother was staring into the heavens. In some inexplicable way she looked different, like a stranger. The change was frightening. It was as if people could slip in and out of their skins, disappear.

"Mamom?"

"You look like him, you know," her mother said in the strange, soft voice. "Very much like him."

The moth circled the light. Something tickled deep in her throat. She wished her mother would go back to naming stars.

"Even as a baby you favored him. His brown eyes. His brown hair." Her mother's hand rested on her head. "And he had a cowlick just like that." Fingers touched the whirl of hair at her temple. "Right there.

"And he had a dimple in his chin," her mother continued in the stranger's voice. "Just like yours."

They sat for what seemed like a long time after that, faces lifted to the heavens. Closer to the porch, fireflies flickered. Soleil's chest hurt. The glider swung to and fro. The pale moth landed on the light bulb.

After a while, Helen rose. "We'd better get you back to bed," she said in a voice returned to normal.

The next morning, Soleil stood before the mirror and studied her face, memorizing her features. Later that summer, she saw an old movie on TV. *Jeanne Eagels*. With Jeff Chandler. Staring at the screen, seeing the dimple in the actor's bold jaw, so like the familiar one in her own square face—*And he had a dimple in his chin. Just like yours*—she decided that her father must look like him. Perhaps her father *was* Jeff Chandler.

At the library, she searched until she found a picture of the actor in a copy of *Life* magazine. She clipped it out and carried it around in her wallet until it was faded. Once she overheard two classmates laughing about her and the grainy magazine picture of an actor who she told them was her father.

For months she fantasized that one day she would meet him. In these daydreams, she was very brave and did not cry, not even when he begged her forgiveness for abandoning her. Neither of them mentioned her mother in these meetings. She loved this father she had never known, this man who had disappeared before she was born, and gave him a loyalty so passionate there could be no room in it for her mother.

She wrote to the studio that had produced *Jeanne Eagels* and asked for an autographed photo of Chandler. She included a five-dollar bill to make sure she would get the picture. The money was returned, tucked inside the envelope with an unsigned photo and a handwritten note saying that the actor had died in '61. 1961. She would have been four.

If she had a father, she knew everything would be easier, better. They wouldn't have to move from city to city, house to house, school to school. She learned to hate September. September meant walking into another new classroom, having a teacher look at her and say, "Class, we have a new student this year. Her name is Soleil Browne." Except they always stumbled over it and pronounced *So-le-el,* as if it were three syllables instead of two, and the class would snicker. Her face would grow hot and she'd have another reason to be angry at her mother. Why couldn't she have been named Jane instead of some stupid French name? Or Judith? Girls named Judith had friends who called them Judy. Or Jude. Girls named Judith had fathers.

By the time she'd turned eighteen, she concluded that her mother's silence about her father camouflaged something shameful. After that she rarely asked about the father she had never known.

Years later, she had watched a talk show about adult children searching for parents who had abandoned them. Prompted by the stories of reunions, she actually hired a detective to find her father. When she sat in his office and told the man the few facts she knew about her father, her hands clutched in her lap so as not to touch the soiled and oily upholstery of the cheap sofa, she had once again felt flushed with the heat of shame.

.   .   .

Now her mother's chest rose and fell in breaths so slight the movement was barely discernible. Only the windy breathing behind the mask and the electronic pulse of the heart monitor reassured her that her mother was alive. She finished clipping her mother's nails and placed her hands gently on the blanket.

The patient in the next bed, a widow named Mrs. Greeley, signaled for her attention. "Could you do mine, dear?" the widow asked, holding out wizened hands, all veins and skin.

Soleil pretended not to hear.

According to the staff, Mrs. Greeley had two daughters and one son, but Soleil had not once, in the four days since her mother's stroke, seen a visitor at her bedside. She checked her watch. She had little enough time with her mother. Let the nurses tend to her. Or let one of her own children.

"Please," Mrs. Greeley said in a little voice.

Soleil sighed and shifted her chair around so she could reach the skeletal hands and the fingers as insubstantial as tissue.

"We're having a party at Christmas," the widow chirped while Soleil clipped her nails. "We always have one. It's lovely. Really quite lovely, my dear. I do hope you can come. You and your mother." She had issued the same invitation several times.

The third patient in the room, an elderly woman named Alice Knowles, was in the midst of a long monologue delivered into the telephone with a conspirator's slyness. Only yesterday had Soleil realized that there was no one on the other end of the wire.

"They stole my purse," Mrs. Knowles whispered into the phone. "I've called the police and they're coming right over. Then I'll get some satisfaction. Imagine. Stealing my purse. I had it hidden, but they took it when I was asleep. You have to watch them all the time. But don't you worry, dear, the police will get it back."

A nurse came in, looked over at Alice, and breathed an exhausted sigh. "Hang up the phone," she said to the old woman. "If you keep this up, we'll have to take the phone away. Do you hear me, Alice?" She took the receiver and hung it up.

At least I've been spared that, Soleil thought. She took a jar of Pacquins from her bag. It was her mother's favorite hand cream. Gently, she smoothed the lotion into her mother's dry skin. The hands held no life, gave no response to her soft ministrations. It was difficult to think of them in life, how busy they had been. Sewing, cooking, cleaning.

Remember all the clothes you sewed for me, Mamom? And the gown you made for my senior prom?

The dress had been exquisite. Pink chiffon with a dropped waist and hundreds of seed pearls hand-sewn on the bodice like opalescent armor. Soleil had lied about the gown, told her classmates she'd bought it in New York. If her mother ever knew about this lie, she never revealed it. She just followed Soleil with hungry, consuming eyes. But then, her mother wanted too much from her, and perversely, Soleil held back. There was not room in her heart for both love and shame.

Now, with her mother lying unconscious before her, she regretted the old betrayal. Now she wanted to connect.

A flash of rage—hot and irrational—seized her. Fury at the stroke. At the doctors. At her mother. And at herself. She fought it back.

She screwed the cover back on the hand cream, returned it to her tote, and took out a comb.

"The strangest thing happened today," she told the blank face. "A taxi driver, a Lebanese man, had a heart attack just as he was dropping a fare off at the museum. He hit a pedestrian. The woman he hit was a night-shift nurse, the volunteer for the new dream exhibit at the museum." She ran the comb through her mother's thin white hair. The scalp was pink. She tried to remember exactly when her mother's hair had turned from gray to white, but couldn't. "They needed someone to take her place. I did it. Can you imagine?"

She studied her mother, searching for a sign she had been heard, but her mother's face revealed nothing.

And what if, miraculously, her mother gained consciousness this minute? What then? Would Soleil return to her old ways and withhold all the details of her life from her mother's over-eager eyes and ears? She didn't know. So for now, she told the slight, silent figure about her day. She told her about Andy, about seeing him again, about the surge of feelings and how shaken she had been. All the while she chatted on, she wondered if, like Alice Knowles, she was only sending her words off into an abyss.

"Andy said it was amazing that I was awake all night just when they needed someone to sleep. He said it was a coincidence. What do you think? Was it a coincidence that we saw each other again?"

She could hear her mother's answer as clear as could be, delivered in a flat Ohio accent.

"There is no such thing as a coincidence," is what her mother would have told her, had she been able to speak.

CHAPTER 5

Shoe watched from the barn window as Shelby Mathews came out of the house. Her neighbor carried a glass of lemonade and headed across the field to Harley. Her going-to-church shoes sank into the freshly furrowed earth. Harley thrust the gear stick into idle, pushed back his straw hat, wiped a forearm across his brow, then downed the drink in a single gulp. He said something to his wife and twisted in the metal seat, indicating the north pasture with a broad, sweeping gesture. Even from the hayloft window, Shoe could tell he was mighty pleased with himself.

It had been Harley's horse had kicked her. White-faced and swearing, their neighbor had swept her up and carried her toward the house. Before he could reach the porch, her pa was there, lifting her from Harley's arms, taking her up as if she weighed no more than a good-sized ham.

There was so much blood, her ma fainted dead away. Later Thomas told her about it. With shaking fingers, he scratched

43

out the words on the chalkboard that hung from a cord around his neck, telling her how her face had been all red and white when their pa carried her into the house. Red from blood and white where the bones showed.

When she returned home from the hospital and the doctor finally removed the bandages, she climbed up on a chair to look in the mirror over her bureau. Her skin was purple and brown with bruises, and the scar of the still-healing wound was livid. She stared at the imprint of a horseshoe on her cheek and jaw. She stopped crying almost at once because the salt of her tears stung so.

That night she took a pair of her ma's sewing shears and cut off her hair. She threw the long, corn-colored braids in the wastebasket in the corner of her bedroom. Then she climbed back on the stool to take a look. She ran her fingers through her newly shorn locks, pulling the strands forward until they hung over her cheek.

A few weeks after the accident, Harley Mathews came to the farm to talk to her folks. She heard the muted sound of voices through the closed parlor door. She knew they were talking about her. As she listened to the words leaking through the door, her heart raced so she thought she'd faint. *There was money to fix her face. Doctors could fix her face with something called an hoperation.*

Weeks went by. She waited, watching for her ma or pa to give some sign. The early peas blossomed. Cottonwoods bloomed and then the far field of hay was cut. In the garden, the tomatoes turned red. Fall crops were planted. At church every Sunday, she glued her eyes to the cross hanging on the wall behind the preacher's head and prayed for a signal it was time for her face to be fixed. All the while she prayed, she could feel Harley's eyes resting on her back.

Finally she could wait no longer. One morning, after her pa had left for the fields, she went in the kitchen to ask her ma.

"Ma, when're they goin' to fix my face?"

Her ma was sitting in the rocking chair, a colander of string beans nested in her lap. Her fingers worked quickly as she snapped off the tips and dropped the beans into a pot at her side. "What do you mean?" she said after a moment.

"My face, Ma. When's the doctor going to fix it?"

"There's nothing the doctor can do, Reba Grace."

Snap. Snap. Snap. The beans fell into the pot. The chair rocked a little faster.

"But," she began, "what about a . . . a hop-ra-shen? Aren't I going to have a hop-ra-shen?"

"An operation?" Her ma's hands quickened at their task. She didn't look up. "Why, wherever in the world did you come up with that notion?"

"Mr. Mathews."

Her ma coughed. She took a gray handkerchief from her apron pocket and spat a wad of blood into it.

"Oh, child." Her ma sighed. Faster and faster went the beans into the pot. The rocking chair squeaked against the floor. Then, finally, "There's not enough money, Reba. Not enough money for that."

Shoe knew for sure she'd be beaten for sneaking and listening to adult conversation, but she didn't care. She wanted her face fixed.

"But what about the money he gave you? I heard him tell Pa. I did."

The sound of her pa's John Deere suddenly rose and flowed in from the field, crowding the room.

Her ma's hands slowed to a stop and her feet settled firm on the floor. She stared at the bean still between her fingers and frowned, as if trying to remember what she was supposed to be doing. "It's gone," her ma said in a tired voice.

"What do you mean? Gone where?"

"It's gone, Reba." Her ma stared at the bean for a long moment, then—snap, snap—she dropped it into the pot. "We got to be practical, child, you understand? We needed it to pay Mr. Roubiam toward what we owe on the farm." Snap. Snap. Snap. "We had to. You understand? So now you know and you can just put this whole business out of your head."

Her ma rose and set the empty colander on the table, wiped her hands on her apron front, then crossed to the stove with the pot of beans.

She followed her ma to the stove. "Gone, Ma?"

Her ma turned toward her and let one hand rest on her head. The stroke touched her forehead, her cheek, so gentle she scarcely dared to breathe. Then her ma's hand froze, as if it caught itself remembering something, and it pulled back sharp. "Now, don't you be goin' and botherin' your pa about this, Reba Grace," she said as she turned back to her cooking. "You understand what I'm sayin'? He's got enough on his mind without you botherin' him about this."

What she understood was that her face was never going to get fixed. Shortly after that, the other kids in Fortune Groves began to call her Horseshoe, and then, eventually, just Shoe.

She was seven years old that year.

Seven years old and she had learned that, in spite of lightning rods or prayers, nothing weak or pretty was ever going to be safe on this farm.

The sound of the tractor engine brought Shoe back to the present. She turned again to the barn window. Off to the left on River Road, the glint of sun on metal caught her eye. A car turned into the drive and pulled up to the house. There was only one such automobile in all of Fortune. Thomas had written its name for her in big letters on his chalkboard: *Packard.*

Its wheels were a pure and astonishing white, its green paint so shiny it hurt to look directly at it. But the thing that always caught Shoe's attention was the radiator cap. It wasn't the ordinary kind, like the one on Mr. Sparks's Model A. The Packard's cap was a naked lady, slim and silvery, with beautiful wings pinned back as if held there by the wind. Even if you didn't live in Fortune, you'd know this was the car of someone important.

The driver's door swung open and a man stepped out. He had the fleshy, thick-through-the-middle look of someone well fed. He wore a pale gray suit, a matching gray hat, starched shirt, dark tie, and two-tone leather shoes. Wing tips. The kind Shoe imagined city men danced in. Just seeing him, she could smell the scent of bay rum.

Mr. Bogeyman.

Long ago, she'd thought that was his name. Not Mr. Roubiam. *Mr. Bogeyman.*

An odd sheep, her pa had said. Born and raised in Fortune, he'd been—as a child—one of those slight boys, an only child of elderly parents, the butt of practical jokes and never able to defend himself. A lot had changed since then.

Mr. Roubiam lived in town in a big frame house, as white as the First Baptist Meeting House. The children in Fortune always crossed the street when they walked by. Except for Ida May Wilson, few folks had ever seen the inside of the house. Ida May cleaned for him and did his wash and knew him as well as anyone. You could tell a lot about a person from his laundry, she said. She explained how he wanted his shirts done up with a double batch of starch and at the first sign of any fraying, she said, they were to be thrown out. No turned collars for Mr. Roubiam. Ida May's rag bag was swollen with his nearly perfect shirts.

He'd never married and rumors stuck to him like houseflies to a coil of flypaper: He drank. He kept women. He frequented a fancyhouse in Cincinnati. He was a mite touched. He had a fortune hidden in that big frame house. Her pa said Mr.

Roubiam was the only man in Ohio who'd made money during the Crash.

Shoe was careful not to press her face too close to the hayloft window. She knew Mr. Roubiam wouldn't take lightly to the idea of someone spying on him.

The kitchen door opened and Shelby Mathews stepped onto the porch. She stopped short—as if frozen by the magnificence of the car—and then descended the steps. Probably inviting him into the house, Shoe thought. *Her* house. Hers and Thomas's. The crown and brim of his gray hat moved curtly from side to side, and Mrs. Mathews hurried off across the field toward her husband, her feet again sinking into the cultivated earth. Mr. Roubiam stood stiff-backed by the Packard and waited.

Harley Mathews left the John Deere right there in the middle of the field and used the walk back to the yard to ready himself. He wiped his face and neck with a blue bandanna, brushed the straw hat against his pants legs, beating off the dust with nervous, flicking swipes. As he got closer, he fixed a smile on his face and stretched out a hand in greeting.

Mr. Roubiam ignored it.

Shoe pictured her pa's body laid out on the dining-room table, and her legs began to shake. "Go away," she whispered. "Go away and leave us alone."

Her hand crept into her pocket, fingers found the square of paper. Her good-luck charm.

She stared down at Mr. Roubiam and his fancy car and his dancing shoes. And she remembered seeing him at the carnival, watching him take Thomas by the arm and lead him into the horrid freak show tent.

Her fingers tightened on the square of vellum as she thought back to the carnival.

CHAPTER 6

The land by River Road was flat and Shoe saw the carnival long before the sound of it reached her, but later, in her memory, it seemed she'd heard it first: the roar of the cycle engine from the motor-dome; the barkers' shrill cries; the piercing screams spinning out from the Whip and Caterpillar.

Like the skeleton of some prehistoric beast, the Ferris wheel stood against the early evening sky. She ran toward the dancing light as if it could take away her fears. The fear Pa would find out about the dime she'd taken from the Mason jar in his closet, fear he'd discover she'd lied about going to baby-sit for the preacher and his wife, fear he'd find her and beat her like he had that time with Thomas, beaten him so badly that even Ma had this once dared to lift her hand to him and say, "Enough."

But as soon as she inhaled the greasy smell of the midway, a blend of chili dogs and french fries, popcorn and roasted nuts, her fears dissolved. She could almost taste the cotton candy, feel it melt against her tongue, coating her teeth. She tightened her fingers around the Mason jar dime.

As she walked by the midway booths, she grew dizzy with the press of people, the rumble of diesel engines, roars that mingled with the music of the merry-go-round, the spiels of the carny men, and squeals from overhead as the Ferris wheel turned in the evening sky.

"Lem-o-nade, ice-cold lem-o-nade, a nice cool refreshing drink for a nickel, five cents, the twentieth part of a dollar." The wizened concessionaire cried on and on with no letup until her mouth felt dusty and parched. She drew closer and heard him say in a much lower voice, as if talking to himself, "Lem-o-nade, made in the shade, stirred with a rusty spade." Although her throat was dry, she walked on.

A crowd milled around the grocery wheel. She dodged arms and elbows, weaving in to look at a basket filled to the top with tins of tomato soup, jars of jelly, and cans of beans and spaghetti. Enough food to last two weeks. The dime felt hot in her hand. Farmers with sun-burnished faces and necks creased with sweat tossed coins onto the faded red and blue squares; their wives watched, hope battling resignation, while the concessionaire spun the wheel. It whirled madly, then slowed and came to rest on number fifteen. No winner there.

She passed the cane stand. A man held out rings. He had a gap in his mouth where he'd lost a tooth, his hair was long and fell in his eyes, and his shirt was undone to his dungarees. There was a tattoo of an American flag on his forearm. He was only a little older than Thomas, but he swaggered as he faced the crowd of farmers. He spoke like his tongue was oiled. "Only ten cents for three rings and the cane you ring is the cane you get." The prizes were cheap—ashtrays, and bracelets set with colored glass, and dime-store cups and saucers. Kewpie dolls hung from a board at the back of the booth. A man

tossed three rings and quit. Shoe watched a farm boy waste thirty cents. She continued down the midway.

An arm brushed against her. Pa said thieves and pickpockets always worked the carnivals. Hired by the owner, he said. She tightened her fingers around the dime.

She approached the rear of the midway now and the crowd had changed. No children here. Several men noticed her. If any of them knew her pa, they'd tell him and she'd be beaten for certain. Ahead a crowd gathered before a platform fronting a long, mud-spattered tent.

A patched and faded banner was strung overhead. A man with a thick upturned mustache stood in the center of the platform. He was so tall, it hurt her neck to look up at him. He wore slim black pants held up by black suspenders, a white shirt with full, billowing sleeves, high-heeled cowboy boots, and a black stovepipe hat, all of which made him appear even taller than he was. But it was his voice that captured Shoe. It was a rolling, liquid voice, promising wonders and drawing her close.

"Beneath yon canvas we have the curi-aw-si-ties and the mon-straw-si-ties . . ."

He swept off the black hat and, with a swift motion that dipped so wide and low the hat brim dusted the platform planks, he directed the crowd's attention to the fading banner and its pictures of the contortionist and tattooed man, the fat woman and the wild man of Borneo.

"We have in yon tent the world's greatest collection of human od-di-ties. The price of admission, la-deez and gen-tul-men, is a dime, ten cents only, the tenth part of a dollar. Buy your tickets now before the big rush."

The flaps of the tent parted and a man emerged. The crowd murmured and pressed closer. He climbed the platform and stood to one side of the barker, who continued his spiel without a break.

"Now look who's to bat." He swept his hat toward the man. "I would call your particular attention to Joe, the amazing one-headed, two-bodied man."

The freak stared calmly out above the crowd. Hanging from the front of his abdomen was the body of a vestigial twin. The body, the size of a three-year-old, was dressed in a checkered suit. A pair of red socks were visible beneath the cuffs of the trousers, and tiny patent leather shoes covered its feet. The body was joined to its big brother by a thick cord of flesh where its neck should have been.

"Now, ain't that the god-damnedest thing you ever saw?" a farmer said, his face alive and eager.

The freak continued to look out, his eyes focused above the gathering that shoved and elbowed closer to the platform. Shoe could not tell if he'd heard the farmer's comment.

The barker motioned Joe back with a wave of the stovepipe hat. Next a dancer appeared, a dark-skinned woman wearing too few clothes—all purple and green and gold sequins. She shrugged a feather boa off her neck and slid it slowly over her shoulders and back, as if drying her body with a towel.

A group of farmhands, their faces glistening with something close to greed, milled in front of the platform.

"Go inside, boys. You can't lose." The barker leaned forward and said in a voice intended only for the farmhands, "She takes off everything, every last stitch, and her body shakes like a bowl full of jelly. She makes a tired man feel like a wild monkey."

Then he dropped his confidential tone and addressed the crowd.

"The price of admission, la-deez and gen-tul-men, is one thin dime, ten cents only, the tenth part of a dollar. There's still time to buy your tickets before the show begins."

The dancer continued to grind her hips and slide the boa over her body.

"Take it off," yelled the bolder of the farmhands.

The dancer winked at the crowd. "You know what's wrong with him?" she said. "When the doctor circumcised him, he threw away the wrong piece." She tossed her head back and laughed, then, with an exaggerated hip thrust, sauntered the length of the platform and disappeared into the tent.

Shoe had never heard a woman laugh like that. Free and open and low. Shoe's neck felt hot and sweaty.

"Go on in, boys," the barker said. "The show starts in a minute."

The farmhands crowded toward the ticket booth, dimes ready. They pushed and shoved, jostling Shoe. Then she saw that the boy at the front was Thomas.

What was he doing here? He was supposed to be at the bowling alley. She waved to get his attention, but his eyes stayed fixed on the dancer up on the platform. Then, before she could push her way to him, a man dressed in a pale gray suit and gray hat approached him from the side of the crowd, took Thomas by the arm, and handed the barker their admission. As she watched, the tent flaps swallowed them.

The Bogeyman.

Why was Mr. Roubiam at the carnival? Everyone in Fortune knew he hated crowds. He didn't even go to church. And he was stingy. Still had the first dime he'd ever made, her pa said. Why would he pay for Thomas to go into the tent?

She felt the thinness of her dime and thought of the cotton candy, the icy coldness of a bottle of Coke. And she thought of Thomas inside the tent with the Bogeyman. She held the dime up to the mustached barker.

She could feel his gaze sizing her up. His eyes lingered on her crushed cheek and jaw with interest.

"Sorry, little lady," he said, not unkindly. "No children allowed."

She had to find Thomas. She ducked around the side of the

tent. Near a stake, she glimpsed a narrow gap. She waited until she was sure no one was watching her, then crouched and
rolled beneath the canvas. Inside the tent, there were no
women. As she searched, she clung close to the folds of musty
canvas. She saw Mr. Bellington, whose wife ran the dress shop,
and Mr. Simms, who was a deacon at First Baptist. Thomas
and Mr. Roubiam stood in front of a raised stage where the
dark-skinned dancer swayed.

The woman wrapped the boa around her back and shoulders
and drew it over her body as if it were her partner.

Shoe remembered the sound of her low, open laugh. She was
glad then that Thomas was deaf. She didn't want him to hear
that laugh. Or what the Koochie dancer woman was saying.

"Take a good look, boys." She laughed as she opened her
knees.

Shoe inched forward until she could see her brother's face.
He was staring up at the woman with a hungry look. The
chalkboard dangled from the cord around his neck.

The dancer shook her body and looked down at him.

"What's the matter, honey? The feathers bother you?"

The other farmhands laughed, a loud, too-long sound of relief.

Thomas reddened.

The dancer bent down. Her breasts were inches from
Thomas. Her voice was bored, her face hard, but Shoe recog-
nized the eager interest in her eyes. Women and girls, even
Shoe's own classmates, always looked at her brother that way.

"What is it, honey? Cat got your tongue?"

Mr. Roubiam was not looking at the woman. His eyes were
fastened on Thomas.

The smell of the tent was heavy, a smell of whiskey and
sweat and something darker that she was afraid to put a name
to. Thomas. She had to save Thomas.

She felt a hand close around her arm.

"Whatcha lookin' for, girlie?"

The pitchman from the cane stand, the one with the tattoo and missing tooth, pulled her from the tent.

"Let me go," she cried.

"Whatcha doin' in there? You lookin' for somethin', girlie, girl? Somethin' I can give you?"

"You let me go," she cried again. She struggled, helpless against his strength, and he pressed her hard against the tent pole. She felt the length of his leg against her body and a dark fear seized her, a fear more terrifying than when Pa took off his belt to whip her.

"Let her go, Louie."

The carney's hand tightened and then he released her, pushing her so that she stumbled. "Just jailbait pussy, anyway," he said as he walked away.

Shoe could still feel where his body had pressed against her.

Off to one side of the main stage, a dwarf was perched on a chair in the center of a miniature platform. Sharp, glittery eyes looked out from a quiet face, eyes that looked straight at her.

"Was it you? Did you make him go away?"

"Are you all right?" The voice was as high as a child's.

The dwarf's feet jutted out from the chair and she saw he was barefoot.

"Thanks for making him go away." She saw he had no arms. There were only stumps at his shoulders. She knew enough not to stare.

The tiny man edged himself forward on the chair. His feet, no larger than her own, reached out toward a stack of cards that rested on a table next to his stool. He took up the top one between the first two toes of his right foot. "Take it and read it," he said in his child's voice.

As she reached for the card, she was careful not to let her fingers touch his foot. She read: "I can write your name on a card for you to keep. The charge is only ten cents."

The handwriting was as graceful as a bird in flight. She traced a finger over the thin, curling, exquisitely shaped letters. She slipped her hand into her pocket. Her fist closed around the dime.

The dwarf lifted his left foot and picked up a sheet of paper, which he placed at an angle on the front of the table. With his right foot, he took up a pen and dipped it into a glass inkwell. "What's your name, missy?"

"Sho—" she began. The writing on the card was beautiful. She had never seen such handsome penmanship. Not even Miss Rogers wrote like this. She put the dime on his table. "Reba Grace Arnett," she said.

When he was done, he handed her the paper. The downstroke of the *R* curled around to form a miniature rose. She would have paid a quarter to see her name looking so beautiful.

She held the paper out carefully so the ink wouldn't smudge. Just seeing her name written like that made her feel pretty, and lucky, too, as if it were a good-luck charm and nothing really bad could happen to her as long as she had it. She wished she had enough money for the dwarf to write Thomas's name too.

Shoe brushed back the memory. Again she peered out the barn window. Below, the green Packard shimmered in the sun and the winged lady looked like ice. As she watched Mr. Roubiam talking to Harley Mathews, a cold dark fear settled in her stomach.

"Go away," she whispered fiercely. Her fist tightened around her good-luck charm, but the paper felt suddenly thin in her fingers.

CHAPTER 7

As Soleil descended the hospital steps, she reached into her tote bag and dug out her Nikon. Its familiar bulk was comforting in her hand. It was her first camera, an F-2, and already it was working its magic, easing her tension.

The streets were still wet from the day's rain and the pavement shone. Splatterings of leaves were plastered against buildings and on sidewalks, forming mosaics of veined yellow, red, and brown. As she walked from the hospital, she automatically began to search for patterns in the cobblestones, bricks, and leaves. The Nikon was loaded with black and white, so her eyes instinctively filtered out color, looking instead for form, shadow.

She had discovered photography in college when she had signed up for a course to fill an elective and almost immediately became hooked. She fell in love with the works of Stieglitz, Strand, and Adams, and had been moved by the artistry of Uelsman and Arbus. One day, during a lecture, the professor said that, literally translated, *photography* meant "drawing with light." She had nodded, understanding at once. Yes. That was it. *Drawing with light.* At the end of the semester, he had called her into his office. You've got the eye, he'd said. The instinct. These things can't be taught. He'd suggested she switch and get a degree in art, majoring in photography. She considered it, but in the end, she had decided to stick with Library Science. She had been afraid that somehow turning photography into a career would spoil it, diminish the magic, as if love had to be kept small or it would disappear.

Still, she never gave it up. Whenever she was tired or worried, she would grab her camera the way another person might reach for a tranquilizer, and would head out to lose herself in shooting. After work and on weekends she would wander the streets, Nikon in hand, capturing the city on film. The Public Garden at twilight on a clear winter evening. Louisburg Square after it had been blanketed with newly fallen snow. The extraordinary details of Isabella Gardner's Venetian palazzo. Trinity Church with its loggia. The city's ancient burial grounds, where grim skulls grinned out from worn slate slabs. Arched doorways on side streets, with iron gates of black lace. Lively street processions in the North End during holy days.

Always, with each change of time and day and weather, she discovered something new. In rain things were muted, hidden, shadows disappeared. The sun made things harsher, more distinct; its glare created shadows. In fog, objects disappeared.

The sun was low in the sky; there wasn't a lot of time left to shoot. She walked by a row of brownstones. Light spilled down the center of a narrow flight of stairs, forming a simple, abstract composition. She shot a couple of quick frames but knew they wouldn't be anything special.

A red light stopped her progress. She heard a squeal of

brakes as two Lycra-clad youths on bikes pulled up in the street next to her. They leaned over their handlebars in identical postures. Their legs and arms, all black angles against the spoked wheels and bike frames, were a study in shapes, reflected on wet pavement. The streetlight shone down on their helmets, creating soft auras around their heads in stark contrast to the slickness of the helmets, the Lycra and bikes, the rainy street. Even as she was shooting, she felt the jolt of pleasure that meant she wouldn't have to wait to see the developed film to know the shots were good. Pleased with herself, she waved to the bikers as they sped off. She slipped the Nikon back into her bag and jogged the rest of the way to the T.

On the first floor, Mrs. Abelini was cooking spaghetti. The smell of garlic and basil and—from the second floor—sesame oil seeped into the stairwell air. "It's like living in the United Nations," Soleil often joked when friends came to visit, but actually she found the aromas welcoming. During the ten years she had been renting there, she had come to associate these cooking smells with home. Ten years. Longer than she'd ever stayed in one place as a child.

Between the ages of one and eighteen they'd moved eight times. Eight houses in seventeen years. Each time she'd cry at the thought of beginning all over again in a new town, a new school, and each time her mother would say the same thing: "We have to go wherever I find a job."

She couldn't remember the earliest places. The first house she clearly recalled was a large brick mansion in Wellesley. She'd been five when her mother got that job. Seven to ten were the Acton years. The Henleys' house. Looking back, she thought that was probably the happiest time. The Henleys' son, settled in Oregon, had hired her mother to nurse Mrs. Henley through the final stages of cancer. Although the couple was quite old, they never scolded Soleil for making noise. They had a collie named Bingo she'd pretended was hers. When Mrs. Henley died, she'd wept and wept until Mr. Henley had put aside his own grief and taken her on his lap. "Don't cry, little lass," he'd soothed. "You know what happens when we cry for someone who has left us?" Curiosity had stemmed her tears. "The person we're crying for has to carry our tears around in heaven, carry them in a heavy sack." She'd tried to picture Mrs. Henley walking around with the angels, a watery sack of tears dripping from her shoulder. Though she didn't want to have her tears weighing Mrs. Henley down, that night she'd cried herself to sleep. She just hadn't been able to bear the thought of leaving Bingo.

The next job was in Beverly on a horse farm. The Bascombe family. They'd had a son named Billy, who was eleven, one year older than she had been. A thin, funny boy with freckles and blond hair who was always getting them both in trouble with daredevil schemes. The week before he would have turned twelve, Billy drowned in the pond out in the middle of the far meadow. When they told Mrs. Bascombe, she'd cried and screamed until finally Soleil's mother had had to give her a sedative. Soleil guessed Mrs. Bascombe didn't know about Billy having to carry around those tears. The old aunt her mother had been hired to nurse still lingered on, but the Bascombes let her mother go shortly after Billy's death. Soleil always thought that Mrs. Bascombe just couldn't endure looking at her anymore.

She forced her mind to go on, away from Mrs. Bascombe and Billy.

Next was a position at a city hospital and a rented apartment in Springfield. Then—her mother back on private duty care—it was Cos Cob, Connecticut. Two months there.

At the thought of Cos Cob, a picture of Mr. Ormston came to mind and the old confusion of shame and sadness settled in her chest. Regardless of the scene her mother had made, she never believed Mr. Ormston had done anything wrong. She wondered if the next nurse he hired had a teenage daughter, too.

She nudged her memory on. Londonderry, New Hampshire. Then, before she'd escaped to Vermont and four years in college, their final move to Boston.

She slid her hand along the railing and headed up to her landing. All those sick and dying people, and her mother was never ill. Not once. "I've got the constitution of an ox," she would tell her employers. "The only time I go to the hospital is to care for others. Why, I even had my little girl at home."

The constitution of an ox. The thought gave Soleil strength. It would take far more than a stroke. Soon her mother would be conscious and beginning her recovery.

She reached the third-floor landing and heard the muffled yipping of Mr. Tannazzo's Welsh corgi coming from his apartment.

As she fit her key into the lock, the landing light flickered and the hall went black. She swore softly. If the bulb went, it would be days before Klietman got around to replacing it. Last winter vandals had smashed the lock on the street door, and it had taken two weeks and dozens of phone calls to get it repaired. She wasn't worried about herself, but the dark could be dangerous for Mr. Tannazzo. The light blinked back on.

"Soleil, is that you?" The door to 3B opened and Mr. Tannazzo peered out.

Her neighbor was thin and slightly stooped, with limp white hair and sharp features no longer padded by flesh that had long ago faded away. He was retired, but he still dressed for the office. The suit, shiny and double-breasted, was neatly pressed. The only time Soleil had seen him without a shirt and tie was the night his wife, May, had died.

"Hello, Mr. Tannazzo." A fat foxlike body waddled across

the floor and yipped at her feet. "Hello, Tootsie," she said, nudging the dog away with her toe.

Tannazzo made a little clicking noise and the corgi waddled back to his side and took the biscuit he pulled from his suit pocket. "You're late tonight," he said.

"I was at the hospital," she told him.

Overhead, the light flickered again.

"Looks like the light's going," she said.

The old man leaned forward with the intent gaze of the slightly deaf. "What?"

"The light," she shouted, pointing at the ceiling. "It's going." She wondered if the fixture was shorting out.

"Oh, my, yes," he said. "We'd better tell Mr. Klietman."

She nodded and turned her key. "I'll do it tomorrow," she said, and twisted the doorknob.

"I was afraid I'd missed you," he said. "How was your mother today?"

"The same." She shook her head. "I don't like her doctor. He asked me about putting a 'DNR' on her charts, like everyone's ready to give up on her."

"Doctors," he said. He'd brought May home when the oncologist had told him she had two weeks left. It had taken nearly eleven months for her to go.

"It makes me furious the way the doctors talk," she continued. "People recover from strokes. I've seen them. My mother nursed some who did."

"What does your mother want? Have you asked her what she wants?"

"Mr. Tannazzo—" She held back a sigh. "She's unconscious. How can I ask her what she wants when she can't hear and can't speak?"

"You ask her," he insisted. "Who says she can't hear? Doctors. With all their fancy tests and medicine, they forget about spirit. Spirit can't be measured and the doctors, they forget.

Remember that. You ask your mother what she wants. She'll let you know. You hear me? She'll let you know."

She pushed her door open. Inside, she checked her answering machine, switched it off, then stood for a moment, experiencing the rush of pleasure her apartment always gave her.

The blue overstuffed sofa and matching side chair had come from Morgan Memorial, as had the carpet, a worn but handsome Persian. A creamy and blue plaid woolen throw was folded over the arm of the sofa. The round table and four mahogany chairs by the front window she had found at an auction and spent one winter refinishing. Built-in bookcases, another winter's project, lined the wall opposite the window. Volumes of books, a near obsession, filled the shelves and lay in stacks on the floor. Eighteenth-century botanist's field guides, books on Roman and Scandinavian mythology, thick novels by South American writers, volumes and volumes of photographic collections. In the middle of the back wall, there was a working fireplace. Above the mantel, she had hung a series of black and white prints, studies she had taken of cathedrals in Europe. At Rouen and Basel and Burgos.

Beyond this room, toward the rear of the building, there was a tiny kitchen, her bedroom, and a second smaller room she had converted into a darkroom.

She slung her tote on the sofa and slipped a cassette into the tape deck. The soothing sound of Mozart's Horn Concerto floated through the apartment. As she headed for the bedroom, the phone rang. For just a moment she allowed herself to think it might be Andy. On the fifth ring she finally found the courage to lift the receiver.

"God, it's good to hear your voice," said a husky female voice. "I miss you."

She smiled into the phone and pictured Mimi. Black hair cut short to frame a small, determined face, slight body dressed like a Gypsy—all colored skirts and scarfs and bangle bracelets. Most people meeting her for the first time mistook her for an artist or a dancer and were disconcerted to learn that she was, in fact, Dr. Miriam Wells, professor of international affairs at Harvard, author of a current best-seller on Russia.

"How's the conference going?" Mimi was in Charlottesville, Virginia, for two weeks.

"According to schedule. Lots of wasted time. Weak coffee and stale apple Danish every morning consumed by scores of professors blurry with hangovers from the night before, followed by afternoons of mostly tedious workshops."

"Sounds pretty ghastly."

"Not as bad as I'm making it. Sour grapes, is all. I just haven't met anyone interesting, eligible, and under seventy. Except Gorbachev."

"Gorbachev's there?"

"In person. I saw him in the hall today and he's incredibly sexy. Really. For him I'd waive the single-men-only rule. He's speaking tomorrow night and there's a dinner after. I'll keep you informed."

Soleil laughed. "I've missed you."

"I tried to call you earlier." Mimi's voice grew warm with concern. "How's Helen?"

"No change."

"Do you want me to come back? I can leave early and fly up in the morning."

"No. Really. There's nothing you can do here." The offer moved her.

"If anything changes, you'll let me know?"

"Of course."

"Well, I hate to cut it short, but I'm late for the evening session. You've got my number here, right?"

After she replaced the receiver, she realized she hadn't told Mimi she had seen Andy again.

At the thought of Andy, she felt an ache in her chest. She

forced herself to be calm. He wouldn't be at the museum forever. Tomorrow she would find out how long *Dreamscape* would
be open. In the meantime, she'd stick to her office on the third
floor and avoid going anywhere near the exhibit.

Her refrigerator was nearly empty. Seltzer. Cheese. Bread. A
half-empty bottle of Chardonnay. Margarine and chili sauce.
Tomorrow after work, before the hospital, she'd have to shop.
She checked the cupboard. There was a can of soup and a
box of pasta, but she wasn't up to making sauce. She took
out the bread and cheese. Toasted cheese again. "Martha
Stewart," she said aloud, "eat your heart out." She sliced
the cheese.

While the sandwich was grilling, she opened the soup and
put it on to heat. The smell of tomato soup and toasted cheese
reminded her of Friday afternoon and grammar school cafete-
rias. WASP comfort food, Mimi would call it.

She turned the heat down on the grill. In the bedroom, she
pulled a fresh pad of paper from her desk. "Call Klietman
about the hall light," she wrote in her precise penmanship. She
stripped and showered. Then she pulled on a pair of jeans and
a pink T-shirt, the shirt Alison had given her at the staff
Christmas party. The purple lettering on the front read LIBRAR-
IANS DO IT IN SILENCE. She supposed, knowing Alison, she
should be grateful it wasn't worse.

She took longer than she'd intended in the shower and res-
cued the sandwich just before it burned. She set her supper on
a tray and carried it into the living room, then took time to
light the fire before she settled down on the sofa.

Before she had taken more than two bites of the sandwich,
the doorbell rang. She shot a glance at the clock. Eight-thirty.
She seldom had visitors. She was aware her throat had gone
suddenly dry. It's only Mr. Tannazzo, she calmed herself. Mr.
Tannazzo with a cup of pudding. She combed her fingers
through her still-wet hair.

George Connolly stood in the hall. "I tried ringing up, but the line was busy."

She flushed, conscious of her wet hair, her face scrubbed clear of makeup.

"You should get call waiting." Like most of Connolly's declarative sentences, it came out an imperative.

She felt a flash of dislike for the director, for his pomposity and mannerisms, his conversations peppered with British expressions as if he'd been born in London instead of only teaching two years there.

"May I come in." Even his questions were statements.

Across the hall, Tannazzo's door opened a crack.

"It's okay, Mr. Tannazzo," she said. Her neighbor withdrew. Reluctantly she opened the door and stepped aside.

Connolly looked at the dishes on the coffee table. "I'm interrupting your tea," he said.

"That's okay. I'm finished." *What could he want? Was something wrong at the museum?* She picked up the tray and whisked it back to the kitchen, away from his eyes. She knew for sure that Connolly didn't dine on canned soup and toasted cheese. Terrine of turnip laced with nutmeg and grilled lamb for him. Things she read about in the *Globe*'s food pages but never bothered to prepare for herself.

She supposed she should offer him coffee, and then rememberd that she had used the last of the tin that morning. *If it was something about work, why hadn't he just called?*

There was the half bottle of Chardonnay in the refrigerator. Probably not up to his discerning palate, but it was better than nothing. She went back to the living room.

"Would you like a glass of wine?" she asked.

"Wine would be lovely," he said. He stared at her shirt.

Jesus. Alison's stupid shirt. LIBRARIANS DO IT IN SILENCE. She could have died.

She escaped to the kitchen. Should she change? Or would

that be worse? Worse, she decided. While she poured the wine, she heard him walking around the living room, pictured him looking at her things. She couldn't imagine what had brought him to her apartment in the first place. He had been there only once before—for an Easter brunch she had had, a somewhat strained party for her co-workers. "Oh, it wasn't so bad," Mimi had consoled her during their postmortem, getting drunk on mimosas.

Why *was* he here? She poured his wine and, after a moment's hesitation, splashed some in a glass for herself. Oh, Lord. He couldn't be here to ask for a date. Could he? Surely not. She sighed. She never handled these things well. The bite of toasted cheese sat heavily in her stomach. She immediately regretted having offered the wine.

He stood by the fireplace, looking at one of the framed photos. "The cathedral at Rouen. Magnificent. You've seen it?" He took the wine from her.

She nodded. She didn't tell him she had taken the picture.

"It's not, of course, as old as Bourges, which is, I believe, the oldest in Normandy."

"I didn't know that," she said, although she had.

"Oh, yes," he said. He held his glass up in a toast.

Blushing, she touched her glass to his.

"I talked to Dr. McKey." He sipped the wine. "He said the opening went smoothly."

"Yes," she said.

He set his glass down on the mantel and brushed his hair back with the palm of his right hand. It was a reflexive gesture. People said he looked a lot like a young Ted Kennedy. On her first day of work, Alison, the intern, had disagreed. "Not Kennedy," she told the staff. "Berenger. He looks exactly like Tom Berenger."

"Who?" Connolly asked when told of the intern's remark.

"Tom Berenger. The actor."

Soleil imagined that over that weekend he had watched videos of the actor's movies. She could picture his eyes narrowed in concentration as he studied the movie star's gestures.

"So you really think I resemble this Berenger chap?" he'd said to Alison on Monday.

"Absolutely," she replied, flirting just a little.

"Really," he had said, pleased.

"Yes," Connolly said now. "McKey said you did a splendid job."

"Well, it's not much of a job." She stared at her wine. "All I had to do was sleep."

"Glad to hear you say that."

"Not that I'd want to do it every day," she added hastily. An appalling premonition took hold.

"Well, as a matter of fact, that's why I'm here. As I said, I tried to ring, but the line was busy."

He's lying, she thought. He wanted to come, knowing instinctively that while she might be able to refuse over the phone, she'd find it nearly impossible in person. Her hand fluttered to her throat. He *was* handsome. She felt suddenly awkward at being alone with him in her apartment.

Connolly smoothed his hair again. "We're in a bit of a bind." He leaned toward her and smiled earnestly, as if speaking to one of the museum's benefactors. "We need you," he said. "Neither of the backup volunteers can jump in on such extremely short notice and we'll need you to fill in. I wanted to catch you before you managed a full night's sleep."

The glass room, the cables, the blue pajamas. Andy. Her stomach tightened. "I can't," she stammered.

"Wait a minute, Soleil. Hear me out." He dropped the earnest tone and smiled, wider this time—the lopsided grin he knew women found charming. "It will only be for a fortnight. One of our two backups will be free then."

"No." She forced herself not to look away from his gaze.

"Just a fortnight," he said again.

She laughed to herself at the pretentiousness of *fortnight.* "I'm sorry," she said more firmly. He couldn't fire her for refusing, could he? Nothing in her contract covered this.

"I'll tell you what," he pressed. "The exhibit is only scheduled to run until the end of the month. Just promise to help us out through the weekend and then I'll get someone else to fill in the following week until one of the trained volunteers can take over." He grinned. "In fact, I'll do it myself if I can't get one of them."

Not in a gazillion years could she picture Connolly sleeping in the glass booth. "Look," she said. "I can't."

"Why?"

"I'm—I'm already behind at work." She wished she had thought of another excuse, one that didn't sound so feeble.

"No problem. I'll get the Northeastern intern—what's her name? Alison?—I'll get her to help you out." He continued to smile, but he had already decided she wouldn't refuse. "Listen. We'll pay you a bonus at the end of the week."

When Helen got out of the hospital, Soleil would need extra money for home care. She hesitated, hating that he'd found an opening.

"And two vacation days."

She was sinking. "Just until the weekend?"

"Absolutely."

Deeper and deeper. "Okay," she said.

"Or next week at the very most."

She wanted to protest this bullying, her old fears, old insecurities set in. Why did she find it so difficult to stand up to him?

He set his glass on the coffee table and got up to go. He'd taken only one sip of the wine.

"Come in early. There's an interview set up with a feature writer from the *Globe* and they'll want to get a photo of you too."

"My picture?" she repeated weakly.

"You're a lifesaver," Connolly said before vanishing into the hall. "A real lifesaver."

She felt weak. *Her picture in the paper.*

She heard Connolly's footsteps on the stairs. There was still time to catch him. Yet she didn't move. It's only for a few more days, she thought. I can do it for two more days. Her heart was pounding. She tried to tell herself that it was anxiety and had nothing to do with knowing she would be seeing Andy again.

CHAPTER 8

The lasers and synthesizer music were not yet switched on and so Dark Space was pleasantly dim and quiet. Andy performed a final check on the polysomnographic equipment, then activated the paper drive. It advanced slowly; the polygraph pens began to move.

In continually changing ripples, the recordings of Soleil's brain waves, of her eye movements and muscle activity, played out on the paper. Andy surveyed the printout, jotted the time in his log, and made a few additional notes. The EOG was thin, with irregular oscillations. The EMG pen scratched out thick, tight waves revealing a high level of muscle tension. The EEG waves were narrow and regular. Fast frequency, low amplitude. A typically alpha rhythm. Soleil was still awake.

Soleil. She'd gotten under his skin more than anyone he'd ever known. More than under his skin. In his blood. He thought of a woman he had known in Santa Fe, a physical therapist named Hannah who read palms and went to ashrams. She had told him every person was literally part of every other. The molecules of air one person exhaled were inhaled by another, she'd told him. Inhaled to be absorbed by blood and bone. None of us is separate, she had said.

He'd felt that way about Soleil. She had become a piece of him. And then they parted. The pain of their separation had taken him a long time to get over.

He forced his mind away from her. He wasn't about to start that again.

He'd get through this. He had *Dreamscape,* a new area of dream research he and his collaborators would bring to the public, touring other cities, other countries. There was even the possibility of a week-long PBS series hosted by Bill Moyers.

Always his work saw him through. Once Soleil had accused him of partitioning his life into separate segments, of caring more about his work than about her. The charge was unfair, but he remembered those words now. If that was what it took to get him through this, focusing on the work, on his exhibit, then that's what he'd do. Compartmentalizing was a way to stay sane, a way to block out painful memories. And of trying to forget that he'd once been wildly in love with the woman lying on the other side of the partition.

He rechecked the polygraph. Soon she would fall asleep. The work, he reminded himself. Concentrate on the work. He had prepared a spiel delineating the stages of sleep for those visiting the exhibit and although he knew it by heart, he reviewed it now.

Four stages of non-REM sleep would occur, to be followed, in approximately thirty minutes, by a brief period of REM sleep. The dream sleep would last five to ten minutes. Then the pattern—non-REM states alternating with REM—would be repeated several times in ninety-minute intervals until she woke. Each dream would be progressively longer, the final one lasting about a half hour.

He glanced at his watch. *Dreamscape* had been open for twenty minutes, but no one had yet entered the exhibit. Connolly had warned him that Tuesdays were the museum's slow day. At the thought of the director an expression of distaste flickered across his face. Earlier he had overheard Connolly talking about Soleil to the assistant director. "The Virgin," he'd called her as he told of visiting her third-floor walk-up in East Boston, of the indifferent wine she had offered him.

The director's remarks irritated Andy. Considering that Soleil was bailing the museum out of a tight spot, he thought she deserved better.

The Virgin. Hardly a word he'd use to describe the passionate lover he'd known.

He fought the urge to look in at her, then gave in. She lay on her back, her body outlined beneath the light blanket.

The recollections streamed in, overtaking him: the two of them together on the Cape, at the Seashore Park, nested close together on the sand, so lost in each other that a beach buggy had been nearly on top of them before they'd heard it; a night in July—impatient, half drunk on wine and each other, thirsty for more, making love beneath the Longfellow Bridge. Jesus, we must have been crazy, he thought now. A miracle we weren't mugged. Another night—her living room, by the fire, Soleil naked, straddling him, laughing. Moonlight shining through the window blinds, falling on her in stripes. Reaching up to trace the bands with his finger. My tiger, he'd said. She, laughing and tossing her hair so it tumbled over her head, pinning his arms to his sides, holding him down, teasing him, tantalizing him, driving him crazy with her hair and her lips and her tongue.

The memories aroused him. "Christ," he muttered, and wondered if the lab coat concealed his erection. He forced himself to turn away from the window. Cold showers, he thought. Ugly women. The square root of two hundred and eighty-seven. He prayed no one would come into the exhibit until he recovered.

He hadn't expected it to be easy to see her again, but he wasn't prepared for the power of her attraction, as if the intervening years had never happened. Did she still feel this way too? She had seemed composed, detached, controlled. Well, he could be cool as well.

He'd stuck a pair of worn paperbacks in his attaché case that morning. He dug them out now. Melville or Thomas? *Moby Dick* or *The Medusa and the Snail?* The whale won. Before settling in with the novel, he scanned the machines again. The EMG reflected lower muscle tension. The EOG displayed slow oscillations. The EEG waves appeared larger, overlapping with bursts of rapid waves. Sleep spindles. Soleil had just entered the first stage of non-REM sleep. He noted the time in his journal. She would spend a half hour in the initial stages before going on to stage four. Delta sleep. Deep sleep. That, at least, was going smoothly. Predictably. The book, its spine spread from many readings, opened obediently in his hands. "Call me Ishmael," he read.

Twenty-five minutes later, Andy's attention jerked back from nineteenth-century New Bedford. The EEG stylus darted across the channel in small, rapid oscillations. The line beneath the EMG stylus flattened out, indicating an almost complete disappearance of muscle tension. The EOG channel registered the distinct waves that corresponded to rapid eye movement. REM sleep. He wrote down the time. The polysomnograph printout could have served as a textbook illustration. Soleil had just entered her first dream.

In the exhibit hall, green, red, and blue laser lights splashed on the walls and the synthesizer music rose and fell. Soleil's sleep made visible. Made musical.

A high-pitched whining circled and spun about her head, pulling her away. Back.

No. She tried to resist.

She didn't want to sit, arms strapped to the chair. Didn't want the mask fitted over her face. She didn't want her tooth pulled.

She tried to say no, stop, but it was too late to stop, too late to prevent the thin, whirling whining in her head, too late to prevent being pulled back into the dark vortex. The tunnel. The long, dark tunnel.

Don't leave me here, she screamed, but her mother was already out in the waiting room with the other parents. She was alone with Dr. Ouinette and his nurse. She thought she heard crying. Thought it was Billy.

At the end of the tunnel, a dim light beckoned.

Now she heard laughter. She believed for a minute that it was Dr. Ouinette. She stepped toward it.

Hurry up, a voice urged. You're late.

As the afternoon wore on, the number of visitors to the exhibit gradually increased. A group of Emerson students, entranced by the laser projections, listened to Andy's explanation of how the two-watt, argonkrypton laser was beamed through a sixty-degree prism to create the laser show.

Two elderly women elbowed the students aside and impatiently scanned the polygraph paper. One, peering nearsightedly, bent closer to the four pens scratching out peaks and valleys on the polygraph paper. Methodically, Andy explained what each line represented. After a perfunctory glance, the women left.

.   .   .

You're late, called the voice. Hurry up.

She stumbled forward, stretched an arm out to prevent herself from falling, and discovered her arms were not strapped down after all. She was not in the dentist chair. Her fingers encountered cold tiles. Clammy with dampness and slime. But she kept falling, deeper and deeper into the tunnel.

A dwarf waited at the end of the light. He motioned for her to hurry. You're late, he repeated.

I'm sorry, she tried to say, but her tongue was thick and she could not speak. I'm sorry. I'm sorry. I'm sorrrrrry. Don't be mad. The words echoed endlessly in the tunnel, as if they were the only thing she had ever allowed herself to say.

You're late, you know. The dwarf reached into his vest pocket and pulled out a gold watch as big as a balloon.

Don't be mad. Don't leave me here. Words spun soundlessly out of her head into the whirling coil of noise from the tunnel.

A man in jeans and a green and white Celtics sweatshirt entered the booth next. A nine-year-old boy wearing wire-framed glasses walked at his side. After a minute, the boy edged forward and touched the paper with a finger, tracing the patterns of Soleil's sleep.

"Is the lady dreaming?" he asked.

Andy examined the printout. "No," he told him, "but she should begin anytime now." He showed the boy the previous periods of REM sleep on the chart.

The boy stared at the oscillations. He returned to the main room, pressed his face against the glass booth, and watched Soleil sleep. His father smiled at Andy. "He's doing a science report for school," he said.

Soon the boy was back. "Why does she dream?" He was

whispering, as if he feared disturbing the sleeping woman in the soundproofed room.

"Well," began Andy, "no one can agree on why. It's easier to answer how." He warmed to the boy's earnestness. "When we dream, the brain stem at the base of the skull fires a barrage of high-voltage impulses." He touched the nape of the boy's neck. "Here. These impulses then unleash a chemical—it's called acetylcholine—that flows to the cortex. These chemicals induce the dreams." He tore a sheet from the drum and handed it to the boy. "Here. For your report."

"Hey, cool."

"Anything else you want to know?"

The boy gazed up into Andy's eyes. "Does she get paid?"

So much for science, Andy thought. "Yes," he said. "She gets paid."

"Neat," the boy said. He tugged at the hem of his father's Celtics shirt. "Come on, Dad. Let's go."

The father pointed to the fluctuations on the paper drum. "She's dreaming now. Right?"

Andy scanned the printout. "Right," he agreed. "She's just begun another dream."

A roar flashed and the sky turned white.

Hurry up.

She could not see who was calling.

She was out of the whirling tunnel at last. Everything was behind her. Mamom. Dr. Ouinette. Billy Bascombe. She spun out into the white sky. She was flying.

Gravity had no hold on her. She was not exhilarated. She was frightened.

From a distance, a tiny figure waved, beckoning her forward.

Beckoned again.

Come, it seemed to call. Come deeper.

No. She tried to say the word, but her mouth wouldn't work. Come.

It was nearly time for the exhibit to close. Soleil had been sleeping for six hours. Andy checked the equipment, noting that she was now in what would probably be her final episode of REM sleep. Beneath her closed lids, her eyes moved from side to side, as if she were watching a play. The recording stylus moved in rapid oscillations. He checked his watch. This final dream state normally lasted a half hour, but she had been in REM sleep for thirty-eight minutes. Any second now she would come out.

She was flying. She looked down and saw a fairground. A carnival. Her eyes focused on a child far below. A blond, thin-framed child dressed in bib overalls. There was a crowd. Amid families and couples and boisterous clusters of adolescent boys, the child was alone.

She followed the child's progress until, abruptly, the small figure was swallowed by the milling crowd.

Wait, she heard herself call. Wait. But the whining of the tunnel drowned her out.

Andy switched off the laser and the synthesizer. He closed his book, put it back in his attaché case, then stood up and flexed his muscles. His body complained from the long day of inactivity, and he managed a few yoga stretches in the confines of the booth. Finally he turned back to the polygraph. His eyes narrowed and he leaned forward a bit. Soleil was still dreaming.

He followed the printout. Her REM sleep showed no indication of abating. He checked the time. She had been in one dream for forty-seven minutes. A faint stirring of concern caught hold. He shook it off. Odd, but nothing more than a freak variation. He checked the EOG. The line was nearly flat. Nothing to worry about. He knew the body went into a sort of paralysis when the brain was actively dreaming. Yet, for the briefest moment, a second, irrational sensation—a feeling akin to fear—brushed by. He had a momentary impulse to go into the glass booth and wake Soleil, but he pushed the thought away. She was only dreaming. Soon she would proceed to stage-two non-REM sleep. Then she would wake.

Through the filmy scrim that cloaked her eyes, she saw a long tent. A crowd of men and boys. Off to one side, a smaller platform. On it a dwarf. She saw the back of the blond child in the bib overalls. She could not see the child's face, but she recognized Billy, knew him from the blond hair. I'm sorry, she shouted. Please. I'm sorry. But the words dissolved, each syllable floating off into space. The dwarf looked up, stared straight at her.

The exhibit was over. Andy watched and debated whether to wake her. In the booth, Soleil dreamed on.

CHAPTER 9

Green Line to Government Center, transfer to the Blue Line. The Orient Heights car was jammed.

Oblivious to the heat and press of bodies, Soleil stared out the night-blackened window of the T. The nausea and dizziness, the faint vertigo she'd experienced on waking from the dream, had left her feeling hollow. A strange sort of hunger.

She was uneasy, still disturbed by the sight of Billy, haunting even after all this time, even in a dream. Needing to shake off his faint, lingering hold, she focused on the other passengers.

They stared grimly ahead, wearing the dazed, slightly shell-shocked expression of public transit commuters. There were more blue-collar workers than on the line from Cambridge. Fewer *Globe*s. More *Herald*s. The man across the aisle unfolded his paper and disappeared behind it. The bold headline filling half the front page caught her attention, pushing away the last remnants of her dreams: POLICE REPORT NO LEADS ON SWEET-HEART STRANGLER.

Since June, the serial killer had murdered three women. After the second murder, a leak in the police department provided reporters with the crime scene clue that connected the deaths. Three foil-wrapped chocolates had been found at each murder. The heart-shaped mint chocolates had been placed on the pillows of the strangled women, as if left there by a room-service maid. They were manufactured by the Sweetheart Chocolate Company. Because of this, the local press had been quick to dub the killer the "Sweetheart Strangler."

Soleil stared at the row of photographs bordering the bottom of the *Herald*'s front page. Three women, pretty in the healthy white-teethed way of Americans, each smiled into a camera lens, unaware that somewhere in her future a man called the Sweetheart Strangler waited with three foil-wrapped chocolates and death.

Why had he strangled them? Lust? Hate? Anger? The ultimate art of possession? Soleil looked at the women smiling out from the newspaper. When they died, they must have been staring directly into his face, his eyes. She wondered what their last thoughts had been. Terror? Regret? None of this showed in their photos. Nor in the name the media had selected for the serial killer. At this she felt a sudden rush of indignation. The newspeople created an engaging persona for crooks and killers by christening them with catchy names, like characters out of a Damon Runyon story. Legs Diamond. Pretty Boy Floyd. Baby Face Nelson. Bugsy Malone. Son of Sam. Hillside Stalker. Even in that Jodie Foster film, the one Soleil had forever regretted seeing, the killer had a nickname. Hannibal the Cannibal. Like a monster in a nursery rhyme. The creation of these names made them less real, less terrible somehow. As if editors and reporters invented the names knowing that horror needed to be kept at a distance. But it diminished those women, devalued them.

She continued to look at the pictures of the victims. For a moment, it seemed that her own face smiled out from the paper. She blinked and the image faded, but fear tightened her throat. She could feel it spread, threatening to take over her body. It was the old, familiar dread, one she could never remember being without, but that she could never name. She dropped her gaze from the newspaper to the row of shoes opposite her. Athletic shoes and work boots, a pair of flats that looked like ballet slippers. She had stopped breathing. She felt her heartbeat increase. Breathe. Breathe, she told herself. It's okay. I am sitting on the T. There are other people here. We are on the T to Orient Heights. She inhaled. Concentrated on it. Nice and easy. Steady. She continued to study the feet of the other passengers, focusing on each inhale and exhale. By the time she reached her stop, the fear had loosened its grip.

She resisted the idea of going home. She couldn't face the idea of the empty apartment, of staring at the telephone and wondering if Andy might call, of trying to occupy herself during the night hours she usually slept, but now needed to stay awake so she could sleep during the day.

She approached her apartment building and walked past it. She'd pick up groceries. Maybe eat out. Then she would go home and use the night to clean the apartment. The darkroom could really use reorganizing and cleaning. And there were half a dozen film canisters waiting to be developed. Remembering the half-shot roll in the Nikon, she fished the camera out of her tote and strolled down the street. She'd finish it off and then grab a bite to eat.

She found herself wandering down unfamiliar streets, snapped a shot of a cat peering through the window grill of a basement apartment. The buildings on this street were old, with recessed doorways. She took some close-ups of architectural details.

She had two shots remaining on the roll when she saw the gargoyle. Half lion, half man, it peered down from the lintel, as if to guard the entry. She stepped back, closer to the building so as to capture the carving in profile. She focused the lens, prepared to shoot, then froze. A man opened the door and stepped onto the top step. He was a cop, big. And ugly. The gargoyle grinned down from the lintel and for a moment—a trick of lighting—they looked almost identical. Amused by the juxtaposition, she snapped the shot. At the sound of her shutter, the cop turned, scanned the street, then found her. Their eyes locked for an instant. He didn't look as ugly now, more mean. She shivered. She didn't need a confrontation now. Not with any macho cop who looked like someone she wouldn't want to meet alone in a dark alley, policeman or not. But this *was* a narrow street, she realized with a nervous, barely suppressed giggle, and she *was* alone. She slipped the Nikon into her bag and hurried off, gone before he could react.

She was hungry. She had not eaten since morning, before the exhibit. She searched for a restaurant and then decided on a small neighborhood place where she had eaten once or twice.

The fedellini was good here. She ordered it with a side salad and a glass of Bardolino. Most of the other diners were older, couples having a night out, she guessed. A single woman sat at a small table near the kitchen door. She was in her seventies and sat sipping her soup as if long ago she had become accustomed to being alone. Soleil stared at the woman and a heaviness settled in her as she wondered if she were looking at her own future. She felt the sadness that always came when she thought of being alone, of never having kids. That was the most painful thought. She wanted children. Wanted them with a desire that was so deep she could feel the pain of it in her breasts and belly. Wanted them more than she had ever wanted any man. Except perhaps Andy.

The Virgin. That morning, screened by the partition of the dressing room, she had overheard Connolly talking with the assistant director. As she'd listened to him describe his visit to her apartment, her face had flamed with embarrassment, then anger. *The Virgin.*

Well, she wasn't.

Robbie Renault. The name came from the edges of her memory, bringing with it a flush of shame. She had just turned sixteen. A junior in high school. Robbie was older, a freshman at Colgate. His attention had thrilled her, made her feel less the outsider. She had begged and pleaded until finally Helen had given in and allowed her to accept a date. With her permission went a midnight curfew, accompanied by the usual lecture about how decent girls behaved, how older men wanted only one thing, how it started with a kiss but that was never enough for the man, how men would say anything to get what they wanted. Before she left the house, Helen had made Soleil change from her new angora sweater into a shapeless cotton blouse.

They went to a drive-in movie. Within minutes, as she stared up at the screen, she felt the pressure of his leg against hers. Awkwardly, she pulled away. Minutes later, his leg again pressed against hers, and this time she did not move. She couldn't concentrate on the film, only on the sensation of his knee pressing against hers, his hard, muscled leg touching hers, a touch that was exciting, but scary too. A touch that made her aware of her own body. Later, in his car, he kissed her and, aroused, she did not push him away. Then he slipped his hand beneath her blouse. She felt her nipples harden, felt his weight as he pushed her down on the seat. His hands slid lower. The sound of their harsh breathing filled the car. She wanted to lose herself in him, in the touch of his fingers on her thigh, the deep shudder in her belly when his fingers brushed against her panties. Then her mother's lecture rushed in, warning her. You'll get pregnant. You'll get diseased. You'll get the reputation of a slut. She shoved him away, sat up, held her legs tight together.

Two A.M. Standing on the front porch. Robbie had driven off in a roar, leaving his last angry words echoing. *Cock-tease. Professional virgin.* Turning the knob, hoping against all reason that the sound of the car engine racing off had not awakened her mother. The shock of the locked door. Raising her hand to knock, lightly at first so as not to wake the O'Neils. Then, louder. Crying. Helen's voice on the other side of the door. Tight with anger. Soleil's voice, sobbing now, begging to be let in. Helen refusing. The scene going on and on. Then another voice inside, Mrs. O'Neil's. The door opening. Her mother's fury. "Whore." The word spat out as her mother's hand lashed out. The imprint of Helen's hand stayed on her face for hours. It was the only time her mother had ever hit her.

In the morning, her mother had come into her room and gone to her laundry hamper. While Soleil watched, she pulled out her underpants and checked the crotch.

That hurt worse than the slap or the shouted words. But her mother was wrong. She wasn't a whore. In spite of all Robbie Renault's pressure and her own desire, she was still a virgin.

That bit of business had been taken care of in college. A picture of Jerome Hester came to mind, as clear as a snapshot. A swarthy assistant professor who smoked a pipe and quoted Yeats. She'd been bewildered by his attention. Later she realized that his choice of her had been an instinctively clever one. Somehow he'd known she would not make a fuss.

They had driven to a lodge near the college for dinner. Roast duck in wild cherry sauce eaten under the mounted heads of antlered deer and a mangy moose. It was the first time she'd ever tasted the cool pine-needle, dizzying taste of martinis. Instead of blurring her perception, the gin had sharpened it. She noticed Hester's untrimmed fingernails, a line of greasy dirt on his shirt cuff, his old—nearly seedy—jacket. After dinner, he had suggested cognac and coffee in a room at the lodge where they could be comfortable. She didn't want to go but didn't know how to get out of it. He already had the key to the room in his jacket pocket. Much later, she wondered how many students he had taken there, and she wondered why no one had ever warned her about him. Inside the room, he had locked the door. For privacy, he'd said. Then he had pushed her to the bed, saying, in a voice that he didn't use for poetry, "Come on, baby. You want it too." The sudden, real surge of fear. As she'd struggled, she'd tried to figure out what had happened to Yeats, the pipe. How had she misjudged him so completely? Yet knowing that in some way it had to be her fault. She'd cried, said no, but Hester hadn't listened. She was aware of his hands on hers, quick, grabbing. Her panties were pulled aside. Then his finger—fingers—were in her. A quick, sharp pain. "You're hurting me," she'd cried. He'd withdrawn his fingers then, but before she could breathe, something else, bigger, more insistent than the fingers, pushed into her. She nearly fainted with the shock and pain. It would have been better if she had. That would have been an escape. From the pain and the knowledge of what was happening and from the terrible sound of Hester's voice in her ear saying over and over, "That's it, baby. Open to me. Open to me, baby."

Later, safe in her dorm, she'd nearly given in to hysteria, but had fought it off and told no one about the whole shameful episode. Not even her roommate. She had showered and thrown her panties into the trash. At least she wasn't home where Helen could find them. In the following days, she'd prayed for her period, terrified she might be pregnant. She wasn't. She experienced no lasting ill effects. Except that even today the smell of gin made her queasy.

The fedellini was cold. She had stopped eating some time ago. She was aware that two waiters were standing in the corner watching her. Keeping an eye on her. Her mother's phrase. *I'm keeping an eye on you.* Or *God's got his eye on you.* Not that her mother was overly religious. She trotted out God only when she would use him as a threat, to keep Soleil in line. *In line.* Another of her mother's phrases.

She pushed her plate aside and signaled for the check. She left the restaurant without looking at the waiters or at the old woman sitting by herself.

Outside, she headed toward the grocery store. Thoughts of Jerome Hester stayed with her. It had taken her a long time to recover from him, to bear the touch of a man's hands on her. Even then, there had been no real pleasure. The true healing had begun with Andy.

She grabbed a cart and headed down the market aisle, selecting items absently. With Andy she had been able to erase from her mind all fear and bitterness. With him there had been laughter and tenderness, passion that bordered on obsession. Even now, just thinking of him as she stood by the dairy case, her throat thickened with desire and she felt herself grow wet. She hurried through the check-out and left the store in a daze.

She stopped in the building foyer to pick up her mail and newspaper, stuffing them in the grocery bag. In the apartment, she set the bundle on the kitchen counter, shrugged off her jacket, headed for the phone, dialed the hospital. She bit back impatience when she had to identify herself to three people before finally being transferred to someone who would give her any information. The charge nurse told her there had been no change in her mother's condition.

Back in the kitchen, she put the kettle on for tea. While it heated, she picked up the *Globe* and went into the living room. There was another story about the Sweetheart Strangler, an in-

terview with the husband of one of the victims, a woman
named Elizabeth Willey. She had been in her early thirties.
The husband said they had planned to have a child. Now she
was dead. Soleil stopped reading. She shivered. *It could have been
me.* The shadowy fear threatened again. Was this it? The fear
that had dogged her for as long as she could remember?
Death? Her eyes flickered to the apartment door. The standard
lock. She felt vulnerable.

Still, she hated the idea of living defensively. Alison, in her
perpetual self-defense campaign, was always after the women at
the museum to carry a canister of Mace or pepper spray in their
shoulder bags. Just last month, the intern had tried to convince her to join the women's defense class at the Y, but Soleil
had refused. She couldn't imagine actually using her forearm or
foot to chop at an assailant's throat or eyes or crotch. She knew
she'd only manage to enrage the man, with the certain result
that what had started as a routine mugging would end up as
murder. Hers.

Her head began to throb. She went to the kitchen and
poured her tea.

She couldn't sit still, as if Elizabeth Willey had brought her
final moments of terror into the apartment. Suddenly Soleil
desperately needed to talk to someone.

She checked the number scribbled on the pad by the phone
and picked up the receiver. The thought of Mimi's voice already
helped ease her anxiety.

"Dr. Wells is not answering," recited an impersonal, front-
desk voice after the tenth ring. "Do you care to leave a message?"

She hung up, forced herself to sit down, to drink the tea. To
breathe.

As she sat staring into space, the grinning, gap-toothed face
of eleven-year-old Billy Bascombe floated before her eyes,
bringing back the dreams.

He had been wearing a pair of bib overalls, dressed just as he had the last time she had ever seen him. The last time she had ever laughed and played with him. That crisp, sunny December day when they had gone skating.

How odd that after all these years she should dream of him. At least it hadn't been a nightmare. All she'd needed was to wake up screaming and crying in the booth while people stared at her through the glass.

The nightmares had begun when she and her mother had moved from the Bascombes'. Terrible dreams that caused her to wake in terror. "It's all right. I'm here," Mamom would whisper. Rocking Soleil's sweat-covered body, she'd try to quiet her so she wouldn't disturb Mrs. Blake, asleep in another room in the house. "You were just having a dream. Do you want to tell me about it?"

"I forgot," Soleil would say. There was no way she could speak about these night visions. Billy with his bloated body. Billy staring at her while the skin dripped off his face like water. There was no way she could talk about Billy Bascombe at all.

Her tea had grown cold and she poured it down the sink.

It was not her fault. There was nothing she could have done to save him. There was no way now, even in her dreams, that she could change history, no way she could, in some redemptive way, return to save his life.

CHAPTER 10

FORTUNE GROVES, OHIO
July 1932

Shoe sat on the bed and watched.

Mrs. Sparks scrutinized the room, greedily collecting things to tell the other women. *Soiled bedclothes. Filthy windowpanes. Why, the girl never even tried to take up with the cleaning after Lydia died.*

Satisfied that she'd taken in all there was to see, Mrs. Sparks marched toward the bed and, with an impatient snap, shook out the garment she carried.

Shoe didn't move.

"Land sakes, child," Mrs. Sparks chided. "Don't just stand there. Hustle up and get dressed. You can't keep the preacher waiting."

Shoe recognized the green cotton dress. It was store-bought with a lace-trimmed collar and a wide white sash, not made from cotton-print grain bags like most farm girls wore.

"I swear, Shoe Arnett." Exasperation put an edge to Mrs. Sparks's voice, and her mouth thinned as she reached the bed.

90

"Sometimes I think you act deaf as your brother. Now straighten up so I can be gettin' you dressed."

Shoe snatched the green dress from the older woman's hands and twisted out of reach. She unsnapped her straps, stepped out of her overalls, yanked the dress over her head. She moved quickly, but that didn't prevent Mrs. Sparks from taking note of the holes in her underwear or of the swelling of her immature breasts beneath her thin cotton shirt. More shaming things for her to carry back to the other women.

The dress was skimpy through the shoulders and there was a brown stain on the front by the hem. It made Shoe's skin itch to wear it.

"The color washes you out some, but it'll do just fine." Mrs. Sparks retied the bow of the white sash. Shoe saw her face wore that pretend nice look people get when they've given you something, making you beholden to them.

Mrs. Sparks glanced at Shoe's hair, ragged where she had cut it herself. " 'Course, there's not a blessed thing I can do about your hair."

Or your face. The unspoken words hung in the air between them.

"I guess we'd best be gettin' downstairs," Mrs. Sparks continued. "The preacher will be wantin' to get started."

Halfway to the door, the woman stopped short. "And don't you be forgettin' to thank Sarah, you hear? It was her idea about the dress so you can be lookin' proper for your pa's funeral." She paused before stepping into the hall. " 'Course, she's goin' to be wantin' it back. Just so you understand that."

Shoe had to grit her teeth to keep from saying something mean. She knew the preacher said it was a sin to hate, but she truly hated Mrs. Sparks.

·   ·   ·

Thomas was waiting for her in the front hall. Someone had taken away his chalkboard and given him a tie. It made him look grown up. Shoe scowled. It was as if by putting her in a dress and Thomas in a tie, people were changing them, turning them into something they weren't, making them lose part of themselves. She stuck her tongue out at the tie, not caring a whit if Mrs. Sparks saw her.

Then Thomas smiled and he was her Thomas again—tie or no tie. Hand in hand, they walked into the dining room.

More people crowded into that room than had ever come to the farm when Pa was alive. Harley Mathews. Shelby Mathews. Homer and Cora Simms. The Archibalds. Miss Rogers. Mr. Gerney. Preacher and Mrs. Hill.

Eyes crawled over her face. Long ago she'd learned to deal with stares. The trick was to stare right back at people, stare straight into their eyes until they had to look away. She always won this battle. Oh, some folks couldn't resist looking again, real quick-like, but then they'd turn away.

Now she had to face a whole roomful of stares. Her insides went all hot and for one paralyzing moment she thought she'd be sick, then hands took hold of her, pushing and pressing until she and Thomas stood directly in front of Pa's coffin.

The pine box stretched out six inches off each end of the table. Still, it seemed too small to hold her pa. The lid was raised, but Shoe didn't look inside.

"He's fixed up right nice, right nice," Jonas Frye had said the night before. Shoe didn't see how any undertaker could mend a man's skull laid open by a slaughtering hook.

The coffin was constructed of rough planks and there were chisel scars in the wood. She concentrated on these, focusing until all the faces, Pa's body, everything in the room turned wavy and blurry and finally disappeared altogether.

She didn't listen to Reverend Hill. She just kept staring at the chisel marks, fixing a picture in her mind of how a living tree could be cut down and carved up to make a bed for a dead man. But even squinting hard she couldn't stop her mind from wandering and wondering. Wondering how long it took for wood to rot and wondering if the open place in the back of Pa's head would be the first spot the worms would crawl into. *Child, you think too much. That's your trouble. You think more than's good for you.* Ma's voice—all she had left of her ma—echoed in her head, but it couldn't stop her imagination.

A drop of sweat rolled down her back; her neck turned prickly hot. She reached a hand out for Thomas and he squeezed her fingers tightly in his.

He kept hold of her hand during Preacher Hill's service and later all the time they stood at the grave. It was hot in the sun and when the first earth was shoveled onto the coffin, her throat ached just like the time she was sick with the grippe. It kept hurting until they returned to the house.

The living room door was ajar. Shoe inhaled the sugary smell of the funeral ham cooking. The clatter of dishes, the high-pitched voices of women fell like brittle notes with, occasionally, the men's lower tones woven through.

The preacher's left hand felt heavy on her shoulder. He grasped Thomas's arm with his right. "The normal thing," he said, "would be for kinfolks to take you children in and give you a home."

Shoe curled her toes under, tight inside her shoes.

"The sad case here is you've got no blood kin."

Everyone in Fortune knew that. Their ma's aunt Grace had died the year before in the influenza of '31. And no one knew where their pa's sister Reba had gone after she'd run off with the Bible salesman, a thin, yellow-whiskered man who limped.

Shoe remembered how the salesman would thump a knuckle against his wooden leg. "Left the other one at Chateau-Thierry back in '18," he'd say to anyone who'd listen. "I reckon by now it's long gone into fertilizer for some froggie's farm." She always wondered how her aunt Reba could kiss a man whose leg made a hollow sound, much less share a bed with him, but from the moment Reba Arnett had driven off with her one-legged Bible salesman, she'd never looked back or as much as sent a postcard.

Preacher Hill turned to Thomas. He spoke slowly, raising his voice a little, the way people sometimes did with Thomas, for all the good it did them.

"Normally, with no family, you'd be sent up to the Town Farm, but the Lord moves in his own mysterious fashion." He smiled at the wisdom of his God. "Mr. Gerney wants you to come and work full time at the alley. He has a place for you to stay. A room above the alley."

Thomas would never leave her. She knew that, but her eyes narrowed suspiciously at the preacher's news. Pa always said nobody ever gave something nice without wanting in return. She wondered what Mr. Gerney wanted from them. The preacher's next words made her forget all about him.

"Shoe." He gestured toward the sofa hidden in the shadows of the room. "This is Mr. and Mrs. Cade."

Shoe edged closer to Thomas. The man and woman stayed sitting on her ma's green sofa. The woman was a tiny thing. Her head barely came to the shoulder of the tall, thin man sitting at her side. She wore men's shoes. Same size as her husband's. Maybe they were a pair of his. He smelled of black grease. Shoe could tell by the way his leg jiggled up and down that he was jumpy, but the woman was still as a brood hen and made her face blank so it was hard to tell if she was mean or stupid or just plain careful.

"The Cades have agreed to take you in."

Her fingers tightened into fists and she pressed into Thomas.

"Do you understand, Shoe? The Cades will give you a home."

"Don't need one," she said. "We live here."

"You can't, Shoe."

"Well, that's what we're goin' to do. Ain't no one can stop us."

The preacher shook his head. "Hear me out, child. The farm doesn't belong to you. Your pa owed money on it. Owed it to Mr. Roubiam. Since there's no money to pay off the debt, Mr. Roubiam owns the farm. It's all legal. He owns it now and he's hired Harley Mathews to work it for him."

"Don't care. I ain't leavin' and no one can make me."

"Get your things together, child." The preacher smiled with just his mouth. "The Cades will wait."

"No," she said. "I ain't goin'. I'm stayin' here with Thomas."

"Maybe you'd like Mrs. Cade to help you pack," he said.

"I ain't goin'," she repeated, and stamped her foot. "I ain't goin' and I 'specially ain't goin' with any pickle-faced woman like her."

The preacher turned red, but Mrs. Cade stared ahead, as unmindful of the outburst as if she'd just been offered a glass of sarsaparilla.

Shoe ran from the room.

"Let her go," she heard Reverend Hill saying. "Give the child time to get used to the idea. Tomorrow we'll come out here and get the two of them."

Raw, copper-toned earth from the graveyard still clung to her shoes. Not bothering to untie the laces, she pulled them off and flung them in the corner. She struggled to get the green dress up over her shoulders and felt a jolt of satisfaction as it ripped. She tossed the dress in the corner alongside the shoes. She couldn't breathe normal until she was back in her overalls.

She listened at the door long enough to make sure no one

was coming, and then she shut it tight. Long ago the key had disappeared.

She opened the bottom drawer of her bureau. Still listening for the sound of footsteps in the hall, she took out a bundle wrapped in an old kitchen towel and carried it to the middle of the floor. Then she sat down and waited for her brother.

She was relieved to see Thomas had his slate board back and the tie had disappeared.

"Thomas." She jumped up and pulled him into the room. She was so proud of her secret, the words spilled out in a torrent. "Oh, Thomas," she said. "We're safe. We don't have to leave the farm. They can't make us go."

She had spoken too rapidly; he hadn't understood.

She began again, slower this time. "We can keep the farm," she said. "Thomas, we can keep the farm."

Carefully, she unwrapped the towel. The Mason jar shone in her hands.

"See," she repeated. "We can keep the farm." Thomas looked at the jar, no longer watching her talk. She remembered exactly how she felt when she'd first seen the jar in Pa's closet.

He stared so long she squirmed impatiently. Finally he took a stub of chalk out of his pocket. It squeaked beneath his fingers as he scribbled. "Where?" he wrote in the shorthand he used for the slate.

"I found it."

He tapped the chalk impatiently on the word. "Where?" His cheeks were pink, like he'd been running.

"In Pa's closet." She could see he didn't believe her. "It's true," she said. "I found it last week."

He reached for the jar and, after a moment's hesitation, she relinquished it. He unscrewed the lid and dumped a pile of change in his hand. He poured it from palm to palm, back and forth, back and forth, just like it was liquid. His face was shiny with hunger.

"Guess how much there is, Thomas," she said. "Thomas? Guess how much."

He continued to handle the coins.

She cupped his chin and made him look at her. "Seventy-eight dollars and seventy cents," she whispered. In the past two days, she had counted it out dozens of times. It seemed astonishing that quarters and dimes could add up to that much money. "Seventy-eight dollars and seventy cents."

He stared in disbelief.

She scooped up the quarters and dimes and funneled them back into the jar. "We're rich, Thomas. We can save the farm."

His eyes went dark and his features twisted with an odd, thirsty expression she'd seen before. It troubled her she could not remember when. "Or we can leave, Thomas." The notion was so bold, it made her laugh. "We could move away. We could find a room somewhere. Then we'd have plenty of money." With that thought came a hope so tender and fragile she didn't dare give it voice. *Maybe there'd be enough money left for an operation to fix her face.*

"Shoe." Mrs. Hill was outside the door.

Shoe motioned to Thomas to be still. Swiftly, she rewrapped the jar and pushed it beneath the bed.

"Gotta go back down," he wrote on the board.

"No," she said. "I'm not goin'. I'm not goin' down till they're all out of our house."

Mrs. Hill knocked softly at the door, then entered the room. "Come on down and eat, Shoe." The preacher's wife tried to hug her, but she twisted away. "You must be hungry, child. Don't you want to eat?"

Although her stomach rumbled and she hadn't eaten since breakfast, Shoe shook her head. She'd faint dead away from hunger, she vowed, before they'd catch her going down and eating their food. She hoped they got sick on the food.

You're stubborn as a mule, child. Just like your father. Stubborn as

a mule. You're stubborn and you're nosy and you're headed for trouble.
Ma's words echoed deep in her memory.

I don't care if I am stubborn, she told the ghost. I still ain't
goin' downstairs.

After Thomas and the preacher's wife left, she lay down on
her bed and stared at the ceiling. She wondered how much her
pa owed Mr. Roubiam and how much money would be left after she and Thomas paid the debt.

Three more times Mrs. Hill came and knocked on the door,
but Shoe didn't answer. The Cade woman never came. Maybe
she'd changed her mind. Maybe she'd taken her skinny, careful
face and her men's shoes and gone on home.

They can't separate me and Thomas, Shoe swore. They can
try all they want, but I ain't going to let them. I'm staying
here with Thomas and that's all there is to it.

Just before she fell asleep, she pictured the look on Thomas's
face as he'd sifted through the quarters and dimes, and she
suddenly remembered where she'd seen it. He had looked like
that at the carnival when he'd been staring up at the Koochie
dancer in the curiosities tent.

CHAPTER 11

It was dark when Shoe awoke. It took a moment before memory flooded in. Pa's funeral.

Stealthily, as if to match the house's stillness with her own, she crept from the bed and lit a lamp. The green dress had been picked up off the floor and placed on the chair. It was folded, too neatly for it to have been by Thomas, and she wondered if the Cade woman had come sneaking into her room while she slept.

Quietly she turned the doorknob and crept down the hall to Thomas's room.

As soon as she saw his empty bed, a blade of fear cut through her. She ran her hand over his sheets. They were cool beneath her fingers. His chalkboard was gone from the stand where he kept it at night.

"Thomas?" Her voice trembled.

Back in the hall—"Thomas?"—to her pa's room—"Thomas?"—through the dining room—"Thomas?"—past the

table that no longer bore the weight of her pa's coffin—
"Thomas?"—to the kitchen where the women had put up the
funeral foods—"Thomaaaaasssss?"—to the living room where
Preacher Hill had told them what was to become of them.

She fled outside, down the porch steps, and out into the
chicken yard. She screamed his name, lifting her face to the
sky. The night threw back the echo. Thomasthomasthomas.
Still she could not stop. She checked the barn, the milk shed,
the tack room, screaming and screaming until her throat
turned raw and she could not recognize the cracked, sore thing
her voice had become.

Back in the house, she crept through the dark to the
kitchen. She sat in her ma's rocker. He'd be back. Of course
he'd be back. He wouldn't leave her. Not Thomas. To and fro
she rocked in her ma's chair. *Not enough money. Not enough
mon-ey,* squeaked the wood.

The Mason jar.

She took the hall stairs two at a time, stumbling once in the
dark.

Her hand swept the floor beneath her bed and one long shud-
dering moment passed before her searching fingers found it.

She felt at once that it was lighter than it should have been.

Half the money was gone.

She unscrewed the lid and took out a crumpled square of paper. She read:

Reba Grace,
    I had to leave. I took my shere of the money. Don't warry.
The Cade folks ull take care of you. I'll come for you sum
day. Promise.

                            Your brother, Thomas

"No," she whispered. And then again, "No." The word
slipped out of her mouth like a sigh. Thomas was the one sure

thing she'd counted on. Even the time Pa'd beaten him half dead, Thomas had never blamed her. Even though their pa had caught both of them together in the barn. Even though she had been as much to blame as he had.

She had to find him.

She shoved the jar under the bed and ran down the stairs. She thought of the bowling alley first, but as she ran across the yard, she realized where he'd gone.

At night, Ames's pasture seemed farther away, but she ran all the way. Her ragged breath pounded in her ears and kept time with her feet. She fell twice on River Road and her knees burned where the gravel skinned them. The warm wetness of blood trickled down her shins. Dogs bayed as she ran past farmyards. She heard squeals that sounded like crying cats, but she knew were owls.

He could've taken the whole Mason jar. If only he had stayed with her, he could've had it all.

"Oh, Thomas," she cried out.

Even when she was close enough to see that the field was empty, she made herself keep running.

Except for the trash—paper cups and ant-covered cotton candy cones trampled flat in the dead alfalfa—the carnival might never have been there. The Ferris wheel and merry-go-round, the midway booths and tents, all had disappeared as hastily as they'd first sprung up. Still she wandered across the pasture, staring at the ground as if it held clues to where the carnival had gone.

When she walked back to the farm, she heard the baying dogs. And the owls. And other noises—whispering, strange night sounds she'd never heard before. The sound of her breathing and her footsteps on the road were very loud. She supposed she'd best be finding herself a knife. Something to protect herself with.

She took a suitcase from her ma's closet. It was stained and battered. A long, long time ago her ma had carried it with her when she'd first come to Hod Arnett's farm. It did not take Shoe long to pack her clothes.

When she was done, she walked through the house and searched for something belonging to her ma and pa and Thomas.

The only thing Thomas had left behind was the cracked cup he used to hold the bits of chalk Miss Rogers saved for him. Shoe wrapped it in a kitchen towel and put it in the suit-case. She found a folding knife on her pa's bureau and took that. Not much in the way of protection, but better than noth-ing. She had the hardest time trying to find something of her ma's. She remembered there'd been a comb and brush set and a brooch with a purple stone, but like most of her ma's things, these had disappeared with her aunt Reba. Finally, tucked in the back of a drawer, she found an old worn handkerchief with a pink embroidered flower in one corner. She didn't pack the handkerchief in her suitcase with the knife and cup, but pinned it inside her shirt where she could feel it against her skin.

It was not yet dawn, but she left the house and sat on the top porch step, her suitcase at her knees.

She did not cry.

Her ma used to say that crying never changed a thing. Once, when she'd been frying up pork rind, the iron spider had slid off the burner. Her ma'd grabbed it with her bare hand and Shoe had watched while the fat had splashed over her ma's skin.

Shoe knew it hurt, could tell by the way her ma caught her breath in a quick, sharp gasp, but right away, before Shoe could even think to move, her ma'd smeared butter on the red-dened skin. Weeks passed before the blisters drained, but her ma never cried.

"What's the good of crying?" her ma had said. "It don't

change a thing." She said it in a sure, quiet way that left no space for arguments, like it was a thing she'd learned a long time ago over something a lot more painful than a hot spider and a splattering of pork fat.

Shoe sat patiently and tried to shut out the whispers of the house and the echo of the rocking chair. *Not enough money. Not enough money.*

She tried not to think about the future, about life without Thomas or where he was heading, or about what it would be like to live in a house without a lightning rod on the roof.

She tried not to think about Harley Mathews going into the chicken yard and taking Red Boy and Broken Beak and Mr. Big Toes, tried not to think of them being chopped up for stew.

She shut out the memory of Harley telling her pa about hospitals and operations because she knew that now there'd never be enough money for a doctor to fix her face.

Finally, she tried to push away the hurtful, cold stone of knowledge that sat inside her chest: She was all alone.

She slipped her hand into her pocket and held the square of paper with "Reba Grace Arnett" written in the beautiful lettering. As night turned to dawn, she tried to summon up the magical scent of fall apples and new-mown hay, but all she could smell was the damp earthiness of a field freshly laid open.

With the smell of the farm filling her head, she sat and waited for someone to come and fetch her.

CHAPTER 12

By the third day of the exhibit, Soleil found the electrodes irritating and fought a nagging, almost childish impulse to pull them off. She turned on her left side and sighed deeply, then wondered if on the other side of the partition Andy had heard.

Earlier, while he had been attaching the electrodes, she had pulled away without thinking.

He had studied her. "You okay?"

"Yes."

"You sure?"

"I told you. I'm fine." She had been unable to keep the irritation from her voice.

"I just thought you might be worried about Helen."

She felt a stab of anger as she realized Connolly or someone on the staff must have told him about her mother's illness. Then guilt, which she quickly reasoned away. After six years, he didn't have the right to come back and voice concern for

Helen. Hadn't he left for California without worrying about her mother or anyone else?

Even now she could feel the betrayal of his leaving, as if there had been a promise made the first night they met when he had told her his parents had lived in one house all their married years. I'm a man, he seemed to be saying, who knows how to stay in one place, not spend life moving from city to city. I'm a man who knows about family. She had been able to picture him as a father for her children. And then he had gone. Her mother had said she wasn't surprised by this, as if his leaving only added weight to her bitter assessment of men. No, Soleil owed him nothing now. Certainly she was under no obligation to tell him about Helen.

She turned away from the glass and rolled onto her back.

Andy scanned the printouts. Soleil had been in the booth for forty-five minutes. "Come on," he urged under his breath. "Come on, Sleeping Beauty. Do your thing."

He looked over the day's agenda. The first of two school groups scheduled to tour the exhibit was due to arrive in thirty minutes.

Another check of the printout. She was still awake.

He keyed the intercom switch. "Hey, Soleil?"

"Yes?"

"You okay?"

"I'm fine."

He paused, checking the EMG. There was a lot of muscle activity. Something was keeping her awake. Probably worried about her mother. It was strange to think of Helen as ill, near death. She was such a strong, formidable woman.

He always connected Helen with a conversation he'd had with Soleil the second week they had been together.

.   .   .

It had been a Sunday morning, the first time he had stayed overnight in her apartment. Soleil was in the shower when the phone rang. After the fourth ring, he answered it. Minutes later, she came into the living room. She wore a terry robe and a towel around her head, turban fashion. Her skin was rosy from the shower.

"Your mother called."

She stared at him. Her smile faded. "What?"

"The phone rang," he said. "I took the message. It was your mother."

"Oh, God."

"What?"

"What did you tell her?"

"About what?"

"About why you were answering the phone here."

"I told her you were in the shower."

"Oh, God," she repeated. She was pale now, disturbed.

"What's wrong?"

"Maybe she'll think you just stopped by. No, she wouldn't. Not Helen."

"Soleil, what's the problem?"

"Don't you see? She'll know we slept together."

He laughed, trying to ease the tension. "Maybe I'm missing something here, but this is 1987, not the fifties. Unmarried adults do sleep together. And you are an adult."

"You don't understand." She was near tears.

"Tell me?"

She shook her head, too upset to respond.

He crossed the room and embraced her. "Tell me," he said again. "Tell me what I don't understand."

"She'll think I'm a whore. She says only a whore would sleep with a man she wasn't married to."

"She told you that?" He felt a flash of anger. "Christ. What time warp is she in? The Dark Ages?"

"You don't understand," she said again. "I know it's weird, but I think she is only trying to protect me."

"Protect you?"

"That was her way of protecting me when I was growing up. 'When a man's hard, he's soft,' she'd tell me, 'but when he's soft, he's hard.' "

"What the hell does that mean?"

She smiled sheepishly. "That when a man has an erection, he'll promise you anything, but after he's been satisfied, all bets are off."

"Nice sex education. I'm surprised you're allowed to have an apartment of your own." He could not keep a defensive note from creeping in.

She tightened her arms around him. "I know it's foolish, but it was difficult for her." She took a deep breath, then told him, "She raised me alone. My father left her before I was born."

"You never knew your father?"

"I don't even know his name."

His anger disappeared, replaced by a desire to protect her. "You poor kid. And she never remarried?"

"No. I know some of the things she told me were crazy, but she only wanted to protect me. I don't know if you can understand, because you've always had your whole family, but it's just been the two of us. We only have each other."

"Not anymore," he whispered in her hair. "Now you have me."

He pushed the memory away. Too painful now. Too sad.

He glanced at the polygraph. She still hadn't fallen asleep. He dug the Melville novel out of his attaché case. "How about if I read to you?"

"Oh, no," Soleil said. "Really."

He wondered if she was remembering the Sunday mornings they had spent in bed together while she nestled into his side and he read from Coleridge, Shelley, Keats, and Hopkins. Or recited the Auden poem he knew by heart. The one about love having no ending.

He flipped the book open and began.

" 'Deep into distant woodlands winds a mazy way, reaching to overlapping spurs of mountains bathed in their hill-side blue.' " His voice was low with a soothing cadence that made each word soft and full. " 'But though the picture lies thus tranced, and though this pine-tree shakes down its sighs like leaves upon this shepherd's head, yet all were vain, unless the shepherd's eye were fixed upon the magic stream before him.' "

Even after he saw that she had entered the first non-REM stage, Andy continued to read, detailing the magnetic, mystical hold of water on the soul of the whaler Ishmael.

When she entered the second stage of sleep, he looked up from the book. On Monday, her dream pattern had been textbook normal. On Tuesday there had been the abnormally extended periods of REM sleep. Just a fluke, he thought. Probably today would show a total reversion to Monday's pattern, just as Stan Whitelaw predicted it would, when he'd phoned his Stanford colleague at the university the night before.

"Unusual, certainly, but not totally impossible. Or even improbable," Whitelaw had responded. "Prolonged REM such as you're describing would most likely occur if your subject is wrestling with a problem in her life."

"Something emotional?" Of course she would be worried about her mother.

"Exactly. Her subconscious will try and assist by working through dreams. In this case, her dreams could last longer than one might normally expect. Most interesting. Keep me informed."

Unusual, but not improbable. Andy forced himself to read a few more pages of the story, on to where Ishmael arrived at the Spouter Inn. When he again lifted his eyes to check the print-out, Soleil had arrived at stage three.

Minutes later, she moved abruptly, curled on her side, then stilled. She had entered stage four. Delta sleep.

Her dream began.

Whirling. Whining. Into the tunnel she fell. A free fall through space.

On the other side—through a veil created of the flimsiest net—she saw the dwarf. He crossed a street, his gait a curious short-legged waddle, and headed toward a white two-story wood-frame house.

He looked back at her, called out for her to follow, his words more command than invitation. She shivered, unable to move. She did not want to go near the house.

When he reached the porch steps, the dwarf grasped the railing and pulled himself up the stairs. At the threshold, he turned and beckoned impatiently.

The door swung in on its hinges. It too seemed to call to her. She held back, afraid.

Come on, urged the dwarf, disappearing into the house.

Wanting to resist, but unable to, she followed.

The students from the seventh-grade science class crowded into the equipment booth, jockeying for position in front of the machines. Andy, fighting impatience, forced himself to answer their questions politely. All the while, he couldn't help sneaking looks at the chart to monitor Soleil's sleep. Finally the science class trooped out and he turned his full attention on the revolving polygraph drum. Soleil was still in REM. Yesterday's experience had not been a fluke. The pens were duplicating Tuesday's unusual extended periods of dream sleep.

She saw she was alone now. She was upstairs in the house, midway down a narrow hall. The walls were covered with dark, floral-print paper. A carpet, old-fashioned, maroon, worn in spots, covered the floor.

Get out, an echoing voice called to her. Go back.

There was a door at the end of the hall. She began walking, her footsteps silenced by the patterned runner. Her eyes fixed on the door-knob in the distance. It was made of amethyst glass.

The long dark hall stretched out before her. She smelled the dust of generations rise from the maroon carpet.

Go back. Go back.

Why? She wondered.

She continued to walk down the hall, moving slowly and steadily toward the room at the end.

Without needing to peer through the square window set into the partition that separated them, Andy could picture Soleil asleep on the bed. Initially, when she first got in bed, she lay stiffly, sheet pulled to her neck. Then as her breathing deepened and she nodded off, she would relax and shift position. Just before she began dreaming, she would turn on her side and pull her knees up slightly, curl one hand into a loose fist, which she tucked beneath the pillow. Strands of hair, pulled free of the single braid, lay loose on the white pillowcase.

He no longer had to glance at the printouts to know when she progressed through the stages of sleep. In the past two days he had become so sensitized to the subtle changes in the music and lasers that he knew instantly whenever she moved in or out of her dreams. In REM, the music was higher pitched, the tempo more rapid, while the laser beams darted across the walls in short, almost violent bursts of color.

She was now on her fourth dream. He checked his watch. It was nearly time for the exhibit to close. She had been dreaming a single dream for forty-seven minutes. The pattern was almost identical to yesterday's. Again his excitement stirred and with it, a flicker of anxiety. He forced himself to be calm. She was only dreaming, after all. As Stan suggested, she was only allowing her subconscious to work things out.

He couldn't help but wonder if he was one of the things she needed to work out.

The door was closer now. She shivered.
Go back.
The glass knob was just inches away. She reached out and grasped it. It was cold beneath her fingers.

The exhibit hall was alive with her dreams.

They flashed on the dark walls, dancing a quicksilver tango on oversized screens.

Their music skirled through the air, curling around the room like tendrils of smoke. Transformed through the synthesizer, their sound was eerie, a tune played in a minor key, like sitar chords mixed with the cries of whales.

During the day a steady flow of visitors wandered into Dark Space. Twice, scheduled groups toured the exhibit. Their voices dropped to whispers as they observed the leaping and singing of the never-to-be-repeated patterns, the experimental multimedia portrait of Soleil's sleeping brain. The darkness of dreams made visible. Then they approached the glass booth. They seldom spoke as they watched her sleep.

.   .   .

Her fingers curled on the cold glass knob.

Go back. Go back. Go back before it is too late.

Ignoring the warning, she turned the knob. The door opened.

CHAPTER 13

Twice staff members spoke to her as she walked down the museum corridor but, still absorbed in her dreams, she only nodded vaguely.

She supposed she must have had several different dreams, but she could remember only one: The dwarf leading her to the white, wood-frame house. The long, dark corridor.

The house had been old, but unfamiliar, one she was sure she had never actually been in.

"Soleil."

She remembered turning the glass knob, pushing open the door. But after that it was blank. Had she actually gone into the room or had Andy woken her just as the door opened? She was slightly dizzy, had been since he had awakened her. Her head ached as she tried to remember the details of the faded maroon carpet and the dark floral wallpaper. She was certain she had never seen them in her waking life.

"Soleil."

But it had been so real.

"Hey, Soleil, wait up."

The persistent shouting broke through her daze.

"Good God," Alison breathed by way of greeting as she caught up with her in the hall.

"What's wrong?" Soleil asked, her voice distracted. She could still feel the cellular memory, the coolness of the glass knob against her palm.

"Wrong?" The intern rolled her eyes toward the ceiling. "She wants to know what's wrong."

Reluctantly, Soleil pushed away the last remnants of her dream.

"I mean, if I'd had any *idea,* any idea at all," Alison breathed, "I would have volunteered in a heartbeat. *In a heartbeat.*"

Soleil fought back a sigh. "Any idea what?"

"You must have wanted to faint on the spot. I mean, he's just to die for. *To die for.*"

"Alison." She grasped the intern's arm. "What in God's name are you talking about?"

"Not what. Who. Andrew McKey. Dr. Andrew McKey." The intern rolled her eyes in a mock swoon. "He's gorgeous. Testosterone city. I mean, how can you possibly fall asleep with him an arm's length away?"

Testosterone city? Soleil shot a glance down the hall to see if any of the staff were within earshot, knowing that if any of this conversation got back to Andy she wouldn't be able to face him.

"He seems nice enough." She resumed walking. The last thing she needed was to talk to Alison about Andy.

"*Nice enough?*" Alison kept stride with her. "Are you blind? He's gorgeous."

"He's good at his job." She stepped up the pace.

"You know who he looks like? He looks like—"

"Alison." Soleil cut her off. "I don't like to talk about co-workers." Gossip traveled through the museum like a virus. You'd think the museum staff would be above that, but they were worse than old ladies.

"Sam Shepard. He looks exactly like Sam Shepard. You know, Jessica Lange's lover."

"I know who Sam Shepard is," she said. It was true, she realized. Andy did look like Shepard.

"Do you know if he's married?" Alison asked.

"Sam Shepard?"

"No. Dr. McKey. He doesn't wear a wedding ring, but that doesn't mean anything. By the way," she said in a maddening switch of subject, "I saw your dreams today. They were intense. *Intense.*"

"You came to the exhibit?" Soleil stopped in midstride.

"It was great. I just loved the way the synthesizer converts the printout into music. It's fabulous. Like sounds from another dimension. I wonder if anyone has ever tried playing dream tapes to whales. You know. To try to communicate that way. I mean, they sound so similar. Have you heard it yet?"

"Not yet." So the staff were coming into the exhibit and watching her sleep. *Watching her sleep.* This was exactly why she hadn't wanted to get involved in the first place.

"Hey, are you all right?"

"I'm fine."

"I don't know. You look kind of pale. You sure you're all right?"

"Really, Alison. I'm fine. How are things upstairs?" She missed the library. The orderliness. The routine. The satisfaction of knowing she was good at her job.

"It's pretty busy without you. They're fascinating, aren't they?"

"What?" Keeping up with the intern's conversation could be exhausting.

"Dreams. Our anthropology professor says that Austra-
lian aborigines think dreams are the reality and that what we
think of as reality is really all a dream. Did you ever hear of
that?"

"No."

"Well, what did you dream about today?"

"I don't remember."

"You should try. Really. Listen, tomorrow I'll bring in some
books about dreams."

"Please, don't."

Alison smiled. "No trouble. It'll give me a reason to drop
by the exhibit and get another look at the gorgeous Andrew
McKey."

"Alison," Soleil said in desperation, "I've got to run. And,
really, don't bother about the books. I'm only going to be
doing this for a few more days."

Outside the museum, Soleil turned right toward the subway.
The September breeze swept in off the harbor.

The thing about the dreams was that they were so vivid.
Perhaps the house was one of the ones she had lived in as a
child, even though she didn't remember it. Some house with a
hall. And patterned carpet, faded wallpaper, a door with an
amethyst knob. She could still feel the sharp coldness of that
knob, the pressure of the facets pressing into her palm. She
saw, too, the overhead light fixture flickering on and off, in
need of repair.

She bit her lip in sudden confusion. The light fixture hadn't
been in her dream. It was in the hall, outside her apartment.
Not in her dream.

It had been on her mind, that was all. The confusion was
just her brain's way of reminding her that she hadn't yet called

Klietman about the light. She made a mental note to do it as soon as she got home. And while she had him on the phone, she'd ask him about replacing the worn carpet.

No.

She rubbed a hand over her eyes. What was happening? The carpet was part of her dream.

A squeal of brakes and the insistent sound of a car horn brought her out of her reverie.

"Jesus, lady," the cabbie yelled. "What the hell you doing? You crazy or just trying to get killed?"

Other horns sounded as cars swerved to avoid her. She stared at the cab, its fender inches from her knee. She stood in the middle of the street two blocks from the museum.

She managed to cross to the curb. Her palms were sweaty and her knees weak as she stepped up to the sidewalk. How had she walked smack into the center of the street without even knowing it?

The cab driver put his car in gear and drove off.

"Weirdos," he said. "The city's fuckin' full of them."

Her mother's condition was unchanged.

"You look better, Mamom," she whispered. "Before long you'll be back in your own bed." There was no indication her mother had heard.

In the next bed, Mrs. Greeley dozed, her dinner untouched on the tray. On the other side of the room, Alice Knowles slept too.

Had they all been drugged? Who was to know if the nurses sedated patients to keep the floor quiet? For that matter, she wondered, how would she know if the doctor had some special notation known only to the staff—a notation that, in spite of her wishes to the contrary, was a code for DNR? She supposed such thinking was paranoid, but she knew these kinds of things happened.

She pulled a chair up close to the bed and began to examine her mother's thin, wasted face. She wondered again when Helen had grown so old. She was rocked by a confusion of emotions. Regret, resentment, guilt, anger, fear. And love. Yes, beneath it all, in spite of everything, there was that too. "I love you, Mamom," she whispered.

Her lifelong struggle to escape her mother's control, her devotion, and the resulting conflicts and resentments that had defined their relationship, all that seemed meaningless now.

Out in the corridor, two nurses walked past the open door. "Well, what I want to know . . ." Their words floated into the room, but they disappeared down the hall before Soleil could hear what it was the speaker wanted to know.

What I want to know . . . What I want to know . . . The words echoed in her head. What *was* it that she wanted to know?

She wanted to know who her father was. And why her mother never mentioned him, had never even shown her a picture of him. She wanted to know where he was. And why he had left.

Once she'd overheard her mother tell a patient that her husband had a job overseas. Soleil had taken that information in, tried to decide what to do with it, but then, on the next job, Helen told her employers that her husband had died in a car accident. Soleil hadn't believed this. She would have known if her father was dead.

The greatest concern of her childhood was that with all the moving they did from job to job, house to house, when he finally came for her, her father would never be able to find them. After each move, she used to send letters to herself care of her last address just to see if they would be forwarded.

What I want to know . . .

No one but her mother could give her the answers she craved, and now, perhaps, she would never speak again.

She took the Pacquins out of her tote and began to massage it into her mother's thin, veined hands. The skin felt drier, hotter than the day before.

"Remember the dream exhibit I told you about? The one that I volunteered for at the museum? I did it again.

"Andy said I had four separate dream periods today, but I only remember having one. I was in a house."

Her mother's hands felt a little cooler now, not as dry. She screwed the lid back on the jar. The particulars of the dream, its vividness, had not diminished.

"It was weird. The house was strange, but it felt so . . . so familiar. Like I'd been there before.

"There was a long hall, with dark floral wallpaper and a faded carpet. At the end of the hall there was this closed door that I needed to open. I felt this sense of danger, but I kept going. I can still remember how the doorknob felt. It was cold. Did I tell you it was glass? Amethyst glass." In the next bed, Mrs. Greeley snored noisily.

"Yesterday, I had a different dream." She paused for a moment, remembering the blond-haired child she'd watched from afar, knowing she would not tell her mother he was Billy Bascombe. "I dreamed I was at a carnival," she continued. She bent to store the lotion in the cabinet of the nightstand.

Turning away, she did not see her mother's eyes move behind translucent closed lids.

CHAPTER 14

Andy drew his stool closer to the equipment and jotted an entry down in his journal. Today, he vowed, he would be meticulous with his notes.

After the exhibit had closed the night before, he had driven to the research center in Worcester and spent nearly three hours poring over case studies of dream subjects. As he had expected, he had found not a single instance of prolonged REM sleep among any of the adult case files. Only babies and very young children experienced REM stages lasting longer than thirty minutes.

He glanced through the narrow window in the partition that separated him from Soleil. While he watched, she stretched, turned on her side, and curled in a tight fetal position. Unexpected longing tightened his chest.

Again today, while attaching the electrodes, he had waited for her to give some sign she still cared about him. He was determined to take his cue from her. But in spite of her cool reserve, he was finding it more and more difficult to stay detached. The sight of her awakened all the old yearning.

Outside, rain coated the plate-glass windows. It was a steady, quiet rainfall, not loud enough to muffle the squishing sound of windshield wipers that beat like metronomes on passing cars.

A man dressed in gray slacks and a navy windbreaker stood apart from the group that huddled by the front entrance of the museum. The Thursday edition of the *Globe* was folded open to the Arts/Living section.

The lead article was lengthy, covering nearly the entire space above the fold, but it was the picture of Soleil Browne that held his attention. He looked up once and checked his watch—10:03—then looked pointedly through the glass. His eyes narrowed with impatience.

Inside, the museum guard inserted his key in the lock. "Nasty morning," he said as he swung the door open.

The man elbowed by.

"Well, hello to you too," the guard muttered under his breath. His tone was mild. He was accustomed to being invisible, unless, of course, someone wanted directions to the rest rooms or help finding a lost child. Within minutes, he had forgotten the man.

In the exhibit, the dream music soared, changed pitch. Andy glanced over at the printout. Soleil had just entered REM.

The whining was faster. The pitch, higher.

She spun through the buzzing vortex into the house, the hall. She saw at once she was not alone.

*At the end of the corridor, by the closed door, she saw the child.
Blond. Clad in overalls. Billy.*

As she watched, Billy reached a hand out to the door's glass knob.

*No. She fought to get the word out. She had to stop him from en-
tering the room. This time she had to save him. No. The word was
muffled.*

She tried again. Stop. No. The soundless cry melted in the air.

*Go back. Get out. She took a step toward him, but as she moved,
the hall began to recede. She fought the fog as it enveloped her.*

A stream of people entered the exhibit hall. Automatically they
lowered their voices. The man in the navy windbreaker separated himself from the group. Walking stealthily, as if not
trusting the padding on the floor to muffle his footsteps, he
passed the pedestal holding the bell jar and the pale, waxen
brain. He ignored the laser lights spilling on the walls around
him and headed straight for the glass booth.

Asleep, Soleil Browne looked younger than in the newspaper
photo. As his eyes adjusted to the dark, he could see the electrodes taped to her temples and beneath her jaw. He noticed
the way the fingers of her exposed hand curled into a fist, the
mound of her hip rising beneath the thin sheet, the shadow of
the curve of her throat. He stepped closer to the booth. His
breath misted the glass. A vein in his temple began to pulse
and his fingers tensed, tightened into fists.

Andy noted Soleil had returned to delta sleep. The first dream
had passed, but, again, it had lasted longer than normal.

He flipped back over the notebook pages and compared
data. On Monday and Tuesday, the initial dream of the series
had lasted ten minutes. On Wednesday it had extended to thir-

teen. Today, Thursday, it had gone on for nearly twenty. Keep cool, he told himself. All this may mean nothing.

A noise from the exhibit's Dark Space caught his attention. A man pressed close to the glass booth and stared at Soleil. Andy forced back a sigh. Soon the man would be coming to the booth with questions so predictable that he could already answer them by rote. He hadn't time for these questions now. He wished Soleil was in a sleep lab where he could witness her dream stages without interruptions.

He turned back to the machines.

Droning.

It was night. She was not in the hall.

The droning, a low hungry sound, swirled in the air like heat. It touched her face with its fingers.

Near her side, there was a wooden chestlike structure. The droning noise was coming from there.

A bee flew from the box. Then another. As she watched, two settled on her naked wrist. She could perceive the touch of their feelers as they moved on her skin. Inside the hive, the buzzing of the swarm grew louder. She groaned.

She took a step away, felt a bee land on her jaw. She moaned again.

Someone was there. She felt his eyes watching, searching. A man. She knew he was more dangerous than the bees. Much worse than the bees. She knew that he too was looking for Billy. A monster man who would take Billy away. Take him below the water and hold him until his body bloated and his face dripped from his bones. A shadow of a man. A shadow man.

Once again, she moaned.

. . .

The man left the *Dreamscape* exhibit reluctantly. He would have liked to stay, to watch the woman sleeping. To observe without being himself observed. But he could not risk drawing attention to himself.

He walked past the bell jar, crossed the padded floor, and went out into the Light Space. He edged through the crowd, careful not to brush against the rain-damp bodies that were filling the room.

Once outside in the long hall of the museum's first floor, he again unfolded his newspaper. Carefully, he tore the front page of the Arts/Living section free and folded it into precise quarters. He looked one last time at the photo of Soleil Browne before slipping it into the inside pocket of his windbreaker. On his way out of the museum, he tossed the rest of the *Globe* into a trash container. He practiced saying her name, the fullness of it inside his mouth. On his lips.

The afternoon went quickly. A steady stream of visitors, including a troop of giggling Girl Scouts, had come through the exhibit. The girls had reminded Andy of his young nieces. He'd seen his sister Nancy's children only once since he'd been back from the West Coast. He decided that after work, he'd call Nan and invite himself up for dinner over the weekend. He needed a break from the museum—and from seeing Soleil each day. A trip to New Hampshire would give him distance, and maybe some perspective.

When the exhibit doors finally closed, he checked the paper drum. The polysomnograph indicated Soleil was still in REM sleep. This time she had been in the final dream stage for nearly an hour.

He switched off the machine and entered the glass booth. For several minutes he stood by the narrow bed and observed her. She slept like a child. She was sweating slightly and a strand of hair lay across her cheek, stuck there with sleep sweat. He resisted the impulse to brush it back.

Daylight. Sounds swirled in her head. She was dizzy with them. The whirling from the tunnel. The hungry droning of the bees.

She looked around for the shadow man, knowing he was the danger, but she could not see him anymore. Then, by a shed, hiding behind a sheet hanging from a clothesline, she saw the child. Billy.

He stood not an arm's length away now. He was thin, terribly thin, as if his bones had grown too fast for flesh to pad and protect.

Then he turned toward her and she saw it was not Billy. Not Billy. It was a girl.

The scrim—a membrane that had separated her from the beginning—dropped away. She gasped. There was nothing to spare her, to soften the horrific sight of the child's disfigurement. The cruelly puckered skin, the ruined bone.

She wanted to escape. This was worse than seeing Billy. But the child looked at her and she could not run.

She did not hear what the child was saying. She gazed at the girl's scarred cheek and then looked into her eyes. Something sharp stirred behind her breasts, deep beneath her ribs.

"Soleil?" He spoke her name gently, but she only curled tighter into herself. Her absolute stillness unnerved him.

"Soleil?" Louder this time.

He reached over and nudged her arm. Her skin was cool. A chill washed over him.

"Soleil?"

She whimpered, then tightened into her fetal sleep position.

Jesus, this was queer. He grasped her arm above the elbow. "Soleil, wake up."

She moved then, unfolded like a flower and rolled onto her

back. Her eyes were unfocused. She stared at him, puzzled. As if, he suddenly thought, she were surfacing from an underground well. Or a cave.

"Sorry to wake you," he said. He realized he was whispering and forced his voice to a normal pitch. "It's time to get you unhitched." He reached out to remove an electrode.

She shrank back from him, fear flashing over her face. He felt a quick twist in his belly. He willed it away. "You okay?"

Her face was pale, sheeted with sweat. She closed her eyes. "I'm going to be sick," she whispered.

"Hold on," he said. Her fingers were icy in his hands. "Just hold on a minute." He stripped off the electrodes, than helped her sit up. All color had drained from her face.

Gently he bent her head down between her knees. "Just try and take some deep breaths," he instructed.

Twenty minutes passed before her color improved and she was strong enough to change into street clothes.

"Better now?" he asked when she came out of the dressing room.

"I don't know what happened to me. I was so dizzy."

Her color was back, but he still didn't like the look in her eyes. "Did you eat this morning?"

She stared out at the exhibit walls.

"Soleil?"

"What? I'm sorry. What did you say?"

"Did you have breakfast before you came to the museum?"

"No. I don't think so."

Andy fumbled with the wires and argued silently with himself. "Listen," he finally said. "I'm just about finished up here. Why don't we grab a cup of coffee and a bite to eat?"

She rubbed her eyes.

"What do you say?" Andy asked. "It's probably a good idea to get something in your stomach before you pass out again."

"I didn't pass out," she said. Her voice was weak.

"I know a place about five minutes from here. They have delicious soup. Groovy soup," he added in an attempt to make her smile. But she only stared blankly ahead.

CHAPTER 15

Soleil inhaled, welcoming the crisp, rain-freshened air, allowing it to clear her head.

Andy unfurled his umbrella. "The place I had in mind is over on Memorial Drive. The Sail Loft. We can walk, if you don't mind the rain."

"That's fine," she said. Memorial Drive. She wondered if he too was remembering that summer six years ago and the walks they used to take along the Charles when it rained. His umbrella drew them close; her raincoat swish-swished against him. His nearness made her shy.

"Have you eaten there before?"

"No," she said. She wondered when he had gone there. Whom he had taken.

They turned left onto Edward Land Boulevard. She felt his gaze.

"Feeling better?" he asked.

"Oh. Yes. I'm fine." Fine. What was it Mimi said *fine* stood for? Fucked up, insecure, neurotic, and emotional. She had to admit that just about summed up how she'd felt since seeing him again.

They continued along the river, an awkward silence between them. She wondered if he was already regretting the invitation.

They approached the Longfellow Bridge, and for a moment the memory was so strong she had to close her eyes. It had been raining that night, too. After dinner, they had strolled along the Charles. Tipsy from wine and desire, he had pulled her beneath the bridge, drawn her to him, kissed her greedily, tugged her skirt above her hips. They had stayed under the bridge for a long time. Could he have forgotten that night?

He took hold of her elbow. "You sure you're okay?"

"Yes. Really." She could feel the press of his fingers through the fabric of her coat. Even after all this time, his touch felt electric. She inhaled deeply. One quick cup of coffee, she promised herself, then she'd escape.

While they waited for the hostess in the lobby, he studied the Stobart prints. "Port of Annapolis," he said, pointing to one. His grin revealed the chipped front tooth. Her heart jumped.

He nodded toward the other print. "Recognize it?"

She realized that he was struggling to find an impersonal topic. It helped to know this. "No."

"Port of New York."

"Lovely," she said. The word sounded inane, like something Connolly might say.

"There's a special appeal to the East Coast ports. Nothing in the West matches them. I guess I'm just a chauvinistic Yankee at heart."

Then why did you leave? she wanted to say.

"It's good to be back," he continued. "I've really missed this place."

She pressed her lips together to keep from asking if he had missed her too.

"Dining room or the deck café?" the hostess asked. "Our deck's enclosed."

He turned to her. "What'll it be?"

She started to say it didn't matter, but it seemed important to take command, to be decisive, even in this small choice. "Deck," she said.

They sat at a table by a wall of glass overlooking both Memorial Drive and the Charles. The soft patter of rainfall played on the awning. She traced her forefinger over the nautical charts that decorated the tabletop. Suddenly the face of the child in her dreams emerged from the chart lines. She raised her fingers to her own cheek. Felt the smoothness of her skin, but the touch did not erase the image of the girl's face. The flesh and bone cruelly misshapen, the skin disfigured by the scar. So it had not been Billy after all. But still, the poor child.

"Can I get you something from the bar?" A young waitress dressed in khaki shorts and a blue polo shirt interrupted her reverie.

She wanted wine, but didn't order it, settling for coffee.

"Only coffee?" Andy said. "That's all you want?"

She nodded. She didn't think she could afford to drink, to lower her guard while she was with him. And she was still slightly nauseated by the dreams.

The waitress recited the daily specials.

"Just the coffee," she said again.

"You sure?" Andy asked. "The fish and chips are terrific here. Chowder's good, too."

The thought of food made her queasy. "No, really. Just coffee."

He ordered the fish and chips for himself, then, for her, clam chowder. "Just try it," he insisted when she argued. "You should eat."

She felt the old ambivalence. Resentment at his treating her like a child and warmth at being cared for. "You can't have it both ways," he'd said once when she had told him this.

The waitress returned with a basket of rolls.

Andy nodded toward the Charles. "Look." A Harvard scull team was training. As their hull knifed through the water, the scullers' bodies bent and arced.

Through the rain, the faces of the rowers looked misshapen. Again she thought of the girl.

"You ever try it?" he asked.

"What?"

"Sculling."

"No." The girl had been so thin. But at the memory of the child's eyes, she again felt something move deep in her breast.

"A quarter?"

"What?"

"You're so lost in them that even accounting for inflation, they have to be worth more than a penny."

"Sorry. Just thinking."

He smiled, but just below the smile, she saw annoyance. Determined to concentrate, she sat up and pulled her mind away from the child. Only a piece of a dream, that's all. And the evil man—for she knew he was evil—was, too, only a dream.

"It's really odd," he said.

"What?"

"I don't know. *Dreamscape.* Our being together. It seems like such a coincidence."

She forced herself to hold his gaze. "You said you don't believe in coincidence. That's what you said the other day."

"Do you?"

"I don't know."

An awkward silence fell between them.

"I was surprised—" He cut the sentence short.

"What?"

"Nothing."

"I hate it when you do that."

"I was going to say I was surprised you never wrote."

"Neither did you." She returned the volley without pause. How easy it was to slip back into the game. Apportioning blame. A game no one won. It had been a mistake to have come with him, but one she wouldn't make twice.

"You're the one who left," she said quietly.

"I had to. I had to go to Stanford. It was a fabulous opportunity."

"Well, I guess we all do what we have to do."

She wondered how many stories ended like theirs because people did what they had to do.

"We're not going to fight, are we?" he asked now. "Aren't we too smart for that?"

"Too smart and too old," she agreed. She felt tired.

Unfinished business lay in the air like stale smoke.

He picked up the salt and pepper shakers and began moving them about the table like chessmen.

She watched him fiddle with the glass shakers. His fingers were long and strong. She noticed, near the wrist of his left hand, a jagged V-shaped scar about an inch across. She wondered how he'd gotten it. Once she'd known nearly everything about him. That he was the oldest of four and doted on his youngest sister, a woman christened Patricia but dubbed Ricky at birth. That he despised experimental theater and loved Marx brothers movies and poetry, especially the Romantic poets. That his favorite breakfast was sliced bananas on buckwheat pancakes and that he hated cottage cheese. That he liked to sleep on his back.

She stared at the tiny scar on his hand. It seemed symbolic of all that had happened to him since they had parted, changing him, marking him in ways she couldn't understand. She wanted to touch the mark, run her finger over it.

"How—" she started, then stopped. To talk about the years apart in any meaningful way would be to open a door and let something in, and she couldn't do that.

Her attention was drawn away as two soaked and laughing students entered the café. The boy said something and his date, a slender co-ed dressed in a neon-green slicker and jeans, laughed even harder. "You're terrible," she trilled, and hugged his arm tighter. Her eyes never left his face.

Andy glanced at the couple. "Young lust," he said. Then added, "Remember?"

Her face flushed hotly. "Don't," she said.

"You're right. Sorry."

She was grateful when the waitress brought their order.

The chowder was thick and hot. She took several spoonfuls, aware of deep hunger, and then was angry that even in this he had been right. She shook her head when he offered her some of his fish.

"Almost forgot." He took a package out of a bag from the museum. "Here. Your intern dropped by the exhibit today. She asked me to give these to you."

God. Alison. *Testosterone city.* Had that conversation already traveled the museum grapevine?

She opened the first book in the pile and saw Alison's sprawling signature. The *i* was fat and loopy and the intern had dotted it with a circle.

She could feel Andy watching her. Her throat closed and she set the spoon down.

"Why didn't you tell me the first day?" he asked.

"What?"

"About Helen. Connolly told me she was in the hospital."

"The doctor said it was a stroke."

"I'm sorry," he said.

The sadness brought on by thinking of her mother threatened to sweep in, drowning her, and she pushed it back.

"Would it be all right to visit her? Or go with you sometime?"

"No." The kindness in his voice—in spite of everything—

nearly broke her, and her refusal was harsher than she'd intended. She saw his face close.

"It's funny," he said, "but I'm not feeling either too wise or too old to fight right now."

Determined not to be drawn in, she resumed eating the chowder.

"Okay," he said. "Subject closed."

"So tell me, Soleil," he said after a moment, "what are they like?"

"What?"

"Your dreams."

The tunnel. The whirling, whining. The dwarf and then hall with the closed door. The bees. She shivered, remembering the faint scratching of insect legs on her arm. "Kind of like going to a movie," she said. "Like watching a play."

He smiled. "You don't know how true that is. When you're in REM sleep your eyes move in unison, from side to side."

A dream play.

"The eyes in REM," Andy continued, "behave almost as if the sleeper were watching a performance."

But it wasn't like that. Not *at* a movie. *In* a movie. She pushed the soup away. "It's like watching something happen, but not being able to prevent it."

"Anxiety dreams," he said. "I had those the night before every physics exam. A colleague of mine says it's by dreaming that we work out what troubles us during our waking hours."

"Do you agree with him? I mean, do you agree with Freud, or Jung? That our dreams are conceived in our subconscious?" This at last was safe territory.

"Electrical impulses."

"What?"

"I think they're electrical impulses."

"That's it?"

He laughed. "I'm a scientist, remember, not a psychiatrist."

She had to laugh too and, at the sound of their joined laughter, sensed that it would be easy to slip back. He set the shakers down and reached across the table for her wrist. A charge surged through her and she knew that in spite of everything and against her best intentions, they could easily wind up in bed. He felt it too. She read that in his eyes. On the pretense of using her napkin, she pulled her hand away.

Her weakness angered her. As easily as a meal together, a touch of his hand, and she was ready to surrender. She knew friendship was impossible, but so was going back. She wasn't about to lose her soul to him again.

"What movie were you watching in your dreams today?" he asked after a moment. Impartial ground again.

She turned her attention back to the Charles. The scull team was closer now. The laughter of the girl in the neon-green raincoat floated through the café.

"I don't remember." But she did, of course. The child had been haunting her, floating in and out of her mind since she had left the museum.

"Hey, I'm not trying to pry," he said. He signaled for more coffee. "Do you want anything else? Dessert?"

She shook her head. Glimpses of the child pressed against her brain until it throbbed.

"You sure you're okay?"

She nodded, turned her face toward Memorial Drive.

"This isn't as easy as I thought it would be," he said softly. "Sitting with you like this."

She didn't answer, hadn't heard him.

"Soleil?"

She stared out the window. Blood drained from her face.

"It's her."

"Who?"

She stood, pushing the chair back abruptly.

"Who? It's who?" He turned to look out the window, but

she had already left the table. She ran across the deck, past the co-ed in the green slicker, through the restaurant, past the Stobart prints.

Outside on Memorial Drive, she squinted against the pelting rain. "Wait," she called, startling a group of students. She'd gone only half a block before her clothes were drenched, her hair plastered against her face. *It had been her.* Strands of hair fell in her eyes and she brushed them back impatiently. "Wait," she cried out again. "Please, wait."

She felt hands on her shoulders. "Here. You left this." Andy drapped her raincoat over her shoulders. "You're soaked," he said, pulling her into the shelter of a doorway.

"I have to find her," she whispered. She twisted her head, scanning the now-empty street, surprised to find herself blinking back tears. She who never cried.

"Hey. What's wrong?" He put an arm around her, took her hands in his.

"I have to find her."

"Who?"

"A child. A girl."

"Someone you know?"

The child *had* been there. She was sure of it. She pulled her hands free of his and pressed her fingers against her temples. Only a dream. Only a dream. Only a dream.

"Soleil? What's wrong? Who is this girl?"

She saw the concern on his face. Tell him, she urged herself. But tell him what? Admit the girl was just a shadowy figure from a dream? And what then? Add that she'd run out in the rain after a nonexistent child? He would think she was crazy.

She began to shiver.

"I have to go," she said abruptly.

Impossible as it seemed, the girl did exist. She had seen her. Right there in the middle of Cambridge. And she knew the child needed her help.

CHAPTER 16

The morning after her pa's funeral, the Cades came for Shoe. She sat on the porch, clutching her suitcase and waiting as the old black car turned into the drive. Mr. Cade was driving. Ruby Cade was perched on the seat next to him. He stayed in the car and kept the engine running while the old woman got out. She didn't speak or smile as she came toward Shoe, just held out her hand, as if everything were already settled. Shoe was glad that she didn't try to take the suitcase from her as they walked toward the car. Springs poked up through the up-holstery of the backseat and she settled herself carefully.

She sat stiffly, her suitcase on her lap, determined not to look back at the house, but just as Elmer Cade turned the wheel and the car pulled out of the drive, she twisted her head and peeked. The farm already wore the empty look of property deserted.

The Cades' place was south of town and just east of the crossroads. The house itself was small, not much bigger than

the galvanized shed perched in the side yard where Elmer Cade
fiddled with engines. The skin around his fingers was rimmed
with black from the engines, a coarse grease that did not wash
out like the garden soil did from Ruby's hands.

Ruby Cade led her to the room she had prepared for her. It
contained a narrow bed and a bureau made of dark wood. It
was cleaner than Shoe would have thought. On top of the bureau there was a glass tumbler with a bunch of wildflowers
stuffed inside. Weeds, Mrs. Sharp would call them. The sight
of them, knowing Ruby Cade had put them there for her,
made Shoe's throat tighten. For the first time since she realized
Thomas had gone, the emptiness in her stomach eased a little.

The Cades weren't Fortune people. They'd traveled up from
Kentucky seven years before. White trash hill folk, Mrs. Sparks
had said.

"Why'd you take me in?" Shoe asked the second night.

Ruby didn't answer right away. She was setting chicken
windpipes out on the porch railing, drying them for knitting
needles. The thin, silvery rods glowed in the dusty moonlight,
looking prettier than what they were.

"Thuh preacher askt us."

They were not churchgoing folks, and the answer left Shoe
frustrated, wanting more.

She thought that houses were either lucky or unlucky, but
she couldn't decide about this house yet. Or about the Cades.
As the days passed, she looked for clues.

Tacked above the kitchen sink was a photo pockmarked
with a splattering of bacon fat. It was a picture of a thin-faced
man in an army uniform whose eyes reminded her of Thomas.
His face seemed to have nothing do to with the people who
lived in this house.

"Mah boy. Jessie," Ruby told her. "He come back from thuh
war whole but died in Kentucky." She gave the story out as

plain and even as if she were reciting the price of chicken feed. "Died when they fired on thuh strikers."

Shoe knew Reverend Hill would say they lost their son in payment for sins, but she stumbled on that thought. Ruby Cade seemed to carry less sin in her mouth than Mrs. Sparks ever did, but God had never taken Sarah Sparks away. Even before she'd been baptized and saved.

Sarah was the first in the seventh grade to be washed clean of sin and reborn to the Lord. In the last week before her baptism, she refused to play with the other girls. She walked around the schoolyard in her green store-bought dress, behaving like she was already saved.

The following Sunday, Reverend Hill called Sarah up to the front of the church. He wore rubber boots that looked like pants except they reached his armpits. As the preacher crossed to the choir loft in a high-stepping, chicken-yard walk, his neck bobbing forward with each step, Shoe felt a dangerous bubble of laughter threaten in her belly and had to bite the insides of her cheeks to keep it in.

Laughing in church was sure to bring on a beating, but sometimes she just couldn't help it. Once Mr. Emery, who owned the grain and feed store and who everyone in Fortune agreed was the finest tenor to ever sing in the First Baptist choir, farted right at the end of a solo. Just as he hit the high note, he erupted, not once but three times, each a long trumpetlike note. With each outburst, his face grew redder, but he held on to the note as if fighting for his life. In the pew behind her one of the Wheeler twins leaned forward until she could feel his breath on her neck. "Beans, beans, the musical fruit," he began. His brother took it up. "The more you eat, the more you toot." Shoe had laughed until she peed her pants.

That had earned her a beating and she was determined not to laugh at the sight of the preacher with his high boots and bobbing head.

Sarah, all dressed up in a white baptism robe, tried to look pure, but the whole congregation could see by the way she carried herself that she was as proud as could be. There were weights sewn in the hem of the robe so it wouldn't float up and cause a shameful display of legs.

The preacher slid open the wood-paneled doors that concealed the baptism room beneath the loft and led her down the steps. With his help, she climbed into the tub and crossed her arms over her chest, still trying to appear pious, but managing only to look smug. Shoe wondered if anyone had ever drowned, and then tried to push the upstart thought straight out of her head.

Reverend Hill got into the tub too. He clasped his right hand over Sarah's crossed arms and placed his left behind her neck. "I baptize you in the name of the Father, the Son, and the Holy Ghost," he said in his important preacher's voice. Then, still cradling her, he lowered her into the water. When Sarah resurfaced, water streaming down her face and dripping from her hair, Shoe relaxed again. Not that she'd ever wished Sarah would die, exactly, but Miss Rogers said thoughts were powerful things and if Sarah was to drown, Shoe didn't want it on her conscience.

The congregation broke into applause and Mrs. Sparks cried, "Praise the Lord," as her daughter climbed out of the tub. "Praise the Lord, praise the Lord," echoed the congregation. Later, outside in the churchyard, Sarah sidled over and whispered, "If my face looked like yours, I'd kill myself 'cause I'd be too ugly to live," and it was clear as could be that baptism hadn't washed Sarah's mean mouth clean.

.   .   .

No, Shoe decided as she stared at the grease-spotted photo in Ruby's kitchen. If the Lord didn't punish Sarah or Mrs. Sparks for speaking hateful thoughts, it didn't seem likely he would take the Cades' son away because Ruby said "ain't" and smoked a pipe. But Shoe couldn't be certain about that. She wasn't sure about much concerning the Lord. So much of what she heard in church didn't set right with what she saw. Like why any fair God would punish the Cades by taking their son and let someone like Mr. Roubiam get rich.

Ruby Cade was nothing like any other woman Shoe knew. She not only smoked a pipe and said "ain't," but she wore trousers and men's shoes. She gave no mind at all to what others thought and was the only adult Shoe knew who worked barefoot while weeding the snap peas and pole beans. "Ah got tuh plant mah feet in thuh earth," she'd say, her hoe chop-chopping the ground between the flowering peas. Before long, Shoe was stripping off her own shoes when she worked beside Ruby. She never knew a chore could be fun. She grew to love the feel of warm soil against her toes.

There was more she liked about Ruby. It was true that the old lady spoke her thoughts straight out, but she didn't have a spiteful mouth like Mrs. Sparks. Once, testing her, Shoe said, "I'm glad my pa's dead." She waited for Ruby to say she was hard-hearted and mean, but the old lady didn't scold or preach. She only reached over with her thin, freckled hand and laid it on Shoe's.

And even when looking her full in the face Ruby never seemed to see her scar. Sometime in the first three weeks she lived there, Shoe even forgot her cheek was caved in.

Still, she'd learned not to count on anything lasting. She kept her suitcase with her heavy coins packed and made plans for the day when she would have to leave.

Most of all, she missed Thomas. She wondered if he was with the carnival and where it had gone after Fortune. Missing Thomas was a hungry ache in her stomach that never let go.

Today, her chore was delivering eggs in town. Before she set off, she refused the hat Ruby Cade held out.

Child, you're just plain stubborn, her ma's voice chided when she'd rejected Ruby's offer.

Now, minutes later, her shoulders were already sore where her overall straps chafed her skin, and overhead, the sun was white. Inside her skull, a pulse throbbed with a hot, liquid beat.

Stubborn, her ma insisted.

"Well, maybe I am," she told the voice in her head, "but I won't be beholden for some old hat." She was already beholden to the Cades for more than she liked, and taking Ruby's hat would only have added to the list. Just thinking of it made her throat hurt. Charity did that, stuck in her throat like a living thing, clotting it so she couldn't swallow or speak.

It had not rained in weeks and dust rose from the road, coating her until she could taste it on her tongue. The egg basket grew heavy and she switched it to her other hand. Twice now she'd walked into town to deliver honey or eggs for Ruby Cade. When she returned home and handed over the cash, Ruby dropped it in the egg jug. After the first time, Shoe was visited with the notion of slipping a nickel out of the change. Once this idea found a home in her head, it settled in, troubling her with its constant buzzing, buzzing. Pesky and persistent as a deerfly in July.

A pickup rattled by. Dust swirled from its tires, stuck to her sweat-sheened legs, made her cough.

The Stonelick ran off to her right, beyond the cottonwood stand. She shivered in spite of the sun and thought of Mattie Lynn Hayes.

The March she turned thirty-nine, Mattie Lynn gave birth

to her first child. A "change baby," the women called it, although Shoe didn't know what kind of change he could be. There were boy babies and girl babies and she didn't know any other kind, least of all one called a change. Maybe it meant bad luck, because one week after his ma gave him life, the baby died. All through the funeral service, Mattie Lynn sat staring straight ahead and Shoe knew just by looking at the woman that whatever she was hearing, it wasn't the preacher's words. After the first thaw, they took the baby over to the graveyard and buried him with the other Hayeses' kin. Two days later, Mattie Lynn jumped in the river and drowned.

Shoe thought of Mattie Lynn whenever she got close to the Stonelick. It seemed to her that by taking a life, the river came alive, as much a creature of the earth as a snake.

In the spring, the water was swollen and, running swift and deep with melted snows, flooded the lower pasture of their farm. In winter, the Stonelick was different, dangerous. Under black ice, it crackled and called; Shoe covered her ears whenever she came near. In summer, it was quieter, a reptile that didn't give warning before it struck.

A mosquito bit her calf. She slapped at it and blood smeared her skin. Her heart beat time with the heat. Through the cottonwoods, she heard the cold, dark water calling. If she wasn't so dry-mouthed and nearly sick from the sun, she would have kept walking to town.

She turned toward the river. Instantly the canopy of green, heart-shaped leaves cooled her. Thousands of silky-haired cottonwood seeds cushioned the earth beneath her feet. The musky smell of decaying leaves, disturbed by her toes, made her sneeze.

She smelled the river before she saw it. Thirst drove her out of the tree shade. Beyond the banks, the water flowed and sparkled with the play of the sun.

She rounded a laurel bush and was so startled she jumped, actually felt her feet leave the ground. The hairs on her arms stood up as straight as a startled cat's.

Sweet Jesus, she thought. He's dead.

A colored boy lay stretched out beneath the laurel branches, as still and lifeless as her pa had been when they'd laid him out on the dining-room table.

Before her brain could direct her feet to run, the boy groaned. Not dead, then, but what? Unconscious? Asleep? Her fingers tightened on the egg basket. She crept an inch closer.

There weren't many coloreds in Fortune. Except for the men who worked in Mr. Roubiam's sawmill and one or two boys who ran errands for him, they all stayed to themselves over in Coaltown. They had their own schoolhouse and church there. Usually white folk had no call to travel over there, but one Sunday after their ma had died, she and Thomas walked clear as far as Ebenezer Baptist. She could still remember the sound of singing floating from the church. It bore no resemblance to the proper hymn singing of First Baptist. It was uncontained. A leaping sound of celebration and sorrow that caused her to laugh even while a hurt settled in her chest. She'd been glad Thomas couldn't hear it, although she couldn't have said why.

The boy groaned again.

Pa had warned them about niggers and hobos. Bunch of lazy thieves and liars, he had said. Said she and Thomas should stay clear of them if they knew what was good for them. She strained to hear a car or truck passing by up on River Road, but the only sound she heard was the mewing song of a catbird back in the cottonwood stand. She took another step closer to the boy.

Curiosity goin' to kill you, girl, sure as it kills a cat, her ma's voice scolded.

She ignored the voice and her own beating heart and took another step. There wasn't any blood on him. No open wounds. He was skinny and, judging by his size, he had to be about fourteen, same as Thomas. She took in his thick, cropped hair, his flattish noise, and the small, serious ears set close to his head. Ash-color streaks ran down his cheeks, like he'd been scratching there.

She was nearly close enough now to touch him. She wanted to, wanted to see if his skin felt as velvety as it looked. It was the color of stove-blacking, so dark another color seemed to be hiding underneath.

His leg twitched and she drew back. Her heart took up pounding. Then he gave a long, shuttering, hiccuping sound, just like Reverend Hill's youngest did when she'd wailed herself to sleep.

She understood then about the smudges on his cheeks. He'd been crying. Her heart settled back into its normal rhythm. She had nothing to fear from a crybaby colored boy.

A reflection caught her eye in the bed of yellow grass and moldering leaves. She set the egg basket down and bent for a closer look. A quarter lay next to the boy's open fist.

"Well, I'll be a hen's first egg," she whispered before she could catch herself. A quarter. What the devil would a colored boy be doing with a quarter? Where'd he get it? *Thieves and liars,* Pa's voice echoed. *They'd as soon steal as breathe.*

She was quite sure it was real, not fake like the foil-covered chocolate coins Miss Rogers had given the class at Christmas. As she reached forward to touch it, a chill rolled along her spine. She felt his eyes on her. The boy was awake.

She stumbled back, had to scramble to keep from falling. He twisted to his feet.

Sweat shone on the muscles of his arms and chest. Crybaby or not, he was a lot bigger than he'd looked lying down. The egg basket sat on the ground between them. He blocked the path to River Road.

Now you've done it, girl, her ma's voice said.

She could run fast, faster than any girl in the seventh grade, and she probably could escape easy enough, but if she ran, it would mean leaving Ruby's egg basket behind.

His eyes flickered toward the coin.

She thought of her pa's Mason jar filled with quarters and dimes. *Just keep your mouth shut, girl, and get out of here,* her ma warned.

"You stole it, didn't you?" she said.

"Ah din't." His eyes widened. His voice was hoarse, like it had been scraped dry.

"Yes, you did."

"Din't."

"Did too."

"Nah, suh, Ah din't."

"Where'd you get it, then?" His denial infuriated her. "Where're you goin' to get a quarter?"

He looked directly into her face, not even stopping at the scar on her cheek. His eyes turned dark and mournful and suddenly he looked much older than Thomas. Fear twisted up out of the ground, coiling round her legs like a berry vine. She should have listened to her ma's warning and kept her mouth shut.

"Ah din't steal hit."

He moved suddenly. She jumped back, but he didn't reach for her. He grabbed Ruby's basket. Lifted it high. She saw he meant to smash it. "Ah says Ah din't steal hit."

Suddenly the outline of his arm against the sun sent her to another time, another place. Their ma lying inside the house, coughing up blood, bright red, not brownish like usual. Thomas running from the house. Out behind the back side of the barn, Thomas standing over his toy wagon, pounding with the rock over and over until there was nothing left but splinters. Later, she'd buried those fragments so that their pa wouldn't find them and beat Thomas again.

The memory faded.

She was no longer afraid of the colored boy, any more than she'd be afraid of Thomas. She could never help her brother when he was hurt either.

"It's okay." She made her voice soft, like she was hushing one of the preacher's young ones. She wished she had something to give him. Something sweet to take away whatever was hurting him. Sweet like Mrs. Hill's barley candy or a square of Ruby's apple cake.

The basket trembled in his hands.

"Please, don't break them," she whispered. "If you break them, I'll get beat."

The basket froze in midair. "Yer pa strap yo'?" he asked in his bruised voice.

"Not now. He's dead."

"Yer pa's dead?" He lowered the basket an inch.

She was quick to see the advantage this information gave her. "So's my ma."

"Yer ma, too?"

"Both of them. I'm an orphan."

"Whut's dat?"

"Someone with no ma or pa."

He hesitated, then handed her the basket. She knew she could have left then.

"What's your name?" she asked.

"Robert. But everybody call me Gee Whiz." He grinned and suddenly turned young again.

"My name's Reba Grace," she said. "But everyone calls me Shoe."

"Shoe. Dat's a funny name."

"No funnier than Gee Whiz," she said. She liked that he didn't stare at her scar like most folks did.

"Whut yo' doin here?" he asked after a minute.

"Gettin' a drink. What're you doin' here?"

His eyes did that peculiar trick that made him look old and scary. He looked down at the coin.

"Did you steal it?"

"Nah, suh."

"Where'd you get it, then?"

"Nowar."

"You must of stole it or you'd tell me where you got it. You stole it, didn't you?"

She thought he wasn't going to answer. The coin twinkled in the grass.

"Hit's—hit's devil money."

She felt a curling in her chest. *Devil's money.*

In one of the cottonwoods, a catbird whistled.

"Devil money," he said again. His voice turned dark and spooky, like he was talking about some shadowy thing not even a preacher could speak of.

She dared a quick look over her shoulder, gauging the distance to the trees.

Get going, child, her ma urged, but before she could run, the boy swooped the coin out of the dry grass and headed toward the river. *Now, child, now.*

He ran with an odd, hobbled gait. When he reached the bank, he walked over the brown river stones and stepped into the water, waded in right up to where it covered his knees. She remembered Mattie Lynn Hayes and wanted to look away, but she couldn't.

The boy drew back his arm. Her eyes followed the quarter's spinning, shining revolutions until it disappeared into the Stonelick.

He threw the quarter away.

The coil of fear came alive in her chest. He had to be plumb crazy to be throwing money away, no matter where it came from.

He started back toward her. She pulled her eyes from his, cradled the egg basket in her arms, and ran for the cottonwoods.

Back on River Road, she walked quickly, no longer mindful of the midday sun or the weight of the egg basket, only trying to put distance between herself and the crazy black boy by the river. She walked to town as fast as she could without causing the eggs to crack.

CHAPTER 17

Mr. Roubiam's front walk was narrow and bordered by a clipped green lawn, though by now most everyone's in Fortune had turned yellow and dry. The porch steps were painted white and looked like they weren't meant to be walked on. Shoe went around to the back.

Inside, the kitchen was cool and smelled of a place not much light got to. The shades were pulled down against the noontime sun. She set the basket on the counter and unloaded the eggs into the wire basket by the sink. Just like Ruby Cade had showed her.

Her chore done, she turned to go. The silence of the house echoed behind her.

She was all alone in the Bogeyman's house.

Even in the quiet, there were sounds. Whisperings, faint creakings, the buzz of a fly crawling on a window, little scratching noises, like the house was trying to tell its secret.

Leave the eggs and git, girl, her ma's voice warned.

Behind the kitchen door, the rest of the house beckoned to her, a delicious, dangerous call.

All the rumors shook inside her head like a rattler's tail. *He kept women. He had a fortune hidden inside his house.*

She took a step toward the door that led to the hall. I won't touch anything, she quieted her ma's scolding voice. I just want to look.

What kind of fancy things had he bought with all his money? With the farmers' mortgage money and money from his sawmill? With the insurance money her pa had paid him, money meant to fix her face?

The hall floor creaked underfoot.

"Mr. Roubiam," she ventured softly. When there was no answer, she called again, louder. The house was silent.

What could it hurt? Who would know?

The living room was twice the size of any she'd ever seen, with furniture upholstered dark purple. There was a lot of furniture for a man who lived alone. Heavy purple and green drapes covered the windows. It felt as if the air in this room never changed. A shiver ran up her back as she thought she smelled him, a lingering odor of bay rum and whiskey.

Stairs led to a second floor. An electric chill of fear and daring brought gooseflesh to her arms.

Thomas would have stopped her. But Thomas wasn't there. She climbed the stairs to a long, narrow hall laid with carpet. The bay rum scent was stronger here. If Mr. Roubiam had any secrets in this house, this was where she'd find them.

She continued down the hall. There were four doors, all closed. It was the one at the end of the hall that drew her. Beneath the bay rum, she smelled a heavy sweet smell she named death.

Get out. Hurry, child. Leave now. Her ma's voice, but somehow not her ma's voice.

The hall was empty, but still Shoe glanced over her shoulder. The voice was so real.

Now, child. Get out now. Now!

The insistent voice frightened her.

She ran down the stairs, stopping just long enough to grab the empty egg basket from the kitchen table before she escaped.

She reached the sidewalk just as the green Packard pulled into the yard. The car's body reflected light as if it were made of glass, not metal, and the winged lady on the hood glinted in the sun. Paralyzed as a fox-struck rabbit, she watched Mr. Roubiam climb out of the car. Before he walked into the house, his hand fell on the fender and floated over his car in a caress.

She was dizzy with the thought of how nearly he'd come to catching her.

I'll never do that again. She trembled to think of what he would have done if he'd caught her snooping. *Never again.*

But by the time she'd walked as far as River Road, she set to wondering what was behind the closed doors upstairs in Mr. Roubiam's house.

"Why does Mr. Roubiam have such a big house?" she asked Ruby. Several days had passed since she had delivered the eggs.

"Whut you wantin' tuh know fer?"

"Just wonderin'," she replied. She couldn't stop thinking about the dark and meager rooms of her ma and pa's farmhouse. The memory of broken balustrades, the porch wanting paint. And she couldn't stop reflecting on Mr. Roubiam's house with its large, purple-furnished rooms and its white porch shining like feet never so much as tiptoed across its floor. "Why does one man need such a big house?"

"Thuh laks of Mr. Roubiam always be gettin' more 'n thuh

rest of us. Thet's the way hit is, so don't you go and be frettin'
on such questions, 'cause ther ain't no answer."

"It's not fair."

Ruby looked straight at her. "And don't you go be lookin'
fer life tah be fair." She took Elmer's long coat and her veiled
hat off their peg by the door.

"I hate him."

"Oh, don't you be wastin' yer hate on him, child." Ruby
opened the kitchen door. "Thet man is jes' so tiny, he's buyin'
big things so he won't be feeling' so little inside. Thet's all hit
is."

Shoe felt better knowing Ruby Cade didn't like Mr.
Roubiam either.

She watched from the kitchen door as Ruby crossed to the
beehive. No amount of Ruby's coaxing could ever get her to go
closer to the hive. Even clear across the yard, she could heard the
sound of the buzzing. The steady droning filled her with dread.

Ruby was protected by Elmer Cade's coat and the wide-
brimmed bee hat with its net that swung down to her shoulders, but Shoe held her breath as the old woman headed
toward the wooden hive.

She'd heard bees could kill a person. Kill a grown man with
their stinging or drive a dog crazy, so mad he'd howl and yip
and run in circles till at last he fell, red-eyed and frantic, bit-
ing at his legs and stomach.

Ruby'd explained how there was nothing to fear, how the
bees' bellies were too full of honey for them to bend and sting.
Shoe didn't believe this for a second. She saw a few bees stray
from the swarm, dipping and darting around the yard, coming
near.

She caught her bottom lip between her teeth and watched
Ruby extend an arm into the box and select a drawer heavy
with honey. The action disturbed the colony and dozens of bees
flew from the hive. Several settled on Ruby's bare wrist.

It was the waiting for the stinging that Shoe couldn't stand. Sometimes she wished the bees would sting just to end the slow waiting.

Slowly, Ruby returned to the house. The comb dripped gold on the honey plate.

In the kitchen, she cut a corner of the comb free for Shoe to chew on. The honey rolled smooth and heavy on her tongue. It tasted like clover and tobacco and a hint of sharpness that Shoe thought was the bravery of Ruby Cade. As she sucked on the beeswax, she didn't care if Mrs. Sparks thought Ruby and Elmer were white trash hill folks, she was glad they had taken her in.

Ruby took a jar off her shelf. "Here, now," she said. "Tomorrow you tek this tah town and drop hit at Mr. Roubiam's."

Shoe set off early in the day, before the sun was high. When she passed the cottonwood stand by the Stonelick where she'd stopped for water the last time, she didn't think once about the colored boy named Gee Whiz. Her mind was on the Bogeyman's house and its secrets.

She went straight around to the back of his house and marched up the kitchen steps as if she had already done this dozens of times. Inside, she set the honey basket down on the table. Once again the silence of the house enveloped her.

Then, as her ears became accustomed to the quiet, she heard the faint, remembered creakings.

He's buyin' big things so he won't be feelin so little inside. Thet's all hit is. Ruby's words echoed in her mind. They made the Bogeyman seem silly and gave her courage to look around again. Snooping, her ma would call it, but she shut out that voice.

She didn't bother looking in the parlor. He'd hide his secrets upstairs. She slid her hand along the banister and her feet carried her up.

No, child. Go back. Now.

No, she told her ma. I'm not a 'fraidy cat.

She looked down the hall to the end door. She would just look in his room, she told the voice. Not touch anything. Just look. And, if she dared, maybe take a quick peek in his bureau drawer. But she wouldn't take anything. Absolutely not. She felt jumpy, as if eyes were fastened on her back.

Now. Go back. Leave before it's too late.

The door at the end of the hall was not closed. A thin ribbon of sunlight fell on the maroon floral carpet; a shaft of yellow light danced on the glass knob. The noises of the house seemed suddenly louder, creaking.

A curling of fear licked inside her belly.

Someone was crying.

It wasn't the Bogeyman. She knew that at once. The weeping was far too soft to be a man's.

She remembered the stories she'd read in Miss Rogers's books. Adventures about princesses who were locked in towers by evil witches, tales of children captured in the woods, taken from their parents to be sold to Gypsies or eaten.

The weeping was soft. Was a woman in there? Or a child? A girl like herself? Or a captured princess?

If the voice in her head whispered another warning, she could not hear it. She *had* to look. She walked toward the end of the hall.

Mr. Roubiam stood in the room.

She should have run, but she couldn't run on lifeless legs, limbs suddenly as heavy as the anvils in Elmer Cade's shed.

She had never seen a man full naked before. Not even Thomas.

Roubiam's back was to her. His fleshy bum, white and dimpled, shone like a moon carved of flesh, supported by pale hairless legs, naked except for the dark gray stockings ringed by garters. Before him, bent over the bed, was the boy. The colored boy she'd seen crying in the Stonelick. Robert. Called Gee Whiz. He was crying. Thin, high sobs like a woman would make.

"Aw, suh. Please, no moah. Ah's hurtin' awful."

She saw what the Bogeyman was doing. What she'd seen dogs do. And cows. What Thomas had told her men and women did to have babies. What Sarah Sparks had whispered about to the other girls in the schoolyard. That's what the Bogeyman was doing.

Mr. Roubiam pushed his hands between Robert's thighs. The boy's crying was dreadful to hear. He clawed forward on his hands and knees and tried to pull away, but Mr. Roubiam kept grabbing his waist and holding him down.

She smelled the copper smell of earth and blood, the smell of darkness and bay rum, the sour smell of sweat and fear, the fetid smell of some dark place in the earth.

The boy's hands tightened against the sheets and the edge of the mattress.

From a very long way off came the hint of spring rain and apples, and a voice, *Oh, child,* but the other black smell rushed in, blotting it out.

"Ah doan want no moah money. Jest let me go."

"Hold still, you black bastard," the Bogeyman said in a voice unlike the oily one she knew.

"Well, Ah's tellin'," Robert cried out, his voice shrill with desperation. "Ah's tellin' mah pa."

Mr. Roubiam froze; the dreadful jerking motion stopped. Robert made use of the second to pull away. He squirmed free and crouched against the headboard. His face was swollen from crying. There was blood on his thighs and it smeared the sheet. "Ah's tellin'," he whimpered.

Roubiam struck him with a blow worse than any her pa had ever landed on her or Thomas.

This freed her.

She ran. She flew down the stairs and through the kitchen. Her hand grabbed the basket off the table. She saw the honey jar fall to the floor, heard it shatter, but she did not stop.

She gulped lungfuls of hot air, tried to wash away the smell of the Bogeyman, but it clung to her like a second skin.

Sounds filled her ears. Sounds of weeping and pleading and the horrid echo of fist hitting flesh. She wondered if Robert was deaf by now.

Like Thomas.

CHAPTER 18

"Soleil, wait."

She didn't stop, didn't look back over her shoulder to where Andy stood.

As she headed for the T stop, she listened for the sound of his footsteps, half expecting to feel his hand on her shoulder.

The doors hissed shut and the car slid away from the platform. A blond boy in a Boston College T-shirt and knee pads, roller blades slung around his neck, slid over to make room for her on the bench seat. She felt eyes taking her in. Her hair hung in wet strands and, beneath her raincoat, her clothes clung to her skin. Her shoes leaked water onto the car floor. But when she glanced at her fellow passengers, each averted his or her gaze. The woman to her left edged away, as if afraid of catching madness.

She searched for a simple explanation, some sane rationale for what she believed she had seen in the restaurant. She supposed that, preoccupied by her vivid dreams and disconcerted by being with Andy, she had for one instant been caught between worlds. Then, when a young blond girl had passed by on the sidewalk outside, a child who from a distance resembled the girl, she had overreacted. That was all.

She was relieved to transfer at Park Street Station, glad to leave the wary looks of the other commuters. On the platform, she wrapped her raincoat tighter and tried to tame her hair with her fingers. By the time she boarded the T for Orient Heights, she was feeling more in control.

She picked up a copy of the *Globe* from the bench. A bold banner dominated the front page. The Sweetheart Strangler had claimed his fourth victim. She looked at the picture of a handsome black woman. The dead woman had been the anchor on the local CBS affiliate. She was the same age as Soleil. There was an editorial next to the story pressuring the police department to solve the Sweetheart Strangler murders.

During the past week, the police commissioner had zeroed in on the staffs of two of the city's major hotels while looking for suspects. These were the only hotels within a fifty-mile radius that used the Sweetheart brand of chocolates for their guests' nightly turn-downs. The identical heart-shaped, foil-wrapped mint chocolates used by the strangler.

The commissioner had also floated the idea of requiring the city's candy stores to register the identity of every male buying Sweetheart chocolates. This had been met with a shop owners' revolt and the derisive mirth of every talk show host in town. "A Keystone Kop" play, an angry Jerry Williams had told his listeners. GUNS NOT CANDY was the predictable headline of the *Globe*'s editorial. The writer decried the lack of gun control in a city where the year's youngest victim of street crime was a seven-year-old girl walking home from grammar school with two friends.

Soleil put the paper back on the train seat, but the fear had taken root again. She could not remember a time when it had ever totally left her. She thought of it as an animal. Occasionally she could lull it to sleep, but she could never be rid of it. Even while she was asleep, it was waiting. Waiting to strike. She wondered if she would feel secure if she moved out of the city. As if feeling safe could be a matter of geography rather than a state of mind.

She got off at Orient Heights and turned toward her street. The rain had stopped, but the pavement shimmered blackly. Her chest was tight with apprehension.

She had gone only a block when she became conscious of the sound of her footsteps on the sidewalk and, behind her, an echoing reply.

What is that? That sound? What is it? Nothing. Nothing.

She chanced a glance over her shoulder. There was no one on the sidewalk behind her. Just her imagination. She forced herself to keep going.

There it is again. Do you hear it? No, it's nothing. Just keep walking.

She strained to hear the sound of footsteps behind her. Her fingers tightened their grip on her canvas tote. A picture of the dead anchorwoman flashed through her mind.

The words "armed and dangerous killer" came to mind. She wondered if that was true. Not the dangerous part. There was no doubt the strangler was dangerous. But was he armed? He must be, she decided. Surely four women hadn't died at the hands of an unarmed man. Surely we are not that vulnerable, that weak, she thought.

She imagined Alison's reaction. This is just the kind of thing I mean, the intern would say. This is why you need to carry Mace. Or pepper spray.

Shut up, she told her. Just shut up. The skin along her spine tightened.

She scanned the street, looking for light, for shops and circles of safety. She passed a confectioner's shop. A CLOSED sign hung on the door. There were trays of chocolates on display in the window. Not heart-shaped. Not foil-wrapped. But still, her throat tightened. She continued on past a deli and a convenience store, both still open. The sight of several customers and a clerk standing at the checkout gave her courage. It was only a block and a half to her apartment. The echo of footsteps mocked the pulse of her heart.

He was following her. Somehow he'd found where she lived. Who? her reasoning self asked, the self who always dealt with fear. There's no one there. Listen. There, see? There's no one there at all.

There is, said her other self, who knew all about fear.

Who is it?

She knew. Knew from the beginning. Not the Sweetheart Strangler. It was the shadow man. The man who wanted to hurt the child in her dreams. He had been waiting for her. She walked faster.

When she reached her apartment, she had her key in hand. A smart, defensive step. Alison would have been proud of her. It took three fumbling attempts, her back stiffened and waiting for the tight clench of a forearm around her throat, before she managed to insert the key in the street door lock.

Once inside the entry, she leaned against the wall until her heartbeat slowed. Several minutes passed and gradually her legs stopped trembling.

The quiet of the hall soothed her. Now, in the sanctuary of the building, the footsteps seemed less definite. *See? I told you so. It was only your imagination.*

She started up the final flight. The landing ahead was dim. Klietman still hadn't checked the wiring to the light.

Had the footsteps been real?

Her mind reached out for something firm to grasp.

The museum. That was real. And her job. Her office in the library on the museum's third floor. Connolly. Alison, real. Andy. Real. She remembered the coffee and chowder, the Harvard crew team. Remembered the firmness of Andy's touch when he'd wrapped her raincoat around her. The warmth of his breath on her face as they stood in the shelter of the doorway. These things were real.

Her mind grew calmer and her hand was steady when she unlocked her door.

She flipped the wall switch, welcoming the light. Her apartment. She touched the fabric of the sofa, ran her hand over a throw pillow, felt the raised stitching—solid beneath her fingers. A birthday present from May Tannazzo.

She stripped out of her wet clothes and pulled on jeans and a sweater, drew their warmth into her flesh. She towel-dried her hair. This was better.

She sat down on the sofa and dropped her head back against the cushions. Her apartment house. Real. The hall outside her door. Tangible. The recitation soothed her. She stared up at the ceiling and continued. The hall carpet with its worn maroon pattern, real. The light fixture, which still flickered on and off despite her call to the super. Annoyingly real. Mr. Klietman himself. Real. She smiled. Maddeningly inefficient, but definitely real.

Wait. Something nagged at her. Go back. Something was wrong.

Her heart began its rapid pounding once again. *There was no carpet in the hall of her apartment. The maroon carpet was part of the dream world.*

Her heartbeat was a liquid pulsing in her ears.

What is wrong with me?

She got up from the sofa and began to pace. She knew the definition of psychosis was the inability to distinguish reality from fantasy. But would she know if she was insane? Did crazy people know they had lost touch with reality? Wasn't it, in fact, this inability to know that made them "crazy"?

Maybe at first they did know. Maybe it starts with confusion, and then progresses to a dark place where it is impossible to know what is invention and what is reality.

Hadn't that just happened when she'd seen the girl outside the café?

The knock on the door was sharp. She jumped, then froze.

Could the man have followed her here? No. There *was* no man. Only in her dreams. The knock persisted.

She kept the chain tight when she opened the door.

"That's a smart thing." Mr. Tannazzo nodded his approval.

"I called Mr. Klietman," she said, unable to keep the relief out of her voice. "About the light." She unhooked the chain. "Last night. I called him last night. He said he'd get right on it."

Mr. Tannazzo stepped inside, Tootsie at his feet. "Mr. Klietman is a lesson in patience."

"I'll call him again tomorrow," she said. Tootsie sniffed at her feet and then scuttled off toward the kitchen. She watched the corgi disappear, hoped it wouldn't piddle anywhere.

"You're late getting home tonight. I was worried. Were you visiting your mother?"

"No. I—we went out for coffee after work." Her mother. She was overcome with a rush of confusion, guilt. She should have gone to the hospital instead of out for coffee with Andy.

"We?" Mr. Tannazzo leaned forward. "A young man, perhaps?"

She felt her cheeks flush. "Just someone from the museum. Someone involved with a new exhibit."

"He has a name, this person you have coffee with?"

"Yes, Mr. Tannazzo, he has a name." She wasn't going to tell him Andy was back. He and May had always thought she had made a mistake when she hadn't followed him out to Califor-

nia. She heard the corgi's nails clicking along the hall, headed
for her bedroom.

"And what does he do, this young man of yours?"

"He isn't my young man." She listened for the sound of
Tootsie in the bedroom. Mr. Tannazzo seemed unconcerned.

He bent forward and narrowed his eyes. "What happened
here?" He reached a hand toward her face.

"What?"

"Your jaw. What happened?"

She ran her fingers over her jaw, felt the tenderness of the
welt. "Oh, that. It's nothing. Really." Her mind was still on
the corgi. "An insect bite. A bee."

"A bee sting at this time of year? It's late for that."

Her eyes clouded in confusion. Had she said a bee sting?

"When we were children, my mother used to put mud on
bee stings. It's hard to find mud in the middle of the city." He
inspected the welt again. "Good thing you're not allergic."

Tootsie reappeared and headed for Tannazzo.

"No," she stammered. "No, I'm not allergic." She willed
him to leave.

When at last he'd gone, she rushed to the bathroom mirror.
The spot on her jaw was red and raised where the bee had
stung her.

She slid down the wall, her back against cold tiles. Her arms
encircled her legs.

The bees were part of her dream.

After a while, she made herself get up. Avoiding the mirror,
she made herself walk to her kitchen. She just had to get control. That was all. Get control. Gradually, her heart quieted.
She opened the refrigerator and took out the Chardonnay,
splashed some into a glass, took a large swallow.

The apartment was too quiet. She wandered into the living

room and slipped a cassette into the tape deck. A Vivaldi violin concerto. She needed to keep busy. That was all. She carried the wine to the darkroom, welcoming the faint sulfuric odor of fixer that always clung to the air. The room was orderly. She had spent the night before cleaning it.

She would have died before she spoke to anyone of her darkroom in such sentimental terms, but she thought it was a place of magic. A place where, like an alchemist, she could make pictures surface from plain paper. She waited now for the room to work its enchantment, to soothe her.

She'd start by mixing a new batch of fixer. She reached up and took a glass beaker and jar of Rapid Fix from the storage shelf. But tonight not even the darkroom could take her mind off the dreams.

Billy Bascombe turned into the scar-faced girl. And the man? Who was he supposed to be? Unbidden, the picture of Mr. Ormston leaped to mind. And his hands—strong-fingered hands with clean, well-shaped nails. Funny how she remembered that. But Mr. Ormston had not been evil. No matter what her mother thought. He'd only been sad. And lonely. Like her.

That had been in Cos Cob when Mamom had been hired to nurse Mrs. Ormston.

One night, her mother's movie night out—a night the Ormstons insisted she take each week because she worked so hard—Mr. Ormston came into her room. To tuck her in, he'd said. He'd worn a navy and gray argyle sweater over gray slacks. The sleeves of the sweater were pushed up slightly. Dark hair on his forearm. Gold watch on his left wrist. The warm, spicy scent of aftershave. *To tuck her in.* A father's words.

He took the book from her hands—*Heidi*—and set it on the nightstand. "How about a back rub to make you sleep?" he suggested. He'd rolled up the back of her pajama tops. The scratchiness of the wool sweater as he reached across her back.

Then his touch on her skin, soothing, his fingers and palms a little rough, not at all like Mamom's lotion-soft hands. This is what a father's hands would feel like; this is what a father would smell like. She wanted it to last forever.

And then the sound of her mother's voice. Mr. Ormston's stricken face. The terrible scene, yelling and screaming, Mr. Ormston pleading, explaining, the rush to pack their suitcases. "Not one more night in this house," her mother yelled. "I should have you arrested." And, through it all, Soleil's own confusion. Wondering what had been bad about the back rub. The hot rush of guilt. Her fault, her fault. There was something wrong with her.

Later, she had relived that night, trying to recall what Mr. Ormston had done and said that would justify her mother's rage and fear. But all she could remember was how kind his voice had been, how good his hands had felt on her back. He had only touched her back. Had she been wrong to let him do that? And had it been wrong to want a father so much, even if it was only pretend?

That had marked the beginning of her mother's lectures. Never let a man touch you. They only want one thing and you'll be the one left to pay the price. The woman always pays. On and on, all through high school and college. Only Andy— that one summer—only he had been able to totally silence the internal repetition of her mother's bitter and frightening sermons.

Andy again. Better not to remember. She concentrated on measuring out the fixer. Then she returned to the kitchen to fill the water bottle and to refill her glass.

As she poured the wine, she raised a hand to her chin, ran her fingers over her jaw, touched the sore raised spot. The bee sting.

The tenebrous fear, never really gone, returned.

CHAPTER 19

After Soleil ran from him, Andy wandered through Cambridge. He thought about going to a movie, but the idea of sitting alone in a theater was as unappealing as facing his sublet. He couldn't stop thinking of Soleil.

Since he had broken things off with her, he had had several lovers, the last a beautiful woman named Jenny, but none, not even Jenny, had slipped into his heart, his soul as deeply as Soleil had. No woman had ever made him as happy. Or as angry. As if with her, every passion was heightened.

What had gone wrong between them? Should he have given up the opportunity to go to Stanford and stayed in Boston? But if she loved him, wouldn't she have followed him to the West Coast? Instead she'd attacked him.

When his acceptance had come through—*Stanford,* the only one of the three grad schools he'd applied to that he had his heart set on—he'd wanted to share the news with Soleil immediately. She alone would know how much it meant to him.

He'd stopped on the way to her apartment to pick up a bottle of champagne. Although they had not yet discussed the future, it seemed to him they had an unspoken agreement that whatever their future held, they would be together. It had seemed natural to him that she would come with him to Palo Alto.

"California," he'd begun, holding the wine out to her.

She had drawn back, the smile on her face fading. "What?"

"How does California sound?"

She'd ignored the champagne. "What do you mean?"

He'd sensed it was somehow going wrong but plunged on. "Stanford. I've been accepted into the doctoral program."

He'd waited for her to share his happiness—she *knew* he was praying for Stanford—but she just stared blankly, her face stony, so changed he wouldn't have recognized her.

"So when do you leave?" she'd asked after a minute, avoiding his eyes.

"When do I leave?" he'd repeated dumbly, totally lost. What did she mean, when did *he* leave? Didn't she want to go with him? Had he been the only one to imagine a future as a couple? To think of marriage? He'd placed the wine on a table by the door, suddenly unsure of himself.

"Listen," he'd begun again, "slip on some shoes and let's go out. For dinner." Whatever had gone awry, they could smooth everything out over a meal, a glass of wine.

She'd pulled back, her face still impassive. "Not tonight. I have film I need to develop."

He had never seen her so cold, so distant. It frightened him.

"Tomorrow, then," he'd replied. "We'll talk tomorrow." He left the champagne on the table. At the door he had hesitated, but she hadn't stopped him.

The next day, she wouldn't answer her phone, didn't respond to the messages he left on her machine. Angry and confused, he'd driven up to New Hampshire for advice.

"Could she have thought you were breaking it off?" Ricky

had asked. "Could she have believed you were coming to tell her you were going off alone?"

"I can't believe she'd think that," he'd replied.

"Why? Had you asked her to go with you?"

The question only made him defensive. "Why are you on her side?" he'd shouted at his sister.

He decided to wait for Soleil to call him. After all, he had done nothing wrong. She never phoned.

"You and Soleil love each other. Don't lose her because you're a hardheaded Scot," Ricky had counseled him. "Call her. Go see her. Get this straightened out." But he hadn't been able to forget the hardness of Soleil's face, her silence. He left for Palo Alto without seeing her again.

Now he needed to hear a sane and cheerful voice, a voice that didn't suggest hidden secrets or complicated pasts.

He found a phone booth in the Galleria. He checked his watch, factored in the time zones, placed the call. He reached Jenny at the restaurant she owned.

"I'd like a reservation for forty. All lacto-ovo vegetarians who don't eat rice? Can you handle that?"

"Andy." He heard the surprise in her voice. Delight too, he realized. It was the first time he had been in touch with her since he had arrived in Boston. When he had left Palo Alto, there had been no promises made.

"How's the weather out there?"

"Rainy," he responded. He could hear the clatter of the sous chefs prepping in the background. "How about there?"

She laughed. "Sunny."

Sunny. Sun. Soleil. He pressed on. "How's business?"

"Great. Hold a minute." He heard her directing someone, pictured her. Tall, tan, standing in the middle of the small restaurant she owned in San Jose, directing the staff with her sure and calm manner. He could envision her as a wife, a partner. He just wasn't sure whether or not it was as *his* wife.

"Sorry. I'm back. How is the exhibit going?"

"Without a hitch. We're getting some terrific attention in the press."

"Have you heard from PBS about the Moyers thing?"

"Not yet."

The line hummed. Hollow. Already he felt as if he had run out of things to say.

"When will you be back?"

"I don't know." He regretted now making the call, as if he were somehow being unfaithful, although he was not sure to whom.

"You're busy. This sounds like a bad time to have called," he said. "I just wanted to say hi. I'll call later."

She heard the change in his tone, didn't try to prolong the call. He left the Galleria feeling like a heel, and angry because he felt that way.

He walked back to the museum, retrieved his car, and drove home. The only thing he knew for sure was that nothing seemed simply anymore. There was something unfinished between him and Soleil, and until he found out what it was, he couldn't go on with his life.

In the morning, when they entered the booth, neither of them mentioned the supper at the Sail Loft or Soleil's abrupt departure. She sat on the edge of the bed while he set things up. Neither spoke. His chest felt tight, a confusion of anger and desire. He had no idea what she was feeling.

He flicked on the polysomnograph, watched the drum begin its first revolution. He penciled in a notation on the chart. He checked the printout, noting the waves of Soleil's eye movement behind closed lids, her pulse surge and irregular breath-

ing, her inhibited motor neurons, all indications she had
entered her first REM stage.

In the booth, oblivious to Andy's thoughts, Soleil slept. She
was curved in the fetal position he had come to recognize as
her dream posture.

The tunnel was short, her fall swift.

The rain-wakened earth released memories. Raw. Dangerous.

*The blood-thick mist filled the air. She had to find the child. That
was why she was here.*

*She searched the streets of the town, looked into the shops of this
strangely old-fashioned outpost, orienting herself by looking at street
signs.*

*She was close, could feel the child's presence. It was the buzzing that
brought her near, so near her heart ached. It led her from the town.
Down a road.*

Andy studied the printout intently. Someone entered the booth
and he bit back impatience. A hand fell lightly on his shoulder.

"Hi, there."

He looked up at a face that was vaguely familiar. The
woman smiled as if she knew him well. He edged aside to give
her room as she leaned in toward the polysomnograph. Her
hair brushed against his cheek as she scanned the printout. He
struggled with his memory and finally it came to him. Soleil's
intern. The one who had brought the books down yesterday.

What the hell was her name, anyway? He wondered how he
could dislodge her hand from his shoulder.

The intern continued to study Soleil's printout. "What's

wrong with her?" she asked. "Why doesn't she move?" Her hand moved slightly toward his neck.

"She's dreaming," he explained. "It's normal, when we dream, for our muscle activity to be very low."

She almost gave up. Almost. Then she heard the sound of sobs. The child was running, had been running for a long time. There were dirty streaks on the girl's sweaty neck. The child ran straight at her.

At the last moment, instinct caused her to draw back. The child ran through the place where she had stood. She felt the breeze stir against her skin as the child passed. Felt it.

The child had not seen her, could not see her. Of course she could not be seen, she reasoned.

But she could see the child's tears, could hear her sobbing, could feel the movement of air as she passed. Could hear, in the distance, the flow of a river and the cry of a hawk, could smell the salty sweet sweat of the girl's skin, and the rich scent of decaying leaves. Could see, see so vividly that it hurt, the child's disfigured face. It was all so real she could not prevent herself from reaching out.

She might have touched the child then, at that instant. But just as her fingers fell on the child's arm, the sound of an engine cut the air.

The child heard it first. Before she could move, the girl disappeared into the woods.

It was an old-fashioned car. She knew, even before seeing him, that the driver was the shadow man.

He looked right at her, his mean thin-lipped mouth drawn tight. Instinct—or fear—made her draw back. She looked toward the woods, knowing it was not her, but the child the man intended to harm.

The intern continued to lean over Andy, her hand still resting lightly on his shoulder. What the hell was her name, anyway?

He ran through a quick roster of feminine names. Wendy? Jessica? Mindy?

He was conscious of her warmth, the pressure of her hand on his shoulder.

Alison. That was her name.

"So, Alison," he said, twisting on his stool so her hand fell away. "What brings you here?"

"A message for Soleil," she said. "Mr. Connolly wanted to make sure she got it before she left the museum."

Andy reached for the folded square of paper. He found himself wondering how well Alison knew Soleil, if they gossiped about their personal lives. It occurred to him that the intern might know if there was someone Soleil was seeing now. He suspected that if he were to actually ask this question, no matter how casually phrased, it would be fodder for the grapevine within minutes.

"It's the hospital," Alison was explaining. "Her mother's doctor called and wants Soleil to give him a call as soon as she's free."

Andy checked his watch. Officially, the exhibit was now closed and he could wake Soleil anytime. Even without scanning the printout, he knew she was still dreaming.

Alison continued to look at the polygraph. "Isn't it odd that the REM stage lasts so long?"

"Not at all," he lied. "Thanks for delivering this. I'll see she gets it." The dismissal was abrupt, but he didn't want her around when he woke Soleil.

After Alison left, he went into the booth.

"Soleil," he said softly.

The green car slowed and the man scanned the woods. Once more he seemed to stare directly at her, but this time she did not pull back.

After a minute, he accelerated.

Far away, a voice called her name, a summons from a lost, un-wanted world. She tried to ignore this call, but it continued. Before her eyes the car wavered like a mirage in the desert sun. She was be-ginning to lose it.

No, she murmured. No, don't go.

"Soleil." Andy bent over her. "Soleil, it's okay. It's me. Andy."

The nausea was intolerable. She was weak with it and her hands trembled.

As he had the day before, Andy lowered her head to her knees. Concern clouded his face. He felt for her pulse. It was rapid, thready.

"You're sick," he said.

"I'm fine," she said, gritting her teeth against the effort of speaking. "Just a touch of flu." *She needs me. The child needs me. I have to go back.*

He kept his fingers on her wrist. Gradually her pulse strengthened, evened out.

"The exhibit's closed tomorrow," he said. "Good timing. I think you're due for a day off."

No. She needs me. Her knees shook when she walked to the dressing room.

Her fingers gave her trouble—as if they were not hers—and it took a long time to get changed. Everything seemed an ef-fort. When she came out of the dressing room, Andy was wait-ing. He handed her a note from Alison.

She scanned it quickly. Fought to dispel the fog that clouded her mind. What could the doctor want? Had her mother awak-ened? She refused to consider any other alternative.

There had once been a time when she'd imagined that her mother's death might bring relief. She would be freed from her mother's control then, liberated from the responsibility of be-ing the only one her mother loved. Away from eyes that asked more of her than she had to give. And the feeling that she had to make up for everything her mother never had. But there was no prospect of relief now. Only fear. And the empty thought of being alone. And knowing that if her mother died, she would never know who her father was.

Helen had to get well.

She could feel Andy's eyes on her face as she read the note, and turned from the concern she saw there. She did not want pity.

"Want me to go with you?" he asked, and she knew he had read the note first and had known she would not phone, but would want to go directly to the hospital.

She wanted him to go with her then. She longed for his strength, his help. Immediately her neediness made her angry. "No," she answered. "It probably would be better if I go alone."

In the cab on the way to the hospital, her mind skittered over her fears of what the doctor could want. But like a frog who lives both above and beneath the water's surface, her mind kept straying, darting from her mother to the child in her dreams as if, no matter how illogical the thought, somehow they were connected.

The pole curtain was pulled around the bed. This small act of isolation seemed to Soleil to be the first of a long series of steps that would only lead irrevocably to her mother's death, and she swept the curtain back against the wall. The head of the bed had been raised.

She brushed a wisp of hair back from her mother's cheek and felt the feverish skin. Beneath the oxygen mask, her mother, face thin and wasted, took irregular, shallow breaths. Her color was not good.

"Mamom?" She noted other changes: purple marks on her mother's arms; badly swollen hands. "Mamom, it's okay. I'm here." She whispered the words over and over as if they were a

mantra, and did not hear Dr. Allen approach. His face was drawn
with fatigue. He wore a Tall Ships T-shirt beneath his white lab
coat. In spite of the exhaustion, he looked too young to be her
mother's doctor. She wished he were older, more experienced.

He took her by the elbow. "Come on," he said, his voice as
gentle as his touch. "Let's get a cup of coffee."

As they left the room, a nurse entered. Soleil heard the
sound of the curtain being whisked back around her mother's
bed.

"Cafeteria all right?" he asked. "Coffee's hot and strong.
Better than the stuff you get out of machines. Not a lot better.
But some."

She knew he was trying to be friendly, but resisted, steeling
herself for what he was going to say.

He chose a table toward the back, away from the tables oc-
cupied by hospital staff or visitors. As they walked past the
other visitors, she noticed worry lay on their faces, like masks.
The only laughter came for a group of four nurses. A lone
woman seated nearby gave the nurses a reproachful stare.

She took the cup from him, spilling some of the coffee.

"Sorry." She reached for a napkin, but he was already wiping
the liquid up. "Sorry," she said again.

He smiled. "No problem."

The coffee was lukewarm, bitter, but she drank it greedily.

"Ms. Browne. Soleil." He smiled again. "I read your name
on your mother's record," he explained. "Pretty."

She didn't tell him that it was French for "sun." Didn't give
him any information.

"Soleil," he said. "Your mother's worse."

She drank more coffee, knew he was waiting for her to say
something.

"She felt a little warm," she conceded. "I thought maybe
she has a fever."

"Yes," he agreed, nodding as if she were a bright student.

"Her temperature is up. There are indications she's contracted pneumonia."

She leaned forward, forgetting he was the enemy. "What can you do? Can you give her antibiotics or something?"

"I've ordered antibiotics," he said.

"Then her temperature will go down? She'll be all right?" She hated the note of panic that had edged into her voice.

"Her blood pressure has dropped. Her condition is deteriorating." He pinched the bridge of his nose, allowed his eyes to close for a minute. "We need to talk about what to do now."

She shook her head, denying his words. She wouldn't let them give up. Her mother was not *deteriorating*. Not dying. No matter what he said.

He took a gulp of coffee. "Listen. I know how you're feeling. I understand."

She looked across the table. He wasn't much older than she was, but they inhabited different universes. He was like Connolly. She knew the type. North Shore family. Mother on the board of the Boston Ballet or the symphony. Father a doctor or lawyer, semi-retired now. How could he possibly understand? Dr. Robert Allen hadn't had to traipse around the country with his mother, moving from job to job, from school to school, living in the houses of strangers, denied all knowledge of his father. Dr. Allen had known where he belonged since birth.

"I won't let you let her die."

"She is dying, Soleil." His eyes were kind. She knew his patients probably commented on his good bedside manner.

"We can't prevent that, Soleil. We can only prolong it."

"No," she said again.

He drained the last of his coffee. "She won't regain consciousness. Why do you want to prolong it? For whose sake?"

She tried to smile, to keep her voice reasonable. It wouldn't help if he thought she was a hysterical female, incapable of judgment. "Please. Just a while longer."

"You haven't asked my opinion, but if this was my mother, I wouldn't put her on machines."

"No." How could she explain to him her need to keep her mother alive? Could he possibly understand? She needed her mother now. She wanted to tell her mother about the dreams. As irrational as it was, she felt that somehow her mother would be able to make sense of them.

"She'll be comfortable. She won't know any pain. I promise you that."

"No."

A flash of irritation showed through. "So you want her on a respirator?"

"Yes."

He knew he was defeated. "If that's what you want."

"It is."

"She can't stay on the geriatrics floor. We'll have to move her to ICU."

"When?"

"Today. Tonight. After the shift change. Or tomorrow." He stood up. "I've got to get back. Anything you want before I go? Another coffee?"

She shook her head. She followed his progress across the room, saw another woman, wearing the lost look of grief, reach out for him, watched him lean down and say a few words, smiling with reassurance. She turned away.

In spite of what he said, she knew she was doing the right thing. Doctors could be wrong. She had heard of people, patients the physicians had given up on, recovering from comas, regaining consciousness. Her mother couldn't die. Not yet.

If Helen died, Soleil would be alone. A rush of sadness filled her chest. Despite everything, her mother had been the one sure thing she had been able to count on throughout her life.

She didn't want to be alone. Unbidden, a picture of the scar-faced girl came to mind.

CHAPTER 20

"Murder," Charlie Dodd shouted over the engine's whirr.

Shoe, half hidden by a bedsheet, sidled closer to the shed. The clothespin trembled in her fingers as she listened to Dodd tell Elmer Cade about the dead body found buried by the Stonelick.

It began with the rain, a rain so welcome, no one believed it could bring any ill.

For three full days and nights, it poured. Farmers watched thirsty fields drink up everything the sky let loose; women saw the furrows in their men's faces ease. For the first time in weeks, livestock lost their dusty look. Alfafa turned green and cornstalks stretched.

Still the rains continued. Gulleys deepened along the road, and down by the Stonelick the rainfall dug rivulets in the topsoil of the bank, etching branchlike patterns in the land.

It was there on the riverbank that the Wheeler brothers, armed with fishing poles and a half bucket of bait, caught sight of a storm-washed arm and hand. The limb's shriveled

179

black fingers poked up through the sodden earth, beckoning like an agent of the underworld.

"Murder," Dodd said again. "The nigger boy was murdered. No question about it. Doc says it was a blow to the head."

Shoe pinched the wooden pin and clipped the bedsheet to the clothesline. The wet, worn fabric rolled in the morning breeze, wrapping around her upraised arm, pressing against her face, filling her nostrils with the clean scent of Fels Naptha. The image of the boy Robert seemed to float on the sheet. *But everybody call me Gee Whiz,* she heard him say. And then: *Hit's devil money.*

Her hands trembled as she reached for another sheet. He was dead. But hadn't she feared that ever since she'd heard the terrible sound of the Bogeyman's hand striking flesh and bone? For days, the memory of it had echoed and echoed, filling her head so thoroughly she heard it even while she slept. *So much like the other sound of her father hitting Thomas, the sound she had long ago tried to make disappear.*

Elmer Cade flipped a switch, cutting short the engine's whine. He reached up and chose a belt from one of scores that hung like cobwebs from the tin ceiling. He ran the rubber between grease-darkened fingers, then, satisfied, attached the belt to the machine. He switched the engine back on, listening with a practiced ear.

Charlie Dodd worked on a chaw of tobacco. In the face of Elmer's silence, his voice grew louder, defiant. "It bein' a nigger, I figure a nigger musta done it. 'Course the dead bein' a child and all, they catch who done it, they'll string him up. The way I see it, they'll have to get to the killer before the nigger's pa. You seen him?"

An arc of tobacco juice landed in the thin patch of grass beside the shed. Dodd wiped his chin with the back of his hand. He took Elmer's silence as a signal to continue. "Big bull of a man. Name's Washington Jewell. Works over at the sawmill.

Blackest buck I ever seen." The farmer smiled his brown-
toothed smile. "He won't wait for the law to break the neck of
his boy's killer. He'll do it hisself with his own two hands."

Elmer gave the belt on Dodd's machine one final adjust-
ment.

The farmer's voice dropped to a whisper, thick and evil.
"Know what else Doc says?"

Shoe slid her hands along the line and edged closer to the
shed.

"He says the nigger boy was—"

A sound from outside the shed cut Dodd off in midsentence.

Shoe got a glimpse of a green fender, the silver flying lady
on the Packard's nose. She pulled back behind the sheet as Mr.
Roubiam's car rolled up the drive.

Charlie Dodd, two months late on payments to Frank
Roubiam, deflated like a pig's bladder poked through with a
blade. "Guess if you're finished up with this, Elmer, I'll just be
takin' the engine and goin' along."

Lugging the engine, he scuttled past the Packard and climbed
into his pickup before Roubiam turned off the car's motor.

Elmer came out from the shed. He regarded the Packard with
interest. Roubiam always took it to a mechanic all the way over
in Cincinnati, not trusting it in the hands of a hillbilly.

Ruby came from the house to stand by her husband's side, as
if to add her strength to his in whatever was to come. There were
two people folks in Fortune didn't want to see coming up their
drive: Jonas Frye, the undertaker, and Frank Roubiam. Grim-
faced, she waited to hear what brought Roubiam to their place.

"Morning, Ruby, Elmer." The Bogeyman's voice was a snake
slithering through the high grass, a reptile so slippery it nearly
disappeared before the ears could fix on it.

"Mornin'."

Shoe could hear the bees working in the hive. The sound of
their buzzing floated through the air and filled her head. She

swallowed; her tongue tasted of metal. She shrank back behind the bedsheet drying on the line.

"Got a problem with one of the machines over at the mill," Roubiam said to Elmer. "Can you take a look at it?" It was one of only a dozen times he'd given work to Elmer over the years.

"Reckon so."

Frank Roubiam studied Ruby, but could read nothing on her closed face. "How long has it been now that I've been buying your honey?" he asked in the slippery snake voice. "Five years, it's been, hasn't it?"

Ruby straightened up. No one had ever had any complaint about her product.

"That's so. Five years."

"Five years I've been buying your honey and eggs and sending work to Elmer." He smiled widely, but this only seemed to make Ruby nervous. "We've never had a problem."

With an almost imperceptible movement, Ruby leaned toward Elmer. "That's so," she said again.

"The honey you brought last time, you delivered it yourself, did you?"

Shoe pressed her face into the sheet.

"Did you hear my question, Ruby Cade? Did you bring it yourself?"

Ruby studied the businessman. "No. Not last time," she finally said.

"Who did?"

Ruby did not let her eyes stray toward the clothesline. "Thuh gal."

Roubiam looked for the lie in her face. "What girl would that be?" he asked after a moment.

Behind the sheet, Shoe closed her eyes, willing herself invisible. In the black space behind her closed lids, she pictured the boy Gee Whiz floating in the river.

Elmer stepped forward. "Thuh Arnett kid."

"You mean Hod Arnett's girl?"

Shoe held her breath, as if even her breathing could give her away. As long as he couldn't see her, she was safe.

Ruby nodded. "We took 'er in."

"After thuh funeral," Elmer added.

"I heard about that." Roubiam looked toward the house.

I know what you did. Shoe clenched her teeth and fought to keep from shouting the words. *I know what you did to the colored boy.*

Elmer stepped forward, but Ruby cut him off before he could speak. "She ain't here now. She's off doin' a chore."

Shoe caught her breath at the audacity of the lie.

Ruby Cade cocked her head to one side and looked closely at Roubiam. Their eyes locked. "What'd you be wantin' thuh girl fer?"

Her feet. The sheet hung three inches from the ground. *If he looked over, he would see her feet.*

Roubiam smiled an oily smile that matched his voice. "I'm not blaming you, you understand, but the girl broke a jar of honey in my kitchen. All over the floor. And I'm going to tell you straight, Ruby, I'm flat-out not in favor of having that girl in my house."

Too much movement would direct his attention to her. Slowly, slowly, *not too fast, not too fast.*

"Everyone in Fortune knows she's a scar-faced sneak," he said, "as well as a lair, and Lord knows what else."

"Well, she ain't said nothin' about any broken jar," Elmer said. He glanced back at the work waiting in the shed.

Shoe's strong, flat-arched feet inched their way back until they were safe behind the laundry basket.

"Not a word," Ruby agreed. " 'Course, Ah'll replace hit. Ah'll git you another jar right now."

She returned with two jars, which he set on the floor of the Packard.

"When will the girl be back?" he asked as he climbed into his car. The question was as casual as an afterthought.

"Suppertime," Ruby said before Elmer could answer.

Shoe waited behind the clothesline until the Packard was out of sight. "We can't be havin' trouble with him," she heard Elmer say to Ruby.

Ruby found her behind the line.

"You shoulda told me about thuh broken jar."

"Yes, ma'am."

Ruby Cade studied her. "Somethin' else you're forgettin' to be tellin' me?"

"No." She bent over the laundry basket and took up a kitchen towel.

"You sure?"

She pinned the cloth to the line and reached for one of Ruby's aprons. The wet cotton felt clammy against her fingers. "Yes, ma'am." Her heart pounded so hard she feared Ruby would see it beating right through her cotton shirt. And who would believe her if she called a rich, important man like Mr. Roubiam a liar? Who would believe the richest man in town had killed a boy?

But it wasn't about the murder. Her heart sunk with this certain knowledge. What Roubiam really feared—more than he feared her telling that he'd murdered the colored boy—what he feared most of all was that she'd tell what she'd seen him doing in the bedroom.

"You wouldn't be takin' anythin' from his house, now, would you?"

"No, ma'am." And then he'd come back. And he'd kill her. Just like he'd killed Gee Whiz. Kill her so that she couldn't tell what she'd seen him do. She turned away so Ruby Cade would not see her face.

CHAPTER 21

Shoe plunked down on the steps of the narrow porch and stared at the rose-streaked horizon. Ruby rocked in the chair behind her, but the friendly, sittin'-in-the-evening smell of Ruby's pipe didn't comfort her.

"Evenin' sky's powerful medicine fer fixin' a worried heart," Ruby said after a minute.

Shoe had no answer for that. Her head and arms and legs were heavy with the knowledge that no amount of evening sky could fix her problems.

"Ruby," she asked, "why's everyone so afraid of the Bogeyman?"

"Who's thuh Bogeyman?"

"Mr. Roubiam."

"Whatcha call him?"

"The Bogeyman. It's what Thomas and I call him." Her heart hurt with missing her brother.

Ruby chuckled, a shallow, chiggering noise, like hens would

make if they could laugh. "A good name fer him, 'cause he's thuh Bogeyman, all right."

"Why is everyone so scared of him?"

" 'Cause he's thuh money man. One way or another, most folk in Fortune's beholden to him."

"Is money bad?"

"Depends on who's havin' hit. Person like Mr. Frank Roubiam, money's like whitewash on a hog sty. Useful fer coverin' shit."

Shoe had to laugh. She knew Mrs. Sparks and Mrs. Simms wouldn't say "shit" if they were sitting in it. She watched the last rays of red sun slip below the horizon, leaving a trail of pink against the sky.

"It isn't fair." She kicked at the porch railing. "It isn't fair for him to have so much money."

"No, gal, hit ain't. But Ah guess you know better than most that life ain't fair." The rocker creaked as Ruby got up. "Come on, gal. Time to be gettin' to bed."

Long after she heard Ruby and Elmer's bedsprings squeak with the burden of their bodies, she lay awake and thought about the Bogeyman and the violent thing he had done to the colored boy. She shut her eyes to close out the memory, but another memory rolled in. Far worse. Far worse.

It had been seven years ago. She was five and Thomas eight. Back when Thomas could still hear. And her face was still smooth, back before she wore the imprint of a horseshoe on her cheek.

That day Barney Saunders, toting his broad-bladed knife in his swollen hands, made his yearly visit to the farm.

Reee-ba. Her ma was calling, yelling for her to come on out of the barn. Reee-ba Grace.

She stayed where she was. It wasn't fair that this year

Thomas got to watch and she didn't. Just because he was older, everyone treated her like she was still a baby. She hunkered down behind the bin and watched as Barney Saunders and her pa led the cow into the barn, watched as the knife glimmered and then turned red.

Still dazed from the slaughter—stunned just like the cow, which stopped its bellowing as the blade cut deep—she watched. What she saw next was more terrifying than the death of the animal. While Barney worked with his knife, her pa knelt by the cow, a bowl in his hands. The wine-colored liquid filled the bowl and ran over her pa's fingers. She grew dizzy watching. Then her pa stood up. He lifted the bowl to his mouth. He drank from the bowl. Like it was filled with milk.

She'd had to run then.

Thomas had found her in the hayloft. "Aw, Reba, Reba, baby. Don't cry. Don't cry."

She tried to hear only him, shut out everything else. But not even squeezing her eyes so tight it hurt could block out the memory of Barney Saunders's blade, of the hanging cow and her pa lifting the bowl to his mouth. She trembled and tried to stop thinking about whether the animal's eyes had been open or shut. Tried not to think about the sound of the cow's terrified bellowing, the sharp smell of urine, and the copper smell of blood. Tried to keep her mind on Thomas. Her Thomas. The heat of him. The sure and sweaty warmth of him.

He held her tight, crooning. Singing her name and rocking her, just like she was a baby. Making everything all right. Her eyes began to feel heavy and she drifted toward sleep. Thomas moved, stood up.

"What's the matter?"

"Got to pee."

She snuggled deeper into the hay while Thomas walked to the side of the loft. She heard the spattering sound of his urine on the hay below.

"Show me how to do that."

He laughed. "You can't."

"Why not?"

" 'Cause you ain't got a pecker."

"How come?"

Thomas fidgeted. "I got to git, Reba. Pa'll be lookin' for me."

"How come I don't have a pecker?"

" 'Cause you're a girl and you got a cunt."

"Let me see," she said before he could go, her face intent and solemn. "Let me see your pecker."

He blushed. "Cut it out, Reba Grace."

"Just let me see."

"Aw, come on, Reba Grace. You know what it looks like."

"I don't."

"Do too. You seen the pecker on ol' Sam."

"Not close. And horse peckers don't count. I want to see," she begged. "I'll show you my cunt."

Thomas considered it. "You first," he finally said.

She pulled down her overalls. Her skin was sweaty and the hay felt scratchy on her bare behind.

Thomas reached a hand out and touched her. It gave her a funny feeling in her belly.

"Okay," she said. "My turn. Let me see your pecker."

She reached out to touch, but he pulled back.

"You got to let me touch it. I let you."

"Okay. But quick. I got to git."

She looked real close. It must be funny to have something like that.

"Why're we different, Thomas?"

" 'Cause you're a girl and I'm a boy. A man's pecker goes in a girl's cunt. It's how they make babies." He was proud of his knowledge.

" 'Tis not."

" 'Tis too. A pa puts his pecker in a ma."

"Liar," she said.

They had not heard their pa come up the ladder. His roar of rage echoed in the barn. He stood over them, his face purple-red, as if filled and swollen with the blood he'd drunk from the slaughtered cow.

Thomas, white with fear, slipped past him and down the ladder. Their pa caught him in front of the barn. Shoe's body shook so, it took her a while to get down from the loft. When she got to the chicken yard, Thomas was already bloody from their pa's fists.

"Stop, Pa," she screamed. Sure as can be, he meant to kill Thomas. "Stop. Please, Pa. Stop." She threw herself at him, pulled at his legs and sleeves, forgetting for the moment that she would be next. Her pa shrugged her off without once missing a blow on Thomas.

Her screams brought their ma from the house.

"No, Hod," her ma cried. "Enough." She raced across the yard and grabbed at her husband's arm, but he shook her off as easily as he had Reba Grace.

"You know what I found them doin' in the barn? I'll beat him until he hasn't got a pecker left."

"Ma, wait," Shoe screamed as her ma ran back to the house. "Ma, don't go."

Still her pa hit Thomas. Blood began to seep from her brother's ear. "Scream, Thomas," she yelled. "Scream." Thomas never cried when their pa beat him. Sometimes she thought if he'd only yell, it would make their pa stop sooner. As if something in her brother's silence made him keep hitting.

"Hod." Her ma stood on the porch. She held their pa's shotgun. Even across the yard, Shoe could see her ma's hands shaking.

"Enough, Hod," her ma said. "Stop." She stood her ground on the porch. Her voice was quiet and low and more scary than all the screaming. "You stop this, Hod," she said. "You hear me? They're just children."

"You stay out of this, Lydia," Pa said.

"Leave them be, Hod," Ma said in the scary voice. "They're children. And you can't be punishin' them for something not theirs to carry. You hear me? Reba Grace isn't your sister and Thomas isn't you. You can't be punishing them for your sins, so you just leave them be."

Her pa's fist made a wet, soft sound like he was beating a sack of grain.

"Enough." The gun grew steady. "Enough," her ma said. "Leave him be or, I swear to God, Hod Arnett, I'll kill you here and now and not waste spit to water your grave."

Her pa stopped then.

He told Doc Baker that Thomas had fallen from the hayloft. "That so?" Doc asked, looking closely at her ma and then at her. She had felt her pa looking at them then, waiting for their answers. They agreed Thomas had fallen from the loft. She felt the lie bind her to her pa.

Four more times that week Doc came to tend to Thomas. "Won't be able to pay him," her pa grumbled after the third visit, but something in her ma's face shut him up.

During the day, when their pa was out in the field and their ma was cooking, she sat by Thomas's bed. She told him he was brave because he didn't cry, but he didn't answer. Just looked at her with lifeless eyes. Reba Grace wondered if she would feel better if their pa had given her a licking too.

"Damn shame," Doc told her pa after the last visit. "Looks like the boy'll never hear again."

Shoe lay in her bedroom in the Cades' house. *It wasn't her fault that Thomas was deaf. It wasn't her fault.* But she couldn't shut

out the voices of Mrs. Sparks and the other women. *Nothin'*
good can ever come of sin.

She remembered Mr. Roubiam paying for Thomas to go into
the tent with him to see the Koochie dancer. A new and terrible thought took hold. Maybe the Bogeyman had touched
Thomas's pecker and then maybe he had killed him just like he
had murdered the colored boy, Gee Whiz. Maybe Thomas
wasn't even with the carnival. Maybe Thomas was lying in a
grave by the Stonelick.

The thought that Thomas was dead hurt worse than any
pain she had ever known. If Thomas was dead, she didn't care
what happened to her.

He just couldn't be dead. She wouldn't even think that.

She made herself lie still and strained to hear the sounds of
snoring from Ruby and Elmer's room. Then she crept out of
her bed. There was only one thing she could do that would
make her feel safe again. She had to find her brother.

She would find him and they would begin again. They
would go where no one knew them. Maybe that was why
Thomas had left in the first place. Not because of the Koochie
dancer with the spangled clothes, but because he wanted to escape from Fortune. In the carnival, next to a bearded woman
and a man with a second body attached to his side, a deaf boy
or a girl with a scarred cheek could seem normal.

She would leave tonight. But first, she vowed, she would
walk over to Coaltown and see Gee Whiz's pa. She struggled
to remember the name Charlie Dodd told Elmer. A big man,
he'd said. Then she remembered. Washington Jewell. He probably looked just like Gee Whiz grown up. Black-skinned and
tall. Before she left Fortune, she would find him and tell him
what she'd seen the Bogeyman do.

CHAPTER 22

"Are you okay?"

Andy was trying to be casual, but Soleil could see he was concerned. It was no wonder. She looked like hell. Her face was drawn and violet smudges beneath her eyes highlighted the pallor of her skin.

He attached the first two electrodes. "We can't have the star of our show conking out, you know."

Unnerved by his unexpected kindness, Soleil's throat tightened. She waited until she was in control before answering. "I'm fine. Really."

"No more dizzy spells?"

"No."

He affixed the final two electrodes. "How was your day off?"

"Fine." She didn't tell him how the day had dragged. She had spent most of the morning at the hospital, sitting at her mother's bedside while arrangements were made for the transfer to ICU. In the afternoon she'd returned to her apartment. Knowing she should keep to the schedule of the exhibit, she had tried to sleep, but it had been a long time before she'd finally dozed off. Even then she'd tossed and turned fitfully and woke feeling edgy and dissatisfied. She did not dream. The welt on her jaw had disappeared.

She watched Andy check the connections and dim the lights.

"How did you make out at the hospital? How's Helen?"

Again her throat tightened. "They've move her to ICU. They're doing everything they can."

"It must be tough," he said. "If there's anything I can do . . ." He let the sentence trail off awkwardly.

She resisted his sympathy, just as she had resisted Dr. Allen's. Mamom was *not* dying. She closed her eyes, but she couldn't erase the memory of the doctor's words.

She could not think about her mother now. The only way to get through this was to keep a tight rein on everything. If she just kept her mind on one thing at a time, she could make it through.

But as she lay in the darkened room waiting for sleep, she could not help thinking about her mother. She turned on the narrow bed and stared out at the one-way glass.

The whisper of the polygraph pens drew Andy's attention to the machines.

Yesterday he'd called Dr. Whitelaw again and given him an update on the curious pattern of Soleil's dreams. The man's response was so quick it irritated Andy that he himself hadn't thought of it.

"Have you checked the equipment?"

He could have kicked himself for forgetting the most basic

tenet of research. Even novice technicians knew that when re-
sults didn't meet validated expectations, the first thing to
check was the equipment.

Early that morning, he had signed out a new polysomnograph machine and installed it at the museum. Next he'd replaced all the wires and electrodes. Then he called the other
members of the team to check the possibility that in connecting the machine to the laser projector and the synthesizer the
polygraph's functioning might have been affected. Both agreed
this was unlikely.

Pens floated across the surface of the polysomnograph drum,
sketching out Soleil's brain waves, eye movement, pulse. Their
patterns gradually changed and, as he watched, she fell asleep.
Outside in the exhibit's Dark Space, the timbre of the music
changed, rose an octave.

*She descended a flight of stairs into a basement and then into a small
room that smelled faintly of damp concrete. She bent over and, as if she
had done this every day of her life, picked up an armload of wet laundry from a wicker hamper and put it into a dryer. She clicked
the dryer on, then turned to go up the stairs. A flash caught her eye.
Then again. A white light, then red, as if sparks played behind
the basement wall, which was now transformed to wallboard, no
longer concrete. A fire, she thought. Somehow it seemed connected
to the dryer.*

*From the head of the stairs she heard a man's voice. What's going
on down there? he inquired. A fire, she answered, knowing even as she
said it that she would not be believed.*

*The flashes now turned to tongues of flame, still behind the wall-
board. She knew then that she had to go through the wall. The only
way to put out the fire was to go through the wall. Fear crept through
her body, possessing her. I can't, she whimpered. If I go through, I will
die. You have to, said another voice. No one else can do it.*

Andy stared at the printout. Soleil had been in first episode of REM sleep for nearly an hour, much longer than any of the previous initial episodes.

That eliminated the possibility of there being something wrong with the polygraph. He was a scientist, he reminded himself. There had to be a logical explanation for the extraordinarily long periods of REM. It was up to him to find it. Perhaps, in spite of what the other members of the team said, there was something screwy with the laser projector or the synthesizer. If not those, something else he had overlooked. He needed to think. He realized that ever since he had seen Soleil, he hadn't been thinking clearly.

Again, he allowed his thoughts to wander back to her and the hold she had on him. He was swept with a sudden wave of annoyance at the act they were playing out. Behaving like strangers. He wanted to storm into the booth and shake her. Forget what happened six years ago, he wanted to say to her. We have to give it another try.

Or maybe he was the one who needed shaking. Just a year ago he had counseled his friend John to stop trying to rekindle a relationship with an old girlfriend who had reappeared in his life.

"Once a relationship has gone sour, there's no saving it," he'd said.

"Love is not milk," John had replied.

"If you've split up," Andy had insisted, "it's almost impossible to go back. It's better to just go on."

These words, so facile, mocked him now. Was it always too late? Might he not have just as easily advised the opposite? If you find one person you love, it's worth working at it, he might have said. It's worth trying. Don't throw it away.

He remembered what it was like to be with her. There was

the physical desire, of course. The passion they shared. A pow-erful sexual attraction unlike anything he had experienced. But beyond that, her tranquillity and integrity attracted him. Her gentleness and her appreciation of beauty. Her vulnerability.

You're crazy to let her go, he told himself. Tell her how you feel. Beg her if you have to. Just don't lose her again. Tonight, he decided.

A high-pitched whining circled and circled her head, pulling her away. Back.
   Back into the darkness, the tunnel. The long dark tunnel.

Andy's attention was drawn from the printouts to a man stand-ing by the glass staring in at Soleil. He wore a pair of chinos and a baseball cap that hid his face. Still Andy thought he rec-ognized him. He was sure the man had been to the exhibit twice before. Neither time had he entered the technician's booth.

It occurred to him that the man might know Soleil. Maybe even dated her. The thought was disagreeable. He looked the man over. He seemed out of shape, with the beginnings of a potbelly. Andy couldn't picture her with someone who let him-self get fat. The trouble was he suddenly couldn't picture her with anyone but himself.

As if aware that he was being scrutinized, the man abruptly turned his back to Andy. Without a backward glance, he walked out of Dark Space.

The dwarf was waiting. The dwarf again.
   He reached into his vest pocket and pulled out a gold watch. You're late, you know.

Before her eyes, the watch grew and grew until it was twice the size of a beach ball.

We're late, he yelled again. You shouldn't have taken so long.

Watching the pens scratch out the pattern of Soleil's sleep, Andy realized that it would soon become apparent to even the most casual museum visitor that the polysomnograph printout of Soleil's dreams with their extended periods of REM was significantly different from the information displayed in Light Space, where typical sleep waves were exhibited. In effect, what the exhibit was telling the public in Light Space was in conflict with what was occurring in Dark Space. He wondered when people would notice it.

He stared through the small window into the glass booth where Soleil lay curled in her fetal dream position.

She was in the town, but the girl was not there.

She was alone on the street. The dwarf was nowhere in sight.

But someone else was there. She could feel his presence and knew it was the evil man.

She wandered down the sidewalk, searching for the child. She needed to find her before the man did.

CHAPTER 23

The man checked his watch. Three o'clock. He figured he had two hours at the most. Better play it safe and figure on one. In the apartment across the hall, a dog began barking.

He pulled on a pair of latex gloves and went to work on the lock. It gave him no trouble. It was laughable how flimsy the average lock was.

He hesitated for a moment before opening the door. The dog across the hall had spooked him. All he'd need was to find a German shepherd inside, though he figured if anything she'd be a cat person, or maybe some kind of tropical fish.

He pushed the door in several inches and listened. Nothing, not even a canary. He quickly checked out each room and then went to the bedroom. He began with the bureau. He pulled open a drawer, fingered her bras and panties. A cold, tight smile twisted his lips.

. . .

This time, Soleil did not surface from the dream world easily.

In the distance, far away, someone was calling her name. She struggled against this voice, but it was relentless. For one heart-catching, irrational instant she believed it was her father.

She opened her eyes, moved slightly, felt a wave of nausea, knew she must lie still.

"God, you scared me," the man was saying. His voice was vaguely familiar. But when she opened her eyes, she didn't recognize him.

"Do you think you can get dressed?" he continued. "Do you want me to get someone to help you?"

She was in a small room. She saw wires and EEG discs. A hospital, she thought. She wondered if she had been in an accident. She closed her eyes briefly and ran a quick inventory of her body. Nothing seemed wrong. Except for the nausea. She opened her eyes again.

The man was looking at her. She guessed he was a doctor. Her eyes fell to the plastic tag he wore. Dr. Andrew McKey. Yes. A doctor. He seemed nice.

"Are you all right? Shall I call someone? Alison? Someone else?"

She couldn't follow his conversation. Didn't know who Alison was. She wondered how she had gotten here and what was wrong with her. A concussion? An accident? It couldn't be too serious if he thought she could go home. She wondered if the girl was here too, if they had been in some kind of accident together, but a gut wariness kept her from asking. She braced an arm against the bed and sat up. Again, the dizziness weakened her. She fought it, not wanting him to see how unsteady she was.

"Listen, are you sure you can get dressed?"

"Yes. Really, I'm fine." She managed a smile and swung her legs over the edge of the narrow bed to convince him. Her feet touched the floor, and as easily and quickly as if she had stepped through a curtain, she remembered. *Dreamscape,* Andy, the glass booth. Everything else had been a dream. The child. The small town. The shadow man. All of it. A dream.

She felt exhausted, as if she had been swimming for a long, long time in deep water and at last, struggling against the tide, had returned to shore.

"I have a few things to do to close up shop," Andy was saying. "I'll do that while you're getting dressed, and then I'll bring my car around to the front."

She stared at him, uncomprehending.

"I'm taking you home."

"No. I'll be all right. Really." She hated the weakness in her voice.

"I'm taking you home," he said again. His voice was so firm, she gave in to it.

While Soleil was dressing, Andy phoned Connolly's office and told the director that she was ill. It's probably just a twenty-four-hour kind of thing, Connolly responded, adding that she'd probably be fine by tomorrow. It's the flu, Andy replied flatly. She could be out for a week. He hung up before Connolly could argue. He didn't mention the abnormal cycles of REM. There was no point now.

The man was reluctant to leave the bedroom, but he needed to get on to the other rooms. He headed for the darkroom next. The faint, unpleasant smell of chemicals erased the memory of the woman's scent he had carried with him from the bedroom. He checked his watch again and swore softly. He had spent too much time in the bedroom. He should have come to the darkroom first. That was the logical place. There were a dozen or so prints hanging from a line and he headed for those. None were what he was looking for.

And he couldn't find the camera.

He fought panic, checked the wastebasket. Empty. He pushed aside developing trays, searched the storage shelves. Nothing. Fear turned to anger. He'd been so careful, only to have her threaten everything. "Bitch." The only witness.

In the museum garage, Andy apologized for the old Volvo. The seat was stacked high with magazines and books, the upholstery mended with duct tape. Takeout coffee cups littered the floor. "My secret addiction," he said as he gathered the cups and shoved them in a litter bag. "I became a real coffee freak at Stanford." He picked up the books and newspapers and tossed them into the backseat.

He pulled out from the museum drive, merging with the rush-hour traffic. She leaned back against the seat and stared out the side window. As they drove to Orient Heights, he cast glances at her out of the corner of his eye.

"You look pale. Do you think you should see a doctor?"

"All a doctor will say is to take a few days off, which I can't do."

He slapped a palm against the steering wheel. "Jesus, how could I forget?"

"What?"

"While you were dressing, I called Connolly. I told him you were sick, that he'd have to get someone else for the exhibit."

"What?"

"You're off the hook. He's getting a backup."

"A backup?"

"Yep."

"But I'll be better tomorrow. I'm sure." Her face was white now.

"Not the way you look right now."

She felt the charge of panic. She *had* to go back to the exhibit. Had to get back to the child. Somehow she had to return to the girl and, as irrational as it sounded, she felt *Dreamscape* was the only way.

He insisted on walking her up to her apartment.

Inside, he led her to the sofa, covered her with the blue plaid throw. "I'm not an invalid," she protested as he fussed over her, but his attention was suddenly comforting.

He crossed to the fireplace. "How about a fire?"

He crumpled a section of the *Globe,* added kindling from the basket. "Matches?" he asked.

"On the mantel, in the tin box."

He ran his hand along the shelf. "Where?"

She frowned. "A little box. It should be right there."

"Here it is." He took it from the bookcase.

"That's odd," she said. She couldn't remember putting it there. She always kept it on the mantel. She watched as he lit the fire.

He came back to the couch.

"Tea?" he asked.

"You don't have to do this."

"Is that a yes or no?"

She wanted him to stay, didn't want to be alone. "I don't want to keep you if you need to go."

"I don't have anywhere I have to be. I can stay." Their eyes locked for an instant. Memories—too many memories—crowded the room. She blushed a little.

"Tea coming up," he said, and disappeared into the kitchen.

She heard the sound of running water, of cupboard doors closing. She sank back into the sofa and stared into the flames. For an instant she felt disoriented again, like the moment at the museum when she had awoken, that odd time lapse when she truly hadn't known where she was. That gap confused and frightened her. She could still see the scarred face of the child, saw her clearly as if she were there in her apartment. Then she saw the town itself, the individual storefronts. They were wooden buildings. Old-fashioned. A general store. A dress shop. Post office. She remembered the name of the dress shop: Mrs. Bellington's. So real.

"Here you go." Andy came in with the tea.

Her hand shook slightly as she brought the cup to her mouth. The tea was weak. He had added sugar.

"My mother always made us milk-toast when we were sick," he said. "I was going to make you some, but I couldn't find any milk." He grinned. "Your kitchen would make Mother Hubbard's look overstocked."

"I'll get some tomorrow." Another storefront from her dream flashed before her vision. FORTUNE GROVES FEED AND GRAIN said a sign on the facade.

He was studying her. "I'm worried about you. You should try to eat something."

"I'll get a bite later." She considered telling him about the dreams. About the frightening confusion on awakening.

"Listen. I've got an idea," he was saying. "Don't move. I'll be back in five minutes."

She didn't want to be alone now. The old familiar fear crept in.

"Five minutes," he said, as if reading her mind. "I'll be right back."

It took him twenty. She stayed on the sofa, pulled the blue throw tight, feeling as if it held the warmth of Andy.

"Best I could do within the time constraints," he said when he returned. He plopped two takeout bags on the coffee table. "Egg drop soup," he announced as he emptied one bag. He withdrew three cartons from the other one. "Chicken lo mein, fried rice, fried dumplings."

There was an easy chair by the couch, but she pulled her

legs up and made room for him by her feet. It felt natural to
have him there, as if nothing had ever changed.

He poured the soup into two bowls, gave her one. It was
warm, a little salty, but, suddenly hungry, she finished it all.

"This is nice," he said as he set their bowls on the table.
"Like old times."

"Yes." Old times. She was terribly conscious of his body at
the other end of the couch. She could feel the heat of him by
her toes. It traveled up her legs to her thighs, her stomach.
Now the dreams, the museum seemed far, far away.

He separated the chopsticks, pulling them apart like a
chicken wishbone, then handed her a pair. He spooned some lo
mein and rice into the bowls and passed her one. Their hands
touched as she reached for the bowl and she felt the familiar
jolt of desire his touch always brought.

"More tea?" His voice was tense. He had felt it too.

"Not yet."

"You're looking better. You've got some color back in your
cheeks."

"You make a pretty good doctor." Again their eyes locked.

"Soleil," he said. He leaned over and took the bowl and
chopsticks from her. He put them on the coffee table. He
reached for her hand. Her skin tingled with his touch. She felt
the heat begin to build in her belly. "Soleil," he said again.
"We—"

No words, she wanted to say.

"We have to talk," he said.

"I know." But not yet, she thought. Not yet. Later. This is too
soon. She leaned in to him, stopped his words with her lips.

Their kiss was tentative at first, then more searching. She remembered the taste of him, grew dizzy with it. His hand came
up, found her jaw, stroked her neck. Then fleetingly, gently,
her breasts. Her nipples grew hard. He groaned, pulled his
hand away.

He closed his eyes and sighed, then got up. Her eyes followed him as he crossed to the fire.

"Andy?"

He took up the poker and adjusted the logs, creating a little shower of sparks.

"What's wrong?" She knew he wanted her. As much as she wanted him. He hadn't been able to hide his desire. "What's wrong?" she asked again.

He jabbed at a log, watching another spray of sparks leap. "Maybe this isn't such a good idea."

"Why?" It was almost impossible to get the question out. She forced herself to ask. "Is there . . . someone else?"

"No," he said. "No one else."

He returned to the couch, sat down, lifted her feet onto his lap. "I'm afraid," he finally said.

"Of what?"

He ran his fingers over the arch of her left foot. "Of hurting you again. Of being hurt."

"I know."

"Maybe we should take take it—I don't know—slow, you know?"

She smiled.

"What?"

"That's what you said the first time we were in bed together."

"It is?"

"Yes," she said. His fear made her feel stronger, calmer. She leaned in to him.

He buried his face in her neck. "I love the smell of you," he whispered. "So sweet."

He kissed her. He tasted of smoke now, from the fire. She opened her mouth for his tongue, felt her body soften, her legs part.

"Jesus," he breathed when he finally pulled away. She traced the outline of his lips. He held her hand still, kissed her finger, took it into his mouth. The heat of his mouth ran through her. She felt it in her toes.

She reached for his hand, guided it to her blouse, helped him unbutton the front, open it.

"You sure?" he asked.

"Never surer." She felt reckless now. She slipped out of the blouse, her bra. He caught his breath.

"I'd forgotten," he whispered.

"What?"

"How beautiful you are."

He caressed her, gently ran his hands over her shoulders and breasts and ribs.

She heard a moaning. Didn't know which of them made the sound. He kissed her eyes, her cheeks, her mouth. She felt his lips on her neck, breasts. He took one nipple into his mouth, sucked. A jolt of hot desire ran directly to her belly, her legs.

"Hold on," he said in a voice she didn't recognize. "Let me get out of these."

While he undressed, she spread the wool throw down in front of the fire. "Come here," she whispered. She ran her fingers along his collarbone, chest bone, ribs. Memorizing. Remembering. Across his belly. She circled his navel with a forefinger, leaned over and circled it again with her tongue. Her fingers continued over his skin, drew patterns over his thighs. Circled his penis. A spasm akin to pain crossed his face. She bent. Took him in her mouth, heard him whisper her name. He pulled her up next to him, kissed her again, while his fingers explored and found her ready.

Their lovemaking was tender, slow. As if too much passion would burn them up.

.   .   .

Andy woke, reached for the table, found his watch. "I don't believe it," he said.

Still half asleep, she snuggled closer to him, wrapped a leg around his. They had moved to her bed sometime after midnight. "What?"

"It's nearly five o'clock."

"In the morning? You're kidding."

He groaned. "I hate the thought of leaving."

"Don't," she said. Everything was perfect with him there next to her. Safe.

He leaned over and kissed the edge of her mouth. "Some of us have to work," he teased.

She tightened her hold. "Stay."

Gently he disengaged his fingers from hers. "I know. I don't want to go." Reluctantly, he got up, reached for his clothes.

Already it felt cold without him next to her. She hated the thought of his leaving.

"I'll be back in time for dinner."

"Promise?"

"Absolutely." He bent and kissed her. "And this time I'm packing a toothbrush and razor."

"Promise?" she asked again.

"Anything," he said. His fingers traced her mouth, her chin, her jaw. "Anything you want."

After he left, she fell back asleep. When she woke, she felt cold. Her head ached. She scuffed her feet into slippers and shuffled into the bathroom. She took two aspirin, wandered into the living room. It seemed empty now.

The bowls and chopsticks, cartons of rice and congealed lo mein were still on the coffee table. They were the only sign that Andy had really been there. That it hadn't been a dream.

She busied herself cleaning up, carrying the teacups and bowls to the kitchen. She squirted soap into the sink, ran hot water, thought about Andy. She felt calmer now, as if being with him had given her strength. She reached for a towel and dried her hands.

Back in the living room, she continued straightening up. She pictured Andy at the museum. He's in his booth now, she thought. She liked that she had a place to envision him while they were apart. She remembered their last words that morning. *Promise? Anything. Anything you want.*

It seemed a miracle that he had come back to her.

She saw the books Alison had left for her piled on the floor by the bookcase. That was over now. The dreams seemed far away. Still, she picked up the top two volumes. Read the authors' names. Ann Faraday. Fritz Perls.

She flipped through one, scanning the text, read about several cases of precognitive dreams. She took them to the sofa. Reading more carefully now, she noted that the author had categorized dreams as precognitive, problem solving, spiritual, or dreams of visitations. She pictured the town of her dreams, the face of the girl, wondered where they belonged.

She reached for another of Alison's books. Minutes passed as she read of dreams writings that ranged from the scientific to the poetic.

In another book she saw the name of Marguerite Young in the text. While in college, she had discovered and loved *Miss MacIntosh, My Darling.* She read more closely. Young told of how she had once dreamed that Henry James had sat in a corner of her apartment drinking whiskey from a top hat. Later, in an entry in an obscure book by a publisher's wife, Young had read that Henry James had visited the publisher's apartment and sat in a corner drinking whiskey from his top hat.

Soleil remembered that Young lived in New York, in the

West Village. She tried to recall if she was still alive, overcome suddenly with an urge to call her and talk to her about her dreams.

She set the books aside long enough to put on the pot for tea. While the water heated, she began reading again. The waking world, according to one researcher, was as much of an illusion as the dream world; all time and space were but illusion.

She did not believe this, of course. Dreams were the illusion. Reality was here. Now. Awake.

A vision of a street floated into her mind. Storefronts. The image zoomed in close, focusing on one sign, as if her mind were viewing the scene through a camera lens: FORTUNE GROVES, OHIO.

Andy. He was her reality.

Her mind knew this, but something else compelled her to reach for the telephone book.

There were two area codes for Ohio. On instinct, she chose the one in the southern section of the state.

Illusion. A dream, she thought as she punched in the number for Ohio information.

"Directory assistance. What city, please?"

The child. The town. Only a dream.

"What city, please?"

She was surprised that her voice was steady. "Fortune Groves."

"Yes. What is the name of your party?"

She held the receiver tightly against her ear. "There is a city named Fortune Groves?"

"Yes, ma'am," said the operator. Her voice was tinged with impatience. "What is the name of the party whose number you wish?"

It existed. Fortune Groves existed.

"Ma'am? What listing are you looking for?"

There had to be a rational explanation. Somewhere. Somehow she must have seen or read the name of that town.

"Hello? Ma'am? This is the Ohio information. What listing are you looking for?"

CHAPTER 24

She couldn't stay in the apartment.

Outside, the city was bathed in the sunlight of one of the city's perfect Indian summer days. She tilted her face up, but not even the sun's warmth could ease the chill. I only have to get through the day, she told herself. Then I'll be with Andy.

The T, in midmorning, had emptied of its commuters, with their hard-bitten energy. Most of the passengers were students or tourists, shoppers. She chose a seat near the door. A heavy man in a Yankees T-shirt and chinos edged past her and sat down, opening his paper. She caught a glimpse of the headline—POLICE CONSULT PSYCHIC ON SERIAL MURDERS—and turned away. She did not want to read about killers this morning.

An old woman, shopping bag wedged between her feet as if she were returning from town instead of heading in, sat opposite her. The woman had sharp brown eyes that darted around the car, studying everything, missing nothing. Monkey eyes. When they fell on her, Soleil looked away.

She had seen eyes like that before. She remembered sitting on a soiled couch, looking across a desk, staring into the street-wise simian eyes of Harvey Stanton, private detective.

Find my father, she'd said as she put a check for one hundred dollars on his desk.

"Tell me what you already know about him," the detective had responded as his fingers slid the check over the surface of the desk and slipped it in a drawer.

What did she know? What had her mother told her about the man whose blood she carried? That he had a dimple just like she did. That he had a cowlick near his forehead. These two facts she trusted for their truth. All else—the conflicting stories she'd overheard her mother tell employers—were not to be believed.

A month following this meeting, Stanton had come back with specific information about her mother—Helen Browne, née Lovering, born in Chillicothe, Ohio, only child of Dr. and Mrs. Charles Lovering (both deceased). A spinster, he said, who graduated with a nursing degree from Ohio University and then returned to Chillicothe to assist her father. Abruptly, at thirty-five, Helen Lovering left home. Stanton had picked up her trail in Boston, where she was Helen Browne, a registered nurse specializing in private duty cases and a mother of a tod-dler. He could find nothing to explain the two-and-a-half-year gap. She lived a dull life, he said. No men. Only her work and her daughter. It seemed the sole act of imagination in her life was the naming of her daughter, Soleil Rae Browne.

Five hundred dollars, he'd said, his tiny monkey eyes—eyes too small for such a big face—studying her, waiting for her to object. She'd paid him—her rent money—and he'd handed over the folder that contained facts she already knew about her mother, and this about her father: William Browne, the man listed as father on her birth certificate, had long ago vanished as easily and thoroughly as if he had never existed. No birth certificate. No marriage license. No military record. No death certificate.

"Here's what I think," Stanton had told her. "There is no William Browne. I think your mother got herself knocked up so she ran away from home, invented a husband and a new life. If I were you, honey, I'd forget the whole thing."

The stir of passengers as they left the T brought her out of her reverie.

As she climbed the stairs from the station, she felt eyes watching her. It was thinking about the detective that had unsettled her.

Nothing prepared her for the sight of the intensive care unit.

The room was brightly lit, with glass walls and futuristic chrome machinery, sterile and impersonal. There were no potted plants or flowers here. The room smelled of death. She knew this was not a place patients like her mother walked away from.

I want out of here. She fought panic as she walked toward the three-walled cubicle.

She focused on the fixtures. Anything but the slight figure on the bed. There was a metal chair. A blue cabinet. She looked away. A machine with a panel of dials across the front sat atop the cabinet. She studied the dials, trying to calm her heart. At last she made herself turn to the bed. She wondered how many people had died on the mattress.

An opaque plastic tube, held in place by strips of tape, went into her mother's mouth. It was connected to a ribbed vacuum hose that was connected to the respirator. There were two I.V.s running into her mother's arm. New bruises covered the flesh between her wrist and elbow.

The rasp of the respirator was the only sound in the cubicle. She fled.

Out on the street, the crowd jostled her like a wave. She walked, dazed. Eventually she ended up at the Public Garden. Park benches were filled with students and squirrels and secretaries from the statehouse eating lunch, enjoying one of the last warm days of autumn.

She took a seat on a vacant bench and sat, swallowing grief. She understood now that her mother was going to die. She felt a spasm of loss that actually pierced her chest.

She thought again of what the detective had told her about Helen. A spinster. Living in other people's homes, caring for strangers, carting her daughter along with her. Soleil suddenly felt a stabbing regret.

She couldn't sit any longer. She walked toward Downtown Crossing, allowed herself to be swallowed up by the throng of shoppers.

The sound of a child's cry cut across the street. She tried to keep walking, to ignore it. It had nothing to do with her.

The cry persisted. She turned and saw a little girl of no more than three or four, pulling at her mother's hand and sobbing as if her heart would break. *Nothing to do with her.*

She walked on, but the child's crying followed her. She escaped into Barnes and Noble. The heavy doors closed behind her, shutting out the echo of the girl's sobbing. Music floated from loudspeakers. Chopin. A mazurka. One of her favorites.

She looked at the shelves and racks of books. A mystery. That's what she needed in order to take her mind off . . . off other things. Things the little girl's sobs had reawakened. She stared at the glossy cover of a recently published thriller. She turned away. Something quieter. Maybe a multigenerational

saga, the thick kind that required a genealogical chart on the
first page for keeping all the characters straight.

"May I help you?"

The salesman was young and wore a suit and tie. She
thought he looked as if he were playing dress-up.

"Are you looking for something in particular?"

She knew what she wanted. Don't. Don't ask, she told herself. Grab a mystery—there, that one by the counter—it
doesn't matter which. Just grab a book and get out. Go get a
haircut. Think about Andy. Stay away from the dreams. "An
atlas," she said.

"U.S. or world?"

Please. It's not too late. Don't do this. Don't do this. "U.S."

A smile, a grimace close to pain, played on her lips as she
followed the clerk to the rear of the store and the reference
shelves. Perhaps she should have called someone. Maybe she
should talk to Mimi. Her friend, so rational, would help explain it away.

Fortune Groves, it was called?

Yes. How could I dream about a town I never heard of?

*But how can you be so sure you never heard of it? You're a librar-
ian. You see words constantly. Maybe your eyes caught sight of it in
a story next to one you were reading in the paper. Or maybe a college
classmate came from there. You're thirty-five. How can you be so sure
that in all the days and months and years of your life, you never overheard the name, never read it somewhere?*

It would be so easy for Mimi to be calm, to try to extricate a
sane, rational meaning from the impossible. Oh, she'd say, the
memory is an acquiring sponge in which we tuck away the
oddest facts. Then, being Mimi, she'd want to dig deeper, see
it as a game. Why have you dreamed this now? What does *fortune* mean to you? She'd stall Mimi at this point. She hated

word games, uncovering meanings hidden behind and beneath each association. Go on, give it a try, Mimi would urge. What does *fortune* mean to you? Riches. Wealth. And Groves? Forest. Woods. Dale. Sparse or thick? Thick. Great, Mimi would shout. So this place you travel to in your dreams is a place of wealth and riches, but hidden, dark. A fortune is there for you.

But Soleil didn't think a fortune waited.

There was a table by the back wall and she carried the atlas over to it. It took her several minutes to find Ohio, locate Fortune Groves. Her fingertip covered the name for a moment. Fortune Groves was a small town in the southernmost corner of Ohio, nestled between West Virginia and Kentucky, situated on the banks of the Stonelick River. She remembered now that she had heard water rushing in one dream. A river. Now she knew its name.

She replaced the atlas on the shelf. She brushed past the clerk on the way out. "Find what you need?" he called out, but she did not answer.

She crossed the street to Filene's and bought a pair of blue-striped pajamas. They were the closest she could find to match the pair Connolly had sent the messenger out to buy on the first day of the exhibit. She gripped the bag holding her new pajamas and headed for the T.

The sound of footsteps rang out when she stepped off the T at Orient Heights. They echoed behind her as she walked toward her apartment. She did not look back or bother to explain them away. It wasn't the shadow man. He did not have to follow her anymore. She was going to go to him.

When she returned to the apartment, she found Andy's voice on her answering machine. He seemed far away now. She erased the tape while brewing tea. She drank it slowly, as if there were plenty of time. She had been calm since the bookstore. It was only fighting it, the struggle to stay away, that brought turmoil. She knew she was descending into, what? Madness, but she no longer fought it.

She moved her bed out into the middle of the floor. Then she lowered the lights until they were as dim as the light in the museum booth. She striped, pulled on the striped pajamas.

Almost ready. She picked up her tote bag. Snapping open the change section of her wallet, she saw a dozen pennies, some nickels and quarters. She fished through until she came up with six dimes.

Carefully, using tape, she placed the coins on her face: two on her temples, two on each side of her jaws, two on her forehead. She thought she had them as close as possible to the spots where Andy had attached the electrodes.

Finally, ready, she climbed into her bed.

She tried to imagine Andy on the other side of the wall by the head of the bed, tried to imagine everything exactly as it had been in the museum.

"I'm coming," she whispered aloud, and wondered if the child heard her. She closed her eyes and waited for the whirling to begin, waited to tumble down the tunnel.

Whirring cushioned her, wrapped her in its silvery, spinning threads.

"I'm worried about her," Mr. Tannazzo said to Tootsie. The corgi yipped once in response.

"You're no help," Tannazzo said as he tried to decide what to do. In the middle of the afternoon, he had knocked on Soleil's door, but she hadn't answered. He knew she was there. He'd seen her come back after lunch. Mother would have known what to do. He tried to think of what she would want him to do.

Tootsie trotted over to the door and began barking.

"Not so fast," Tannazzo said. "Maybe she's resting. Or doesn't want to be disturbed."

Tootsie pawed at the door, half yipping, half whining.

"Come over here and stop your noise. Give me a minute to figure this out." The dog ignored her master and scratched at the hall door.

"What's the matter, girl?" He had already taken her out for her walk. "You hear something out there?"

He opened the apartment door.

"Hello."

The hall was dark. He stepped out and peered into the shadows. He felt someone there. He motioned Tootsie back into his apartment and swung the door nearly shut behind him so she could not follow him. Through the narrow opening, a ribbon of light cast a band in the hall.

"Hello. Who's there?"

He cursed his failing eyesight, cursed Klietman for neglecting to repair the light.

His apartment door swung shut behind him, cutting off the last blade of light. Through the door, he heard Tootsie whining.

Off to the left, near the door that led to the roof, he heard a noise.

"Who's there?" he demanded again. A shiver of apprehension went through him. There had been a group of boys hanging around the street lately, tough-looking and, to his way of thinking, in need of a father's hand to straighten them out. He knew no son of his—if he and Mother had been blessed with children—would hang around the streets frightening old gentlemen. "I don't know who you are or what you're doing here," he said into the darkness, "but you better stop your sneaking around and get out of here before I call the police."

The form in the shadows moved then, darting across the narrow hall so quickly that the old man didn't have time for a yell or a prayer.

CHAPTER 25

Shoe waited until she heard the harsh sound of Elmer's snoring, the softer counterpoint of Ruby's.

She gathered her suitcase, her clothes, and her pa's Mason jar from where she had hidden them in the closet. *Not enough money,* cried her desperate heart as she picked up the half-empty jar. After a moment's deliberation, she dug three quarters and two dimes out of the jar and slipped them into her pocket. Then she wrapped the jar and carefully packed it in the suitcase.

She crept into the kitchen. There was no telling when she'd eat again. She chose a loaf of bread, a jar of honey, and one of the gooseberry preserves, taking a moment to stow the food in her suitcase. As she rose, a shaft of moonlight cut through the kitchen window and reflected off Ruby's money jar. It beckoned her.

I need more money. I need more money.

She hesitated. The Cades were the only folk who'd ever given without wanting in return.

More money.

She'd need a lot of money to find Thomas. She crossed to the sink and picked up the jar. Ruby and Elmer were nothing to her, she told herself. Not kinfolk. They weren't even from Fortune. *More money.*

She tried to dredge up dislike for Ruby, something to make it easier to take her money. But all she could think about was how Ruby had given her a home when no one else in Fortune would. And how Ruby always looked her straight in the face, as if no scar marred her cheek and jaw. And last, she remembered how Ruby had lied for her to Mr. Roubiam. Not even her own kinfolk had taken her side against the richest man in Fortune.

She set the jar back on the shelf. But now she knew she couldn't leave Ruby flat, without a word of explanation. She took a pencil and paper out of a kitchen drawer. "The Bogeyman killed the colored boy," she wrote. She folded it once and wrote Ruby's name on the front. Maybe no one would take her word against his, but now Ruby would know why she had to leave.

She was careful not to let the screen door bang as she left. She crossed the side yard. The half-eaten face of the moon shone down on her, throwing long shadows, turning every silhouette into something to fear.

Fear could take the shadow of a tree limb falling across a wall at night and twist it into a monster's arm, give it life even though she knew full well monsters didn't exist. Fear could turn your ears trickster too. So that an owl's call was the cry of the goomar woman, who fed on sleeping children. Your head decided what to fear. Once you got to understand that, the only trick was mastering your head.

"There's nothing to fear. There's nothing to fear," she breathed. It might take along time to find Thomas. She couldn't start giving in to terror now.

CHAPTER 26

The tunnel was dark, the whining high-pitched and eerie. It was night. Her eyes adjusted to the moonlight. She stood in a yard. Blades of grass bent beneath the soles of her feet; night dew cooled her skin. This yard was not a place she had ever been before, but understanding came instantly, as if it were part of a song she had learned long ago. She had returned to Fortune Groves.

A flicker of movement off to her right caught her eye. A slight figure—white shirt catching moonglow, turning it silvery gray and ghostlike—circled the shed. It was the girl. She tried to move toward her and felt a peculiar and frustrating limbolike paralysis.

She heard a car door open and turned toward the sound. She saw the man slide out of the car, close the door so softly it didn't make a sound. Look out, she called to the girl, but as soon as her tongue nudged them out, the words evaporated, dissolving into the mist.

CHAPTER 27

Shoe started across the yard when she caught the glint of moon on metal at the foot of the drive. She drew back, edging closer to the cover offered by Elmer's tin shed, waiting for her eyes to adjust to the dim lunar light. She saw more clearly now. In the shadows of the maple tree at the end of the drive, the Packard waited. Like a green monster.

Maybe he doesn't know I'm here. But the notion was more prayer than thought, for the metal glimmered as the car door swung open and Roubiam got out. She inhaled sharply. She still might have escaped, but as she jumped back, her suitcase struck against the side of the galvanized shed. The clang sounded across the farmyard, echoing fiercely, cruelly, as if it would never end.

She turned from the shed, back toward the safety of the house. Roubiam wouldn't dare hurt her in front of the Cades. That was her only hope.

Immediately she saw that before she could reach the steps, before she could wake Elmer or Ruby, he would cut her off. She ran in the other direction.

Roubiam walked up the drive.

CHAPTER 28

She watched helplessly as the man walked up the drive. Run, she called to the child. Run. But again her words fell into a void, dead before they left her lips. The girl darted across the moon-dappled yard, stopping in the shadow of a small wooden structure.

CHAPTER 29

Shoe's hands brushed wood. Not a tree. Too smooth. And square, she realized as she ducked behind it. Of course. Ruby's hive.

From its shelter, she watched Roubiam's shadow.

His steps were stealthy, noiseless as he crept toward the shed, searching for her.

When Pa would come up the stairs after her or Thomas, he bellowed their names, promising a whipping. But the silence of Roubiam as he came for her was far scarier than her father's shouting. The threat of giggles—worse than any fit she'd had in church—tickled in her chest, moved up to her throat. She fought them back, bit her cheeks hard.

The hive, night silent with sleeping bees, released the smell of honey-soaked wood.

"Please." She whispered the word. No more than a prayer. But who did she think could help her? In whom did she believe? Then, for just an instant, from beyond the honey, beyond the raw smell of rain-wakened earth releasing dark memories, beyond the sour smell of her own fear, from beyond all these Shoe inhaled another smell. It curled around her and comforted her. For an instant she felt nearly safe.

"Mama," she cried. Then, "Ma," although she knew her ma could not be there, knew it was not the smell of her ma's sickness, but something lovely and sweet.

Her cry was not loud, but it was enough. Roubiam turned toward the hive. His breath, harsh and brutal, echoed across the yard.

CHAPTER 30

Ma.

For a moment, in confusion, she thought she was hearing Billy Bascombe. His last cry before he disappeared beneath the dark surface of the ice.

Ma. Not Billy. The girl. Her child's voice no louder than a whimper, but shrill enough for the man to hear.

She reached out to the child, to hush her, comfort her.

She heard the sound of the man's breathing as he made his way across the yard, coming toward the child. Toward her.

CHAPTER 31

"Ma?" Shoe cried again. The apple-tinged sweetness was still with her. "Ma?"

She reached out to steady herself. Beneath her fingers she could feel wood vibrating as the hive came alive. The bees were waking.

Roubiam saw her clearly now. His steps were bolder as he came for her. The moon glinted and danced on his face and she saw meanness settle there.

"I just want to talk to you," he said in his slippery snake voice. "That's all. Just talk."

Fear paralyzed her.

"I have something for you," he said. "Something to give you."

Shoe shivered at the sound of his oily voice. Go away, she directed him silently. But curiosity slipped in, fighting fear, caution. What could he have for her? What would he want to give her?

CHAPTER 3 2

*She could not allow him to hurt the child. She slid closer to the girl,
even as the man drew nearer. Again she reached for the child, and this
time her hand did not slice through air. This time, so naturally she
didn't even think it odd, she felt the girl's rough skin against her
own. Smelled her sweet and childlike sweat.*

*The man came closer. His voice, when he spoke, was slithery, soft.
But beneath the slippery tone, held in tight rein, she heard cold rage.*

*She drew the child closer, willed all her strength into her. Don't
worry, she said. I won't let him hurt you. She prepared to step between
them, tightened her muscles to accept the blow he intended for the girl.
She was weak with fear, terror she had known all her life. But she
had to save this child.*

CHAPTER 33

"Don't you want to know what I have for you?" His voice was dangerous, slipped in where it was not wanted.

"No," Shoe whispered. But of course she did.

He was so close that he could have reached out and touched her. Instead, he slid his hand into his pocket.

Shoe stiffened. Did he have a knife? She thought of Barney Saunders's broad-bladed knife. Ruby's kitchen knife. The folding knife her pa had kept in his pocket.

But his hand, when it reappeared, was filled with crumpled bills. "Here," he said. "For you. Money."

Their eyes met in the moonlight. His were black and as oily as his voice. Her gaze was drawn to his hand.

"For your face. I'll pay for the doctor. And the hospital." He did not have to tell her the terms.

Her hand slid up to her cheek, her jaw, felt the puckered skin, the caved-in bone. She used the tips of her fingers to imagine what it would feel like to be healed and whole again. The longing was so deep it hurt.

The voices started up in her head. *Careful, child,* warned Ruby. *Don't be beholden,* added her ma. She stared at the money and tried to shut them out.

"All the money you need," Roubiam was saying. His eyes pinned her.

The boy Gee Whiz spoke next. *Hit's devil money,* he said. His voice was louder than her ma's or Ruby's had been.

"No," Shoe cried. "No." But she didn't know if she was answering the Bogeyman or the voices in her head. Then she pushed them all away, pushed with all her strength.

Roubiam was caught flat-footed.

Shoe felt the hive rock beneath her hands, and then she felt it topple. She heard the droning rise. A thick and angry humming.

"Sweet Jesus," Roubiam screamed. And then, "Get them off. Get them off." The screaming was horrid.

She picked up the suitcase and ran. From the bees. From the high-pitched, frantic sound of Roubiam's voice.

Ran down the drive, past the Packard, out onto the River Road. She turned right—not toward Fortune—and ran on. She ran until her legs begged for her to stop and still she kept running. She got no farther than the bridge by the Stonelick when her lungs began to burn. A hot, stabbing pain grabbed her side, as if the Bogeyman had kept a knife in his pocket after all and had slid it between her ribs. Her feet struck the ground in steady slaps and she felt the jolts run up her body. Her breath, when she gasped air, caught on the pain in her rib. The suitcase was heavy and banged against her leg. Inside, the honey and jam rattled against the Mason jar.

She kept going, past the Town Farm, past Coaltown. A couple of farm dogs woke from sleep and barked as she passed by, but they did not leave their narrow porches. No time now to think of Gee Whiz or to find his pa to tell him what she knew. She remembered the note she had scribbled for Ruby and hoped that the old woman would find the man and tell him. She continued on until she reached the woods near Overton.

She was afraid of the dark and what might live in the woods; but, more afraid of what she had left behind by Ruby's overturned hive, she curled up at the base of a cottonwood tree, slipping in and out of a restless sleep, haunted by the echo of Roubiam's awful screams.

CHAPTER 34

Before she could stop her, the child darted from her side. *Wait*, she said, but Soleil's voice had again turned silent and when she reached for the child, her arm again encountered only air. *No*, she cried, *willing herself to reach the child. But it was all fading.*

She heard from a distance the echo of the man screaming. "Sweet Jesus. Sweet Jesus."

She was flying now. Above the scene, looking down as the child ran down the drive.

Wait, she called, but she could not keep her. The farmyard, the evil man, the girl. Everything grew dim.

Long after it had all vanished from sight, she heard the sound of the man's screams. Shrill, penetrating, pulling her back, away from Fortune Groves.

CHAPTER 35

Mists. Swirling, thick, enveloping. Then—penetrating the mists—a scream.

Soleil pulled the pillow tight against her ears and tried to fall back, to surrender once again to the shadows, but the shrill sound pierced the pillow as easily as it had the dream haze.

Still she fought it. It was bringing her back too soon.

Back? her drugged brain asked. Back from where?

To where?

She opened her eyes, careful not to move her head, knowing that if she moved too quickly, a terrible nausea would overcome her.

Nothing in the darkened room was familiar. She reached out for the girl, but her arm encountered only empty space.

From somewhere outside the room, she heard the shrill sound again. It rose, louder, then stopped abruptly, as if cut. She recognized it then. A siren. She moaned. Had something happened to the girl? Was she hurt? But the child was back there.

Back where?

She lifted a hand to her forehead as if to wipe away the confusion and her fingers encountered tape and a hard round disc. She peeled off a strip of tape and a dime came with it. She ran her fingers over her jaw and cheeks, found the other coins, which she quickly pulled off. The sight of the dimes disturbed her.

A sound broke the silence. After a minute she identified it as a phone. She heard a click and then a woman's voice speaking in a hurried, self-conscious manner. "Hello, this is Soleil Browne. I am unable to answer your call right now, but if you leave a message I will get back to you."

Another click, a beep, and then a man's voice. "Hello, Soleil, French-for-the-sun. This is Andy, Scotch for Missing-you-at-the-exhibit today. Just wondering how you're doing and if you're feeling better. Give me a call."

She stared at the ceiling; memory returned. She was in her own apartment, lying on her own bed. Bit by bit, she remembered it all. Buying the pajamas. Taping the dimes to her face and jaw. Each step a mechanical effort to return to the child. And she had succeeded. But she had come back too soon.

Back from where? The question echoed.

Fortune Groves.

She shook off the thought. Of course, she hadn't really gone anywhere. She was in her bed, in her apartment. It had only been a dream. Hadn't it?

She bit the insides of her cheeks, the first hint of suppressed hysteria.

Her doorbell rang, two short summonses. And then, when she didn't answer, a longer one.

She sat up slowly and threw back the blanket. Her hand,

unclenched, released a dime that rolled across the mattress, landing in the folds of the bedclothes. The doorbell rang again.

She turned deliberately and reached for her robe. Her fingers were icy.

"Miss Browne?"

The policeman's face was earnest, young, too young to be a policeman.

"I'm sorry to disturb you," he said, "but there's been an accident."

"An accident?" Something hot, like failure, moved in her chest. So the child hadn't escaped after all.

"Your neighbor," the cop continued, "Mr. . . ." He glanced down at his notebook, "Mr. Tannazzo, Samuel Tannazzo, has had an accident."

"An accident?" Her hands unclenched.

"Have you heard anything?" The cop was looking at her oddly. She began to perspire.

She shook her head, not trusting her voice.

"You sure?" He narrowed his eyes. She had the feeling there was more he was keeping from her.

"I've been fighting the flu," she stammered. "I was sleeping."

He looked beyond her into the darkened apartment.

"I see."

What did he see? For one frightening instant she wondered if there was a dime still taped to her jaw or temple. She couldn't resist raising a hand to check.

"So you didn't hear anything? A little more than a half hour ago?" he prodded.

"What happened?"

"Your neighbor fell down the stairs."

"The stairs?"

"We're checking with everyone in the building," the cop

said. "Anyone who knew him. Anyone who might have heard anything."

"But Mr. Tannazzo," she interrupted. "Is he okay?"

He avoided her eyes. "Just a few more questions. I understand he lived alone."

She realized then that the cop had been speaking of Mr. Tannazzo in the past tense.

"Is he . . . I mean, is he all right?" she asked again.

He replied quickly, "He's dead."

She felt the blood rush from her face. The room grew dim. She was aware of the cop supporting her, leading her to a chair. "God, I'm sorry," he was saying. "I shouldn't have told you like that. With you sick and all." A frown of concern creased his face, making him look even younger.

"But I just saw him."

"You okay now?"

"I just saw him," she repeated dumbly. "This morning."

"Do you want some water or something?"

She shook her head. "How did it happen?"

"He fell down the stairs."

"Oh, no," she said. She felt heat flush her face. It wasn't my fault, she told herself.

In the distance, she heard barking. Tootsie. She wondered what would happen to Tootsie now.

"Do you know if he had been ill? Did he have dizzy spells?"

"No." She wasn't up to this. His questions were confusing her.

The cop jabbed his pencil toward the still-open door and the hall beyond. "I noticed the light fixture was out. That been out long?"

"About a week." Was he blaming her? It wasn't her fault. Not her fault she couldn't save Mr. Tannazzo. Or Billy. Or the girl. "I called Mr. Klietman to get it fixed," she said.

"Klietman?" The cop scanned his notepad. "Oh, yes, the

building super. He's a lucky guy. If Tannazzo'd lived, he'd probably end up owning the building."

She felt a headache begin to build. The shadow man, she thought. He did this.

The cop was studying her. "What is it?" he said. "Did you see anything? Hear anything usual? A shout or call?"

"A man."

"A man?" He looked up from his pad. His voice betrayed an edge of excitement, one he'd kept just below the surface until now.

Lord, what was she saying? The shadow man was in her dream. Not real.

The cop was waiting.

"A man was outside the building," she began, wondering where the lie would lead. "Yesterday. He was probably looking for someone."

"What did he look like?"

"I don't remember."

He pushed her, asking for details of clothing, height. She gave vague answers.

"Is that all?" she pleaded. "I'm really not well. Dizzy." She willed him to leave, followed him to the door. There she edged the door shut, narrowing the opening.

"Yes. Sorry to keep you," he said. "You remember anything, give us a call."

She heard faint scratching at Mr. Tannazzo's door. "What will happen to Tootsie?"

"Tootsie?" The cop checked his pad again.

"Mr. Tannazzo's dog."

The cop flipped his notebook shut. "The guy had no relatives. My guess is the dog gets put down."

Her throat tightened. She would not cry. Not now.

After the cop left, she returned to her bedroom. She thought about Mr. Tannazzo, his kindness. She felt the futility of regret.

She sank down on the couch and dropped her face into her hands.

The hair on her neck, her arms, stiffened. She jerked her hands back from her face, dropped them to her lap.

She stared down at her palms. After a moment she slowly brought them up to her face. She cupped her fingers over her nose and inhaled, drew in the smell from her dreams. The thick, clovery scent of honey and, over that, the sweet and salty scent of girl sweat. An icy chill swept over her body. Her skin held the smell of the child in her dream.

No. Not possible.

Her hand itched. She crossed to the bathroom. She ran the water until it nearly burned her. Then she lathered her palms, holding the soap tightly and scrubbing until her skin was red. As if it were possible to wash away the madness.

The bed was still in the center of the room where she had pushed it. She sank down on the mattress. A ray of light fell on the rumpled bedclothes. A glimmer caught her eye.

A dime was nestled in the blankets. She picked it up and moved to place it on the table with the other coins and the tape and then paused.

She looked more closely. But instead of seeing Roosevelt's familiar face, she saw the winged head of Mercury. She flicked on the bedside lamp. The dime was new and shiny. She read the date stamped beneath the winged Mercury. 1931.

"No," she whispered. She dropped the coin on the bed, as if shrinking from something contagious. "It's not possible." Impossible. Impossible. There was a ringing in her ears, high-pitched, like the sound of the tunnel.

Impossible. Impossible. Even as she chanted her denial, she remembered.

The feel of the child's slight hand in hers. The hard thinness of the coin, sticky with the girl's sweat.

The girl had given her the dime.

CHAPTER 36

Andy swiveled on his stool and scanned the paper rolling off the drum. The new volunteer was just coming out of REM sleep. The woman was a forty-four-year-old fire department dispatcher who worked the night desk at a station in Quincy. She had a hearty laugh that matched her cheerful Irish face. She snored slightly when she slept. She wasn't Soleil; her dreams were the placid, rolling ones that kept people sane.

Soleil.

At the thought of her name, his body warmed. He waited impatiently for the exhibit to close so he could be with her again.

Across the city, a man sat on the edge of his bed, unaware that he was rocking back and forth. He was thirty-three. His name was Louis Grunner. He was a cop with the Boston force, currently on night patrol.

Grunner continued to rock. An icy edge of fury circled his forehead. A too-tight headband. If the old grandpa hadn't been such a meddling bastard, everything would be all right. He forced himself to be calm. He felt his heart beat slow. Always, he could control his emotions. Even when he was a child in his father's home, he could control himself.

He always knew when the beatings were about to start. For a week before, his mother would taunt his father. When his father came home from work, she would set their plates on the table, then sit, hands folded primly in her lap, and watch him eat. "Watch your manners, Louis," she'd begin. "You don't want to end up like your father. A no-mannered slob."

He'd feel his stomach go tight and pray she'd shut up. Stop it, he'd shout silently. Just this once. Stop it. His father was important. An officer at the Bristol County Jail. A big man. Handsome. "A slob," his mother would repeat. He'd wait for his father to say something. But Otto Grunner would just keep eating, as if he had not heard his wife's scorn. "You're no better than the lowlife down in the jail." She'd keep at it. "Maybe it's a mistake, you being a guard. Maybe they should put you on the other side of the bars." Still his father would take the abuse.

And later, after he had gone to bed, he'd hear their voices through the wall, hear his father begging his mother, begging to get what was rightfully his. And he'd listen to his mother's harsh response, knew it by heart. "Your hands aren't fit to touch a decent woman. Go find one of those whores you like so much. Take one of your cheap whores to bed, but keep your hands off me." And still his father would plead. Louis would cover his head with his pillow just to shut out the sound of his father begging.

Three or four nights in a row, his father would plead with

his mother, take her refusals, inhale her disdain. And then, one
night, finally tired of it, he would use his fists where his voice
had failed. Then it would be his mother's turn to beg. Louis
wouldn't cover his head with his pillow those nights. He'd sit
up and hold as still as possible so he could hear every blow his
father landed on his mother, could hear her voice, no longer
proud and contemptuous. On these nights, listening in the
dark, he would be able to breathe again.

Finally the blows would end. Then the only sound that
would slip into the bedroom would be the sound of his mother
weeping. And his father grunting. The bedsprings groaning,
squeaking. The sound of the headboard pumping against the
wall. "You're just like them," his father would say. "Just like
the rest of the whores. You like it same as them."

The next evening, dinner would be quiet. His mother would
leave them to eat in peace. As if the night before had cured
something gone wrong. And after dinner, his father would say,
"I brought you a little something, Margo." And he'd hand her
a box of candy. A heart-shaped box of chocolates.

Grunner stopped rocking. He crossed to the desk and lifted
out a leather scrapbook. With his forefinger, he carefully wiped
a tiny smudge from the cover. A slight movement caught his
eye. A spider, with delicate lines of green in a nearly translucent body, inched along the desk. He flicked it to the floor and
crushed it underfoot. He opened the scrapbook. His collection.
His women.

Sometimes women laughed at him. He knew they thought
they were too good for him. Just like his mother.

These women, bitches who wouldn't have bothered to give
him a smile on the street if they walked by, these bitches had
groveled for him in the end.

He smiled at the memory of how the women had begged.
Even the newscaster, so haughty, so arrogant when he'd first
appeared at her door, had, at the last, offered him anything.

Said she'd do anything if he would let her go. But he couldn't do that. They were liars. Not to be trusted. After he left, they would have turned on him.

No one understood. The reporters, a dull, sheeplike lot, called him the Sweetheart Strangler. A vulgar name. He would have preferred something subtler. But then he should not have expected imagination or understanding from that bunch. Certainly they were not a threat. Only one person was a danger.

He remembered turning on the steps, just after he had killed the reporter. Hearing the click of a shutter. Turning to see the woman with the camera. The only witness who could connect him to his last victim. Bad luck. Until then he'd had only good fortune.

He had taken this as a sign that it was time to move on. Move to another city. Dallas, perhaps. Or to New Orleans. Her shooting him like that was a sign of luck turned sour. But then, proving luck was still with him after all, he had seen her picture the next day.

He opened a drawer again, fished in the desk, and removed the creased newspaper clipping. Soleil Brown stared up at him.

Twice, although he knew it was dangerous, he had gone to see her sleeping at the museum.

He remembered the smell of her apartment, her bed. This one would be special.

The headache had eased, but he felt jittery. Waiting made him nervous. He should have had her by now. It should all have been over. Except for the nosy, meddling old man, he would have been with her by now, would have heard her plead.

The old man was just a minor setback. Luck was still with him. He'd wait until he was sure the precinct cops were gone and then he'd go back for Soleil Browne. This time she wouldn't escape.

CHAPTER 37

Soleil turned off her answering machine. Twice she heard Klietman out in the hall. She could hear the clicking sounds of his screwdriver as he repaired the light fixture. Before he left, he called her name and knocked insistently at her door, but she stared ahead with indifferent eyes until he gave up.

She was aware of being hungry. She moved to the kitchen—a vague, sleepwalker's progress—returning to the bed with a handful of crackers. She wondered what would happen to her. A cramp—deeper than hunger—knotted her belly.

She had not changed from the blue-striped pajamas. The cotton fabric carried the slightly metallic odor of sweat and fear. She curled on her side. The dime in her hand was hot with her sweat. Slowly she unclenched her fist and looked. Of course the date on the coin had not changed. 1931.

Her mind closed and she retreated to the dim, shadowy, half-conscious place where thinking stopped. She hummed a soft, tuneless sound, but was unaware of doing so.

She needs you.

She heard the voice as clearly as earlier she had heard the ringing of the telephone, the sound of Klietman repairing the hall light. "There is no one there," she said aloud, a prickly feeling on her scalp.

She needs you. The voice was steady, emphatic.

She didn't deny it this time. She knew what it wanted. "I can't," she said desperately. It was more than she could give.

But you did earlier. Earlier you were willing to help.

"That was before."

Before what?

"You know what." The dime burned in her hand. She dropped it on the bed.

Oh, before you knew it was, what? Real? Before you knew it was real? What kind of courage does that call for?

"I can't. Don't you understand? I can't. I'm afraid." Each word was thick, urgent.

You're the only one.

She began to rock in the bed, swaying back and forth. She was cold now with a chill that snaked up her spine and crawled across her scalp.

No. She began to hum again, as if to drown out the unwelcome voice. Soon another melody, counterpoint to her humming, circled in the back of her brain. A Frank Sinatra song her mother had played over and over one year. Let's fly, let's fly, let's fly. The words echoed like a needle caught in a groove. She stopped humming and covered her ears with her hands.

Coward.

The voice was a stranger's, but the noun was familiar, a mocking, one-word echo that had followed her all her life, trailing her, shaming and deriding. A voice she thought was Billy's.

She bit her cheeks to keep from crying out. If once she be-

gan to scream, she knew she would not stop. She forced herself
to stop rocking. She frowned with concentration as she looked
around the room. Her eyes fell on the bedside clock. 5:35.
That was good. Specific. An anchor in time.

Please help me.

She inhaled sharply. This was a different voice. She knew,
even while dread knotted her chest, that it was the child.

There was no child. It was a dream.

She began to rock again. Let's fly, let's fly, let's fly, Frank
sang on in her head.

She climbed out of bed and crossed to the dresser. The roll
of tape and dimes were on top where she had placed them the
day before.

"My name is Soleil Browne," she said as she reached for the
coins, "daughter of Helen Browne." She picked up the tape. "I
am thirty-five years old. I live in an apartment in Orient
Heights, Boston. I am a research librarian and I work at the
Museum of Science. I am in love with Dr. Andrew McKey."
She recited these facts like a child dropping bread crumbs so
there would be a path to follow back out of the woods.

She tucked her hair behind her ears and taped a dime to her
left temple. Then one to her right.

Her hands froze as she began taping a third dime to her jaw.
She heard the sharp, frantic sound of Tootsie barking.

Not my problem, she said. She tried to shut out the barking, but it persisted. She heard, too, the echo of the cop's
words: "My guess is the dog gets put down."

She sighed, gave in. One final thing she would do before she
went to the child. Tannazzo's key was in the kitchen drawer, in
a box holding rubber bands and twist ties. "For emergencies,"
he'd said when he gave it to her.

The rays of the ceiling light reflected on the painted walls.
She hesitated and then stepped out into hall, peered down the

stairwell. There was no one there. She noticed a sweet odor, too faint to identify. She crossed to Tannazzo's door.

"Tootsie," she called.

From inside the apartment, she heard the corgi's soft whining.

The room was crowded with furniture and every surface held an assortment of little bells. Tootsie was curled up on the sofa. "Come on," she called. The corgi whined and looked at her with watery eyes. There was a bowl of untouched food by the door.

"Come on, girl," she urged, but the corgi did not budge. When she lifted her, the small body trembled.

"Poor old thing," she said. She hugged Tootsie closer and left the apartment.

Again in the hall, she picked up the faint, sweet smell. Her brain identified it just as the hands grabbed her shoulders. *Chocolate.* The hands were rough, pushing her forward into the apartment.

Tootsie wriggled free, half fell, half jumped to the floor. Somewhere in her brain, she heard the deep-throated growl. Behind her, a sharp movement. Tootsie's responding yip of pain. The grasping hands, which had loosened their grip momentarily, tightened again.

Absurdly, then, she thought of Alison. Alison and all her warnings.

Fight, she heard Alison say. It was enough to break through the paralyzing shock. She struggled, broke free, and stumbled forward, sucking in air. The shadow man. Here. Not in her dreams.

But not the dream man at all.

He blocked her path to the kitchen, the hall. She ran toward the window, screamed. It was the first sound she had made since he had grabbed her in the hall. He hit her then, and the shock of the blow cut off her scream. He hit her again. This time the force knocked her against the bookcase. A lamp crashed. A light bulb exploded. He was speaking to her now, but she could not understand the words.

His hands found her throat again. She twisted away, nearly escaped before his hands grabbed her again and pinned her against the floor.

Light and darkness played and swam before her eyes. He had come for her after all. This is what I was afraid of, she thought.

This is what she had been afraid of all her life. She was going to die. She couldn't save herself, any more than she had been able to save Billy Bascombe. Or the child in her dreams.

"I'm sorry." She tried to speak, but fingers tightened around her throat, shutting off her words. And then . . . "Mamom." But the room was already turning black.

CHAPTER 38

Shoe huddled in the woods near Overton, falling in and out of a restless sleep.

Bees could drive dogs crazy and kill grown men. Just what he deserved, she told herself. He got just what he deserved for killing Gee Whiz. Her stomach ached liked she'd been eating green apples.

"I ain't sorry if he's dead," she said, but the defiant words could not make her belly sickness go away.

She waited for daylight. She missed Ruby. She even missed Fortune. Once or twice, she caught herself praying. She cut these prayers short. Prayers couldn't go as far as spider spit to fix her face, she thought as she watched the sun being born. She didn't believe in God and she didn't believe in miracles.

She shook the old leaves and dirt off herself. She would be strong, not weak. She'd start by making plans.

The sun was higher now. She took a moment to open her suitcase and get out one piece of Ruby's bread. She used a twig to spread a little jam on it. She took small, careful bites. When she was finished, she was still hungry, but she didn't take another slice. The food from Ruby's kitchen would have to last her. She didn't know how long it would be before she found Thomas.

When she first went to the Cades', she had asked Ruby where the carnival went after it left Fortune. "Usually heads west," Ruby had told her, "goes from town to town for most of the summer." It had been more than a month since Thomas had disappeared. She figured he could even be as far as Cincinnati. The next thing to do was head over to Danville and buy a train ticket going west.

She walked along the road and thought about her brother. Soon they'd be together. Then a picture of him in the sideshow tent looking up at the dancer flashed in her head.

She knew girls liked Thomas. All the girls in her class giggled and showed off whenever he was around. He pretended not to notice, but she knew that he liked the attention.

One of her classmates told Shoe that her older sister snuck out at nights to meet him behind the bowling alley. Shoe knew who the girl was, a tenth grader with buck teeth who wasn't even pretty. She couldn't imagine Thomas kissing such an ugly girl. But then she couldn't imagine that her brother would have ever taken the money from the Mason jar and run off, even if he had promised to come back for her.

She just had to get to him soon. She quickened her pace toward Danville. Twice she had to leave the road to hide in the long grasses growing alongside the road because a car was coming.

Fortune was no more than a crossroads with a half dozen stores, but Danville was a real town. There was a post office and a beauty parlor, a hotel, picture show, a café, and across the street from the café, a railroad station. It was nearly noon when she arrived, but things were quiet. She headed for the depot.

A weathered wooden baggage cart stood down the platform from the station and she slipped behind it. She took a minute to look things over before she entered the depot.

Cool, dusty air greeted her as she opened the door. The only furniture was a long oak bench that looked like a church pew. A tired dark-haired woman sat on the bench, holding a toddler on her lap. As Shoe walked past, the woman looked up at her, then quickly averted her eyes. Shoe pretended not to notice when the woman sheltered the child's sleeping face from hers.

Her footsteps echoed as she walked across the slate floor to the ladies' room. After she'd peed, she went to the basin and splashed cool water on her face. A loop of worn linen hung from a bar next to the basin. She tugged it around full circle, but it was grimy and damp. She pulled her shirttail out from her overalls and blotted her face dry.

The ticket clerk peered at her through a barred window, just like in a jail. Behind gold-framed spectacles, his eyes were sly, like one of Harley's sheep. She looked straight back at him, but he did not drop his gaze from her face. She felt heat creep up her neck and spread over her cheeks.

"Can I help you, little lady?" he asked. His eyes seemed to narrow.

Her belly lurched. Maybe there was a law against traveling alone if you were a child. She'd never heard there was, but she'd never traveled anywhere before. She wondered if it required special permission. She wished she had given these matters some thought before.

"Can I help you?" he asked again.

"I need a ticket," she ventured. "To Cincinnati." She didn't figure that Thomas could be farther west than that.

"That'd be on the Crescent."

"Yes." She hadn't known that trains had names.

His eyes narrowed. "One way or round trip?"

"One way," she said.

She heard, behind her, the sound of the heavy station door opening, then closing. Involuntarily, her back muscles tightened.

The sheep eyes flickered over to the door and back to Shoe. She risked a glance, saw with relief that it was only an old couple. The clerk separated a ticket from a large roll on the counter and slid it along the shelf beneath the iron-barred window.

"That'll be thirty-five cents," he said. His fingertips still held the edge of the ticket.

Carefully she took a quarter and a dime from the money in her pocket. She wondered how long the Mason jar money would last. Long enough, she prayed, for her to find her brother.

The ticket man pushed the ticket toward her. He told her it'd be an hour before the Crescent came through.

In spite of Ruby's bread and jam, she was hungry. Outside, she looked up and down the street and then headed for the café directly across from the depot.

The place wasn't much. Two booths and four swivel stools at a counter. Four men perched on the stools. They turned toward her when she entered, then turned away, as if they had seen something shameful. She regretted she hadn't thought to take Ruby's veiled bee hat with her. She set her suitcase down under the booth and slid in on the bench, choosing the right-hand side so that the scar would be turned away from the men.

The waitress was a huge woman. Old Cora Simms was the biggest woman in Fortune and the waitress made her look small. Huge breasts that looked like they'd be a lot of trouble to lug around pressed against the waitress's stained uniform. Her name was spelled out in faded pink thread above her pocket. Maybelle.

The sign on the wall behind the counter said the Blue Plate Special cost twenty cents. She rolled the words in her mouth.

Blue Plate Special. She didn't know what it could be, but it sure sounded pretty.

"You got money?" the waitress asked. Her voice was squeaky, as if it belonged to a much smaller woman.

Shoe pulled a quarter out of her pocket and set it on the table. Satisfied, Maybelle took Shoe's order for the special down on her pad. "You be wanting the cornbread or the biscuit?"

Shoe's mouth watered. "Cornbread," she said.

Maybelle headed back toward the kitchen. When she walked, her hips jiggled up and down in a rhythm independent of her feet.

Minutes later, the waitress reappeared and slapped a plate down on the booth table. Shoe stared at the dish—beans, hot dog, a mount of slaw, and square of cornbread and a biscuit— and tried not to let her disappointment show. *Beans.* This was the Blue Plate Special? If she owned a café, she decided, she'd make sure the food matched up to the way it was advertised.

Maybelle looked back toward the kitchen, where a wrinkled man stood over a grill. She lowered her little voice so only Shoe could hear her. "Thought you looked hungry, so I brought you both the cornbread and the biscuit," she said.

The unexpected kindness made Shoe's stomach hurt almost as much as the hunger.

"What will you be wanting to drink?"

She looked over at a red and white sign hanging on the wall by the counter. "How much for a Coca-Cola?"

"Five cents."

She'd need to be practical. "I'll take a glass of water," she said.

Maybelle, walking like her feet hurt, returned to the counter, where she refilled the men's mugs and then busied herself wiping the counter, all the while looking across the café and watching the booth. Shoe tried to slow down, but she was so hungry, it was hard not to gobble. She wiped the bean juice up with the slab of cornbread. For a few minutes she was even able to forget about the Bogeyman.

Maybelle came back and set a glass of water on the table. "Where's your folks?"

"They're dead." She had spoken without thinking and immediately wished she could take the words back. Her story was nobody's business.

The fat face softened at once. "Both of them?"

Shoe nodded.

"You poor thing. You sit right there. I'll get you some ice cream."

Shoe felt a strange surge of something like power.

Maybelle brought her a silvery little dish holding a ball of pink ice cream *and* a glass of Coca-Cola.

She'd eaten too much, could feel the food weighing heavy in her belly, but nothing in the world could have stopped her from eating every spoonful of the ice cream.

When she finally left the café, she had tucked in her pocket a lard-and-tomato sandwich Maybelle had given her to take along on the trip to her aunt's. The lie about going to see her aunt, easily told, had satisfied Maybelle. Shoe wished she had thought to tell it to the ticket clerk at the station.

Meeting Maybelle and ordering a meal by herself, topped off with ice cream, seemed part of a grand adventure. As she returned to the depot and swung her suitcase up on the baggage cart, she felt the swell of anticipation. The road ahead, starting with the ride on the Crescent, seemed filled with possibilities. She had never traveled on a train before and couldn't even imagine what it would be like. And Thomas. Soon she would be seeing Thomas again.

She was still smiling at this thought when the long green Packard pulled up in front of the station. She shrank behind the baggage cart. "No," she whispered. A man got out, and for one moment she didn't recognize Roubiam. His face was fat and splotchy. Lumpy. Then she realized—the bee stings. He walked toward the café.

She felt the platform tremble beneath her feet and knew before she saw it or heard its drawn-out, lonely whistle that the Crescent was coming down the tracks.

There was no way she could get on the train without crossing in front of the station. Soon Mr. Roubiam would leave the café and cross to the station. He would question the sheep-eyed man, would know she'd been there. The ticket to Cincinnati—useless now—fell from her fingers and fluttered to the platform. The breeze took it up and it skidded like a dried oak leaf across the boards and down onto the train tracks.

She pictured Gee Whiz throwing the quarter into the Stonelick, pictured him crying upstairs in Mr. Roubiam's house, pictured him dead and buried by the river.

Please, she begged. Help me. Help me get away from the Bogeyman and help me find Thomas.

She knew she had stolen from her pa and told lies; she knew she'd sinned. She remembered how the women after Pa's death had talked about how nothing good ever came of sin, but still she prayed, harder than she'd ever prayed for anything, harder even than all those Sundays when she'd knelt and prayed for her face to be fixed, but she knew her prayers wouldn't be answered. There was no one who could come. No one who could help her.

CHAPTER 39

As the publicity for the exhibit ran, the crowds grew. Today there had been a line waiting when the door first opened, and now, at the end of the day, the visitors were reluctant to leave.

Andy flicked the lights in *Dreamscape,* signaling that it was closing time. As the last person straggled out, he switched off the laser and synthesizer. This afternoon, he'd found the dream music annoying, grating.

As he reached over to shut off the polysomnograph, he checked through the window and saw the volunteer had just awoken. He knocked on the glass. When she looked up, he drew a forefinger across his throat to signal that the exhibit was over. He heard her laugh through the partition.

She gave him a thumbs-up. She woke quickly without needing time to adjust. He supposed that came from her dispatching job at the fire department.

While she dressed, he locked up the booth. It seemed to take longer than usual, though when he checked his watch, it hadn't.

His stomach felt funny, the fluttery, hollow feeling he associated with trips to the doctor's and the nights before his college swim meets. His mind was on Soleil. He was eager to be with her again, to know that last night had not been a fantasy.

He thought he could still smell her perfume in the car, but knew he must be imagining it. He drove up the garage ramp, pulled out onto Mass Ave, and headed toward Orient Heights. The fluttery feeling intensified with each block he drove. He parked a block away, jogged the short distance to her apartment.

As he lifted a hand to ring the street bell, an Asian couple climbed the steps behind him. He backed off to make way for them, waited while they slid their key in the lock. The woman eyed him nervously. He smiled. "Nice evening."

He grabbed the door before it could shut behind them. The woman edged closer to the man. "I'm visiting Ms. Browne," he explained. "On the third floor."

He followed them up the first flight of stairs. They had reached the second-floor landing when they heart a crash from the third floor, followed by a scream cut short. Then another scream. Soleil.

"Get help," Andy said as he headed up the final flight.

The man shielded his wife and muttered something in a language Andy couldn't recognize. His hand trembled as he rushed to unlock his apartment.

"Get help," Andy yelled again over his shoulder. "The police. Call the police." It occurred to him that perhaps they didn't speak English. "The police," he repeated, holding an invisible phone to his ear.

From above came the sounds of a piece of furniture falling, glass breaking.

He took the rest of the flight two steps at a time.

Her apartment door was open. Over by the window, a cop crouched over Soleil.

"Soleil," Andy cried, his voice rough with fear. She didn't move.

The cop rose.

It took a moment—an instant of confusion and fear—for it to register that a cop was attacking her. The sight of the uniformed man paralyzed him. Some part of his brain told him to stay put, to wait for the police to arrive and straighten things out. This guy was a cop, after all.

A split second passed. Cop or not, the man was attacking Soleil. *Wait,* the sane, cautious voice urged Andy again.

But he dove, aiming for the cop's waist. The attacker let out a surprised grunt. The force drove both men back against the wall. Surprise had given Andy an advantage and the cop fell back, his mouth open, his arms limp by his sides. Andy reached out and grabbed the man's head with both hands, snapping it back, exposing his throat above the uniform collar, cutting off the startled rasp of exhalation.

He smashed the head against the wall and felt the man go weak. Behind him there was only silence. Terribly aware that he could not even hear the sound of her breathing, he risked a quick look back at Soleil. She had not moved.

This brief distraction gave the man all the time he needed to recover. A blow—a hard, sharp jab—caught Andy on the side of his jaw. He tried to tighten his hold, but the cop, no longer stunned by surprise, was twisting away, punching with renewed strength and fierceness. Andy stumbled back, fighting wildly.

The cop broke off and Andy watched in horror as he reached for his holster. With a cry he lunged for the cop's right hand, held on ferociously. The cop jerked away. Fists landed on Andy's ribs, his face. He fought back, his breath coming in labored sobs as he felt the blows strike his shoulder, neck, his left temple. Black specks danced behind his eyelids. He inhaled the hot, animal scent of the man's sweat.

Hands reached for his throat, tightened there; cruel fingers dug in, clawed. He brought his forearms up and broke the hold. The cop dodged, crouched, and his hand swept the floor, searching blindly. Andy caught a glimmer of light. Saw the hand come at him, felt a sting of coldness on his neck, like a point of ice had drawn a line there. Felt wetness. Warm. Blood.

The attacker held a shard of the broken lamp in his hand and slashed it again, this time catching Andy on the forearm. Hot, searing pain spread up his arm. Fury rushed through him. He pulled back, then punched the attacker full in the jaw. The man exhaled, collapsing like an inflatable toy. Andy hit him again. Both of them were on the floor now. Again Andy struck out. Felt the satisfaction of something breaking beneath his fist. Finally, aware that the cop no longer fought back, that his head rolled limply, he stopped. The man's face was wet with blood.

Andy rose and stumbled toward Soleil.

She law unconscious. Her pajama top was torn, exposing her right breast, where already a bruise was forming on pale skin. "Soleil," he whispered, pushing her name out past the raw hurt in his throat. His gaze fell on the rug beside her head. His breath caught as he saw three bright red spots. It took him only a moment to realize the red wasn't blood. He stared at the spots, metallic spots that were not spots at all. They were three small foil-wrapped hearts.

"Jesus," Andy said. Real fear, much worse than when he faced her attacker, tightened his chest. He lifted his eyes to Soleil's throat. Was she breathing? She *had* to be breathing.

"Come on, Soleil, my sun girl," he said softly. "Hang on. Just hang on." He crawled toward her.

Now he heard the sounds of footsteps running up the hall stairs. He reached an arm out to cradle Soleil, brushed her hair back from her face.

"What the hell," he gasped.

Dimes were taped to her temples.

"Jesus Christ," he said.

CHAPTER 40

The steps sounded from the hall. Quickly, Andy peeled the dimes from Soleil's temples, slipped them in his pocket. Bruises were already darkening the skin of her throat. He held her wrist, felt for her pulse. Her heartbeat throbbed steadily against his fingers. With his other hand, he pulled her pajama top closed.

At the door, a cop, gun drawn, glanced at the patrolman lying by the window. He edged in, his revolver covering Andy.

Andy nodded toward the unconscious man. "He tried to kill her."

The gun remained pointed at Andy. "Okay, just keep your hands where I can see them. Now stand up. Nice and easy. No quick movement."

Andy could not let go of Soleil.

"He tried to kill her," he repeated. "She needs help."

"Get the fuck up." The cop's voice was tight. "Get up before I blow your fuckin' head off."

Andy stood up, held his hands shoulder height, palms out. The gun barrel was pointed directly at his chest.

"Now, who the fuck are you?"

"Andy McKey." He struggled to keep his voice calm. The cop looked ready to explode. "Dr. Andrew McKey. I'm a friend." He nodded toward Soleil. "We work together at the museum."

"Got any identification?"

Andy fought the impulse to scream. Moving gingerly, careful to do nothing that could be misinterpreted and cause the cop to shoot, he reached for his wallet, flipped it open, offered it for inspection.

The cop scanned his license.

"Him?" The gun barrel waved toward the uniformed man.

"I don't know. I was on my way here, heard her scream. When I got here, she was like this. He was kneeling over her. He was strangling her. I tried to stop him."

Still holding his gun on Andy, the cop crossed to the unconscious man. A second cop appeared at the door. "You called in yet?" he asked his partner. He picked up the phone. Andy heard him speak to a dispatcher, heard him request an ambulance. Outside in the hall, the Asian couple and an older black-haired woman, breathing heavily from either the excitement or the three flights of stairs, bunched together.

"Better have them send two, Tony," the first cop said. "This guy's in rough shape."

"You know him?"

"Seen him around. His badge says Grunner."

Aware the cop's gun was still unholstered and the cop was still watching his every move, Andy scooped Soleil up in his arms and headed for the sofa. Blood flowed from the cut on his forearm, staining her pajamas. The wound on his neck burned.

"Let me do that," the cop named Tony said.

"I've got her." Andy didn't want anyone else touching her.

"You sure? That arm's going to need stitches."

"I've got her," he repeated.

The cop backed off. His gaze dropped to the floor where Soleil had lain, took in the foil-wrapped hearts. "Jesus H.
Christ," he said. His voice throbbed with excitement. "Davy,
look at this." He pointed at the three chocolates.

The tone in the room changed. "Don't touch anything," the
cop named Davy said, his voice edgy again. He raised his gun,
pointed it at Andy.

An older woman, black hair dyed so often it was flat and
lifeless, pushed past the Asian couple and came to the couch.
The cop tried to turn her back, but she nudged past him,
brushed Andy aside, and took Soleil's hands in hers and began
briskly chaffing them.

"Davy, get her the fuck outta here," Tony ordered.

"Terrible, terrible," the woman said. "A person can't be safe
in her own apartment." She continued rubbing Soleil's hands,
ignoring the cops. "You take care of that cut," she said to
Andy. "I'll watch her."

"Jesus Christ," the cop said. Andy headed toward the
kitchen. The second cop followed him, watched him find a
dish towel and wrap it around his arm. It didn't stop the
bleeding.

Andy returned as Soleil regained consciousness.

"Mrs. Abelini?" she asked. Her voice was thick, raspy.

"I'm right here, dearie."

"Just lie still," Davy said. "The ambulance is on its way."

She saw Andy then. Her face, already pale, turned white at
the sight of his arm, his neck, the blood. "My God," she
breathed.

"You know him?" Davy asked.

"Oh, Andy. Oh, God, you're bleeding."

"You know this guy?" the cop asked again. "Was he the one
who attacked you?"

She clung to Andy's hand. "No." She pointed to the uniformed body, unconscious. "He did."

"Shit," said Tony.

"What a fuckin' mess," his partner said.

In the distance, they heard the sound of sirens. Within minutes, the room was crowded with cops. The ambulance attendants arrived, and a man carrying what looked like a doctor's case but proved to hold brushes and jars of power. Another cop began to photograph the room. The first detectives arrived.

Andy sat next to Soleil, held her hand. "It's going to be all right," he told her.

She saw the blood seep through the towel on his arm, took in the cut on his neck. "Oh, God, how bad is it?" she said in a thick, bruised voice.

"Not serious."

They both watched as the attendants carried Grunner out on a stretcher. One of the detectives pulled on rubber gloves and picked up the foil-wrapped hearts.

Soleil shuddered. "It was him, wasn't it?" She began to tremble, felt again the pressure of the fingers on her throat. The shadow man. Here.

Then she allowed herself to be taken away. She wouldn't let go of Andy's hand all the way to the hospital.

The emergency room was a nightmare.

They sat for what seemed like hours answering questions. First from the admitting nurse, then from the doctors.

She refused to allow them to separate her from Andy, insisted on being with him even while an emergency-room doctor stitched up the cuts in his arm and neck. She held tightly to his hand while the doctor checked her bruises.

The police hung around in the background, waiting until the doctors were done, then they began their questions. They

showed her a photo of the man who had attacked her. She
stared at the fleshy face, shivering as she remembered his hands
on her neck. She noticed his uniform. "He's a cop?" she asked.
Her eyes darted back to the picture. She recognized him then.
The man beneath the gargoyle.

She must have seen him, taken his picture just after he had
killed his last victim. "I should have known," she said to
Andy. "Somehow I should have known." It seemed to her that
a murderer should have some visible mark that set him apart
from others, a stigmata that singled him out. She told the detective where to find her camera—still in her tote bag—and he
went off to phone the information to the police back in her
apartment.

When he returned, he told her more about the killer. "He's
a night patrolman in the city. His name's Louis Grunner."

She repeated the name. It meant nothing to her.

"You're one lucky lady," the detective said.

Her head ached.

The emergency-room staff tried to talk her into admitting
herself overnight. Just for observation, a doctor said, but she
refused.

"You sure you're not making a mistake? You'd be better off
here, where we can keep an eye on you. Just overnight."

"No," she said. She needed to be with alone with Andy.

They caught a cab. "Shall we go to my place?" he asked.

"No." She began to shiver. "I want to go home."

"You sure?"

"Please," she said. "Take me home. Let's just go home."

"You're cold." He reached for her hand.

"Yes." She wondered if the chill would ever go.

Vans from two of the city's television stations were parked in
front of her apartment. A crowd of reporters and photographers

gathered on the sidewalk, just beyond the yellow tape the police had used to cordon off the front entrance.

"You can't stay here," Andy said. "This is a circus."

"There's a service entrance in the alley behind the building. We can go in there."

"Why don't we go to my place?"

She needed to be in her own apartment.

It was after midnight before the last of the detectives left. Their imprint still remained in the apartment, just as the attacker's touch seemed burned in her neck. The Sweetheart Strangler's touch. She began to shiver again. *He had come into her home.* He had nearly killed her. She pushed the thought away.

Her eyes flicked from the smashed lamp back to the front door. The lock looked suddenly fragile. "Will you stay?" She was shaking harder.

"Of course," Andy said. He paused awkwardly, as if unsure of what to do next.

"Hold me?" she asked.

"Yes." He could feel her trembling, tightened his arms around her. "It's going to be all right," he said.

"I'm cold."

"Listen," he said gently. "Do you want to take a shower? Or a bath? I'll stay right here. I'll just sit here until you're done. Take as long as you need."

She wondered how he knew she needed Grunner's touch washed from her body.

She stayed in the shower for nearly a half hour, letting the water stream over her body, plastering her hair to her scalp and soothing her bruised neck. She opened her mouth and let the water stream in and then spit it out in a gush. But even when she finally turned off the water, she couldn't seem to erase the smell and touch of the man, the faint odor of chocolate.

She slipped on a robe.

Andy sat on the sofa. Tootsie was nestled in his arms.

"Tootsie," she said. "I forgot about her."

"I heard a noise. She was hiding under your bed."

"Is she all right?"

"Scared. Her side seems tender. Other than that I think she's okay. I'm pretty sure nothing's broken."

It was dark. Andy had closed the blinds and straightened the room. A fresh pot of tea sat on the coffee table between two mugs.

She sat on the couch. As she dried her hair with a towel, her fingers discovered a sore spot where her head had hit the floor, and she winced.

"You okay?"

"Bruised. What about you? How's your arm?"

"Numb. Thank God for Novocain."

"He was the man," she said after a moment.

"The man?"

"The one who was following me. I thought I was imagining it, imagining that I heard footsteps. I was confused with the dreams, but now I know he was the one. He's been *following* me."

She began to shiver again.

"Don't," he said. "Try not to think about it. Come here." He took her hand, led her back into her bedroom. She lay beside him, unable to relax, straining to hear sounds from the front room.

"Try not to think about it," he repeated. And then, "It's okay. It's over."

He touched her neck gently. She winced and cried out when his fingers stroked the bruised spots.

"I should have killed him," he said fiercely. "If anything happened to you—" He couldn't go on.

"Shhh," she whispered. It was her turn to comfort him.

She reached up and ran her fingers over the bandages on his neck, his forearm. It had taken five stitches to close the gash on his neck, eighteen for his arm. Her touch was light, but he winced. "God, I'm sorry," she whispered.

"I love you, Soleil."

She curled against him, allowed her eyes to close.

"I love you too." She was warmer now. Safer.

He bent over, kissed her mouth, her cheek, then brushed his lips over her neck. The bruised spots. She shivered.

"Did I hurt you?" He pulled back, looked at her.

She shook her head. She needed him to make the other man's touch fade, to make her safe. "Does your arm hurt?"

"No."

He kissed her again.

He looked at her, the gaze a question. "Maybe we'd better wait." She took his hand, guided it to her belt, helped him un-tie the robe, open it.

"Jesus."

Bruises, larger and darker than those on her throat, made dusky shadows on her ribs, spread across one breast. There was another on her thigh. He started to draw the robe together.

She stopped his hands. "It's okay," she said.

"You're so bruised. I'm afraid of hurting you more."

She took his hand, led him to the wetness of her.

This time he did not pull away.

They lay curled in the darkness for a long time. He got up once, brought them each a glass of water. She found it hurt to swallow. Her throat was hurting more now than it had at the hospital. Her body was stiff and sore, reminders of the attack, but she now crept into the safety that Andy had created.

"He was here," she said, remembering.

"Don't talk about it," he said. "Not tonight. Later. But not tonight."

She knew he was right. This was where she belonged. She would be safe with him. Nothing else mattered. Not even the dreams.

"What's wrong?" he asked.

"Nothing."

"You just shuddered."

"It's nothing." She pushed away thoughts of the dreams. She couldn't go back to them. She reached for the security of his hand.

But once recalled, the dreams were not so easily banished. She thought of the girl, and the heaviness of failure settled in her chest.

"What is it?"

She considered telling him then, but she couldn't risk losing him.

"It's okay, Soleil," he said. "Whatever it is, it's okay. Just tell me."

"I don't know how."

"Just begin. Trust me."

"You'll think it's crazy." She laughed a shaky laugh. "Even I think it's crazy."

He didn't respond, just waited for her to continue. Finally he reached over and pulled his jacket free from the pile of clothes next to the bed. "It's about this, isn't it?" He fumbled until he found the jacket pocket, the length of tape. The dime was still stuck to it.

"Yes." She began to turn away. He held her.

"Whatever it is," he said, "you can tell me."

She stared at the dime. Her voice was low, nearly a whisper. "The dreams began at the museum. Very vivid. Very real."

A vision of her REM printout flashed in his mind, and he nodded.

"There was a house. A carnival, once. And a child. I thought at first it was someone I knew when I was a little girl. A boy named Billy."

"Then you found it wasn't." Unconsciously, he made his voice low, matching hers.

"No. It was a little girl. A girl who had some kind of terrible injury to her face." She paused. It was hard to continue. "This is where it gets kind of crazy." She stopped again. "I'm afraid to tell you."

"Soleil, I swear. Whatever it is, you can tell me."

"Well, I started to get confused. Things from the dreams got mixed up with everyday stuff. And the girl—"

He held her, let her take her time.

"You remember the night at the Sail Loft? When I ran out into the street?"

"Yes."

"I saw her. I swear I saw her on the sidewalk."

"Dreams can seem real," he said carefully.

"There's more. A man. A shadowy man who is stalking the child. And there's a town. An old town, rural. I saw a sign in the dream. Fortune Groves, Ohio. I checked: There really is a town named Fortune Groves in Ohio. It exists. But I never heard of it before the dream."

"There's an explanation."

"Andy, I know it's nearly impossible to believe, but I never in my life heard of that town. And I went there. In the dream. I touched the child."

She remembered the smell of the child on her skin.

"I think you had a very vivid dream," he said softly. "So vivid you got confused."

She needed him to believe her. "Wait," she said. She got up

and went to the bureau. "The last dream I had, I held her hand. I mean I really held her hand." Her fingers tightened around an object she had taken from the shelf. "She gave me this. Here." She handed him the dime.

He hesitated, then accepted the coin.

"Look at the date," she said.

He read the year. 1931.

"Old," he said, his voice carefully neutral.

"When I woke up, it was in my hand."

He continued to stare at the dime.

"Do you understand? She gave me this. I was with her. Don't you see? Really with her."

His voice was gentle. "You know that's impossible, Soleil."

"I know it sounds nuts. But it happened. I swear it." She needed him to believe her.

"I'm sure there's a rational explanation."

On the floor by the bed, Tootsie trembled in her sleep, chasing rabbits.

He put the dime on the nightstand. He avoided her eyes.

"In the exhibit," she began, "there's a quote on one of those posters in Light Space. By Friedrich Hebbel. 'Dreams are the best proof of the fact that we are not as securely locked inside our skins as it seems.' "

"That's philosophy. Not reality."

"But how do we know?"

"For God's sake, Soleil. We know. You are quoting poets, philosophers. I'm a scientist. I know what's possible."

He flashed back to the picture of her lying unconscious in her living room, the dimes taped to her temples.

"There's an explanation," he said again. He forced himself to be calm, keep his voice steady. "Listen. You thought you were being followed. This shadow man from the dream. Well, if what the cops say is correct, this maniac who attacked you has been following you. Your subconscious picked up on that. Maybe it was trying to warn you in your dreams."

She hadn't heard him. "All my life," she said. "All my life I've been afraid."

"Everyone's afraid, Soleil."

"Not like me. It's like every day, every step, I walk on the very edge of a canyon. It's just one short misstep to falling in." Her voice was matter-of-fact, as if they were discussing the weather.

"We all have fears."

"I have been running all my life. From everything. From my mother. From the knowledge that I don't even know who my father is. I'm like one of those kids who have that disease—you know, where they have no immune systems and so they live in a bubble? The 'Bubble Kids,' they call them. Well, I'm like one of them."

"Don't . . ."

"When I was ten, we lived in Beverly, on a horse farm. My mother had a job there as a nurse. The family had a son about my age." *You don't have to tell him. You don't have to tell anyone.*

But she knew she did. Keeping it inside didn't work. Nothing worked. There was no way to hide, nowhere that was safe. Because of the fears, the shadow men would always find her.

"There was a pond way in the back of the property. That winter, after school Billy and I used to go skating. Billy Bascombe.

"We weren't supposed to go without having an adult check the ice first. That was the only rule they had about skating. Billy said it was a baby rule and we were old enough to know if the ice was thick enough. He kept calling me a baby and said I was a 'fraidy cat."

Andy reached over and took her hand. "It's okay," he said.

She shook her head. "I mean, I was so tired of being afraid.

Of everything. Of all the new jobs, the new schools, new kids. Of the night and what might be waiting for me in the dark. So tired of it all. And he was so brave.

"We knew enough to stay away from the center where the river flowed through because it never froze solid there. But that day Billy kept skating closer and closer and calling me a 'fraidy cat until I began to skate out there too."

She shivered and he tightened his grasp on her hand.

"The ice began to crack. Little noises. But Billy still kept going. 'It's nothing,' he said. 'Ice always cracks.' Then there was a louder noise. Like a whip. Billy stood there laughing, and then the ice sort of folded right up beneath him. One minute there was ice there, and the next there wasn't. I was close enough to see his face. I'll never forget how his eyes got. So surprised. He looked right at me. 'Get my dad,' he said. He didn't scream. Not even then. He just said, 'Mom?' His eyes didn't look surprised anymore. They looked scared.

"I couldn't run. I couldn't do anything but stare at Billy. I kept staring even after he disappeared. I couldn't move. I was afraid the pond would take me too.

"It took me a long time to get home. I told my mother. She called the fire department. I heard the sirens, but I didn't go back while they tried to find him. They even had a diver with them, but they didn't get him.

"We moved after that. I think Mrs. Bascombe couldn't stand the sight of me after Billy died. She blamed me. *She blamed me.*" Her voice broke.

"It wasn't your fault."

She always remembered the way Billy's mother looked at her. And she remembered how her own fear had paralyzed her.

She let her hand lie in his.

"So you see," she said, "I have to go. This child needs me and I have to help her. Please."

"It's—"

"Please. I have to." He saw how hard it was for her to ask for help. "I've never done anything for anyone. I have to do this for her."

He knew what she was saying about going to the girl was unthinkable. Absolutely inconceivable. There was a sane explanation for the dime. The rest was the workings of an overwrought imagination.

He saw the plea in her eyes. "All right," he was amazed to hear himself agree. He regretted it almost immediately.

"Thank you," she said. Her eyes were grateful and he knew he couldn't back off now.

She held very still while he taped six dimes to her temples and forehead and jaw. It made him queasy to do it.

Then he sat in the darkened apartment and held her hand until she drifted off. He watched her sleep and wondered if they had both gone crazy.

There was no tunnel this time. No whirling noise. Almost immediately she was in the land and time inhabited by the child.

She stood on a wooden platform that fronted a building. A wooden structure painted mustard yellow and red. A sign on the roof read DANVILLE. *A railroad station. She did not see the child.*

In the distance, a long whistle sounded. Three people came out of the station and lined up on the platform. A woman—no more than thirty but already worn out—carried a child in her arms. She struggled with a brown suitcase. There was an older couple waiting for the train. The man looked toward the young mother but did not help her. She could see, even from a distance, the trace of tears dried in furrows on the toddler's dusty cheeks.

Then she saw the green car. A long, shiny, old-fashioned car. She knew the girl must be nearby.

CHAPTER 41

Shoe peeked out from her hiding place behind the baggage cart. She was sick from the Blue Plate beans and the ice cream. Across the street, the green Packard drew a small crowd to the curb. Two boys edged closer, itching to touch the car, peered through the windows. Their mouths hung open.

Roubiam came out of the diner. He shouted something to the boys, but Shoe could not hear what he said. Maybelle appeared in the doorway behind him and, hands on huge hips, looked down on the car and the crowd. In three quick strides, Roubiam was in the street, grabbing one of the boys by the arm, yanking him away from the Packard. The boy shook himself free, and without waiting to see if his friend or any of the townfolks would come to his defense, he ran. The other boy took off after him. Soon the rest of the onlookers sauntered off. A tall, long-limbed man spit a stream of tobacco in the street near the car's rear tire, close enough to spatter, and gave Roubiam a hard, daring look before he walked away. Maybelle shook her head, as if she'd seen everything now, and returned to the café.

Roubiam stood by his car protectively.

"Git in the car and drive away," Shoe whispered.

He turned back toward the station. She couldn't hesitate. Still shielded from sight by the baggage cart, she darted across the tracks. A row of dusty, half-dead shrubs bordered the rail line and she ducked down behind them. She felt as if she had been running from Mr. Roubiam all her life. She pulled two branches apart and peeked out. He crossed the street and headed into the station. In the distance, she heard the long, lonely sound of the Crescent's whistle as it approached.

As Roubiam entered the station, the dark-haired mother and her child came out, followed by the old couple. They lined up along the edge of the rails.

Shoe's eyes swept the platform, measuring her chances. Her suitcase was still on the baggage cart. Forget it, she told herself. Leave it. But she couldn't leave it. The Mason jar and money were inside.

CHAPTER 42

Across the tracks, the girl. The train whistle sounded again; she could hear its wheels rolling along the metal rails. Hurry. Hurry. Hurry. Their rhythm echoed in her heart.

As she watched, the girl ducked out from behind a bush and darted toward the platform. Halfway across the tracks, the child stumbled. Soleil's heart leaped and pounded more fiercely. She watched the station door, willing the shadow man to stay inside until the child could escape.

CHAPTER 43

Roubiam was still in the station. Shoe gauged the distance from her position behind the shrub to the baggage cart. There was really no decision. She'd have to have the money. Without the money there was no chance of escape.

The Crescent's whistle sounded again, closer now. She couldn't wait anymore. She darted across the tracks, stumbling once and twisting her ankle. She grabbed her suitcase from the cart.

She didn't look back. Down the street, past the café, past the green Packard, she ran. She could hear the sound of the train rolling closer, the whistle sounding its sharp, lonely cry.

Her twisted ankle slowed her down. She ran unevenly, trying to think as she ran. The fat waitress must have told Roubiam she was taking the train. The sly-eyed clerk would remember selling her the ticket to Cincinnati. Roubiam would wait until the Crescent came, to see if she got on.

She had a few minutes, maybe five or six, until the train

pulled in. Then he'd know he had missed her. She wondered if any of the passengers had seen her and would tell him she had run off.

As she ran, the suitcase banged against her leg with a rhythm that pounded in her head. *He's coming. He's coming. He's coming.*

The ankle she had twisted back on the tracks began to throb. She willed the panic away.

Roubiam wouldn't want a scene. He wouldn't want to give her a chance to tell her story.

If he meant to kill her like he'd killed Gee Whiz, he'd have to do it when no one was around. *Run, girl, run.* If he got her into the green car, she was dead. As dead as the colored boy the Wheeler brothers had found buried by the Stonelick.

The road ahead yawned like an open mouth. A hole. A grave. Like the one he must have dug by the Stonelick. He couldn't have hired any help to dig that grave. Mr. Roubiam, with his soft hands, hands that had never seen labor before, had to dig all alone by the Stonelick. She thought of her ma and pa. Already dead.

Don't think like that. Don't think like that. Her ankle throbbed insistently now. It hurt to breathe. All the food she'd eaten churned in her stomach and burned her throat. She strained to hear, above the sound of her ragged breath and the flapping of her feet against the road, the *ruhr-ruhr* of a car on the road behind her, but there was only the call of a crow overhead.

Please, she prayed, please come and help me.

CHAPTER 44

She ran beside the child. They would need a place to hide. Ahead the road swept on, rolling against the open landscape. To the left there was a house, and behind it a lean-to of some kind. Go to the barn, she urged the child. Go hide behind the barn. The child paused in her running, tilted her head, as if listening. Go to the barn, she repeated. She heard, in the distance, a whistle and knew the train was beginning its slow roll out of the station.

CHAPTER 45

Shoe felt her breath catch at the faint smell—so faint she hardly dared speak for fear it would go away. The smell of fall apples. She heard the voice speak in her head, and without hesitation she obeyed. She crossed the yard and ducked behind a barn.

She leaned against the barn boards, sucking in air. She heard the buzzing of flies. That's all it is, she comforted herself, flies. But the buzzing grew louder until she knew she was hearing the unmistakable sound of a car engine hurling past on the road.

CHAPTER 46

She was being called away, back. No, she pleaded, not yet. I can't leave her yet. She needs me. Not yet. Not yet.

The child, the farm, the landscape all began to fade.

She was in the mists. Whirling mists. She couldn't find the tunnel or the child or anything that was familiar. She knew she was lost.

CHAPTER 47

What am I going to do? Tell me what to do. Shoe swallowed to fight off nausea. Her ankle wobbled and she knew it was swollen. She was afraid to look at it. She inhaled deeply, needing to catch the scent of fall apples.

All she could smell was the odor of manure and sour milk. She was alone again.

Come back, she pleaded. Please come back. But she didn't know whom she was calling to.

CHAPTER 48

Andy's apprehension, faint at first, turned to fear.

Soleil's skin was waxen, white. Her pulse was faint, her skin cold to his touch. He didn't know what was happening, but whatever it was, it was scaring the hell out of him.

"Soleil?" He nudged her arm, but she did not respond to either his voice or his touch. She looked alarmingly close to being comatose. It occurred to him she might be in some kind of self-induced hypnotic state. He realized his hands were trembling.

Tootsie crept closer to the bed. The corgi had begun whining almost as soon as Soleil had fallen asleep.

"Soleil?" Andy took hold of her shoulders, shook her. She did not respond.

He shook her again, rougher this time. Still she did not react. He swallowed, his throat suddenly dry. He slapped her face. Her head rolled to one side from the blow, lifeless as a doll's. He felt sick to his stomach.

In a mixture of panic, confusion, and fury, he pulled the strips of tape off her face. An expression of disgust twisted his mouth and he tossed the coins and tape on the floor.

How had he let himself be talked into this? He wasn't even sure what *this* was. He didn't have a clue to what was happening to Soleil, but he was certain what it wasn't. People didn't—*couldn't*—leave their bodies when they dreamed.

The thought was cut short by a sound from Soleil. He bent his head close, heard what he thought was a single word. "No."

"Soleil?"

Her eyes fluttered open. She looked up at him; there was no sign of recognition.

"Soleil? Hon?" A cold dread took hold of him. "Hon, it's me, Andy."

She stared at him, her eyes empty, lifeless.

Then she began to tremble, a deep tremor that shook her whole body. He took the blanket from the end of the bed and tucked it around her.

"Listen, hon. Just lie here. Stay quiet. I'm going to call a doctor."

"No." She whispered the word. She reached out and took his hand in a tight grip.

"I'll be right back. I promise. I'm just going to call a doctor. I think someone should see you."

"No. Please."

The dreadful blankness lifted from her eyes, but he still wasn't sure she recognized him. He sank down on the bed by her side. She still clung to his hand. The light from the kitchen cast shadows in the darkened room.

Gradually she returned to full consciousness. He watched her come back, watched comprehension return to her eyes. It seemed to take a long time.

"Why did you bring me back?"

That's what she'd said: Bring me back.

"I had to." Nausea closed his throat.

"No."

"Don't talk. Just rest."

Sweat sheened her face. "I think I'm going to be ill."

He remembered the times in *Dreamscape* when she woke from REM sleep disoriented and nauseated. "Take a deep breath." He got a facecloth from the bathroom, wrung it in cold water, and returned to the bedroom. HE folded the wet cloth and placed it on her forehead. The pattern of the bruises on her jaw and neck was spreading, like a stain.

"I have to go back," she said. "He's going to kill her."

"Stop it. Just stop it." Fear made him angry.

Tootsie whined at the foot of the bed.

"I'm sorry," he said after a minute. "I just don't know what the hell is going on here."

"I—"

"I couldn't wake you."

"I—" she began again.

"I was scared when I couldn't wake you."

"I have to—"

"Don't. Don't talk about it."

"I have to go back."

"No."

"I *have* to. She needs me."

"Listen, Soleil, I don't know what the hell this is all about, but I don't want any part of it. I don't know what you're doing, but I think it's risky. You don't know. You couldn't see yourself, but for a minute . . ." He hesitated, but anger forced the words out of him. "For a minute, I was afraid that you were going to die. Whatever is happening, I think it's dangerous. So just stop now."

He had taken her hand in his. She let it lie there.

"It's not dangerous," she said.

"How do you know?"

"I just know." But she didn't really.

"Tomorrow," he said, buying time. "Let's talk about it tomorrow. Okay? You've been through too much today. Why don't we try and get some sleep now?"

She studied him, saw his fear and anger. "All right," she agreed after a minute.

He was relieved, but the concession seemed to have taken the life from her. Her face was dull, expressionless.

"I'll stay with you," he said. "We can talk in the morning."

"Okay," she said in a tired, resigned voice.

He pulled back the blanket and slid in beside her. Earlier he had put on his slacks and shirt and he kept them on now.

"Hold me," she said.

He wrapped his arms around her, felt a dull bolt of pain in his forearm, groaned.

"What?" she said.

He eased his arm free. "The stitches. I guess the Novocain is wearing off."

She sat up, concerned, ran a forefinger lightly over the bruise that was forming on his cheek.

"Maybe I'd better sleep on the sofa," she said.

"No way." He reached up with his free arm and pulled her close. Another groan escaped.

"Let me get you an asprin." She felt edgy, nervous. Worried.

"I should be taking care of you."

"We can take care of each other. Why don't you get out of those pants and get comfortable while I'm getting the aspirin?"

"Insatiable," he said, smiling sleepily.

"I promise I won't lay a hand on you."

"Shit," he said. "I was afraid of that."

She brought him two aspirin. He drank the water, handed her back the glass. She turned to set it on the nightstand. The winged Mercury coin was lying there. She didn't touch it. To-morrow. She glanced at Andy. His eyes were already closed.

"You okay?" he asked after a moment when she had not joined him. He sounded exhausted.

"I'm kind of edgy. Reaction to everything, I guess."

"Come here," he said. His eyes were still shut. "Let me hold you."

"I don't know if I can sleep," she said. "I might heat some milk, see if that helps. Do you want some?"

"I don't think so." He was drifting off. "Do you want me to make it for you?"

She leaned over and kissed him lightly. "No. You're already half asleep. I'll be right back. Just keep the bed warm."

She went into the living room, checked the lock on the door, made sure the chain was in place. She tested the lock on the service door in the kitchen, made sure that too was secure. She had forgotten to buy milk. There was a package of cocoa mix in the cupboard, but she didn't want that. Didn't want tea either. She wandered back to the bedroom.

She picked up the dime from the nightstand. The head on the coin—winged Mercury—reminded her of the radiator cap on the long green car.

She returned to the bed, lay down next to Andy, careful not to bump his arm. She reached over and stroked his forehead.

"Feels good," he mumbled.

"Good."

"Better get some sleep," he said, trying to pull back from the edge of sleep, to stay awake for her. "We'll have to be ready to face the onslaught tomorrow."

"Onslaught?"

"Mmmmm. Reporters. Police."

"I can't even think of facing them."

He reached a hand over and rubbed her back. "I'll be with you."

"Yes." She clung to that idea.

She watched him fall asleep. Held his hand in hers.

Andy had assured her that it hadn't been her fault that Grunner had entered her apartment and tried to kill her. It was nothing she had done. She knew now that no matter now carefully you lived, there was always a shadow man out there. Waiting. Beneath black ice or on a city street.

But if you knew he was out there, sometimes you had to try to fight him.

Sometimes there wasn't any choice. She knew then that she had to go back. No matter what she had promised Andy.

She gently withdrew her hand from his and got out of bed. She found the tape on the bureau.

"Soleil?"

He was awake, watching her.

She turned to him, "Andy, I have to."

"Jesus."

"I know you can't understand, but I have to go back."

He fought to keep his anger, his fear under control.

"I thought we agreed we'd talk about it tomorrow."

"I can't wait. I need to go now."

"What the hell do you mean, 'go'? Go where?"

"I don't know. Fortune Groves."

His arm pulsed with pain and his head ached. He felt unable to resist her.

"You're still going?"

"Yes."

She remembered losing him before. She didn't want to lose him again. "I have to," she finally said.

He saw the determination in her face. And something else too. He realized she looked calm, no longer afraid.

"I have to," she said again. "And I guess I want . . . I want you to be by me. I'll understand if you can't, but I just want you to know I'd like you to be here." To help me back, she wanted to add, but didn't.

Her calmness helped him decide. "I'll be here," he said.

"I need you to promise. This time—no matter what—promise you won't wake me."

He didn't answer. Finally he spoke. "I'm afraid for you," he said.

"Will you promise?"

"Yes," he said.

He couldn't watch while she taped the coins to her jaw and forehead and temples.

CHAPTER 49

Shoe was tired and frightened. She huddled behind the barn; every sound held terror. After a while, she slept. When she woke, the sun was low in the sky. Before long, it would be dark. She didn't want to sleep in the woods again, as she had the first night. Tonight she'd have to find another place to go. She stood up, then sank down again. Her right ankle was swollen from where she'd twisted it running across the train tracks. It hurt just to stand and she couldn't think about trying to walk.

She remembered once one of the men in the crew who came for the haying had wrenched his ankle. Her ma had wrapped strips of sheet around it and the man had been able to work. She opened her suitcase and took out a shirt, ripped it into strips. She tied them around her ankle. That helped. She poked around behind the barn until she found a length of wood she could use as a cane. She'd have to leave the suitcase behind. She slipped her pa's knife in her pocket. Thomas's cup she'd have to leave behind in the suitcase. She took part of the torn shirt and dumped the money from the Mason jar into it, then tied it in a knot. She put this in her other pocket. The paper the dwarf had written her name on she tucked in her pocket with her pa's knife. She held the ribbon she'd won in the spelling bee and ran her fingers over the blue satin. Miss Rogers and her school seemed far away. She thought about all the things a person worked hard for that didn't really matter. She left the ribbon with the suitcase.

She didn't know how far away the next town was, but she started out. Even bandaged, her ankle hurt when she walked on it. Don't be a baby, she scolded herself as she hobbled along the road. Think of other things.

She fell into a rhythm, step on left foot, half-hop on right. Step on left foot, half-hop on right. The road stretched out in front of her. The fields and sky were aglow in the fire of the morning sun. The edges of the fields and road were softened in the light. She'd lived in Ohio all twelve years of her life, but she'd never seen it looking like this, all glowing and beautiful. In spite of her ankle and the fear, the sight made her hopeful. She never thought land, just plain, sweet land could look so pretty, like she was walking into a painting.

She thought about Thomas. He was out there somewhere. Waiting for her. She thought about how brave he was and how he never cried, even when their pa beat him. She wanted to thank him for all the times he'd comforted her and protected her. She had long ago forgiven him for leaving her, for taking half the money.

She thought about her ma and how the only time she had seen her ma cry was just before she'd died. Ma had looked right at her and said, "Come closer, baby." It had been a long, long time since her ma had called her baby. Then her ma had made her lie down on the sickbed right at her side. Shoe remembered the smell of her ma's skin, sour touched with the heavy sweetness of something gone bad. She'd looked at her ma's dried lips—all cracked and thin—and waited for her ma to scold her for being too noisy, but her ma had hugged her tight and cried. Her ma, who never cried. "I'm sorry, baby," she'd said. "I'm so sorry."

She thought about her pa. How silent he was. She remembered the weight of his silence as he climbed the stairs of the farmhouse, remembered waiting to see if he would stop outside her door, hers or Thomas's, remembered praying that he would not be coming to give them a thrashing for some wrong they had done during the day. Then—in the midst of these memories—she suddenly heard the sound of his whistling. The whistling man seemed to have nothing to do with the man who beat her and Thomas with his belt.

Thinking of her family made her throat feel thick and funny.

Her ankle was buzzing now. Like bees had settled in there.

Thinking of bees brought Ruby Cade to mind. She thought about how a person could talk all she wanted about God and sin and churchgoing behavior, yet it wasn't what a person said but what she did that counted. She pictured Ruby's bare feet firm in the soil of her garden as she hoed the rows. Pictured her standing by the beehive while the bees swarmed around her and knew that Ruby Cade understood secrets none of the women in Fortune would ever know or learn. She was glad she hadn't taken any of Ruby's honey-jar money when she left.

The bees in her ankle were angry now and the buzzing was so loud she could scarcely think. She pursed her lips and, for the thousandth time, tried to whistle like her pa. She almost got close. Close enough to shut out another sound she heard coming up on the road behind her.

She whistled louder, louder, louder, but the low dangerous sound of a car engine drew closer to her. Closer.

CHAPTER 50

She was sucked into the vortex and then, almost immediately, was fly-ing. She followed a road past fields, and then she saw the child. The girl was tiny against the landscape. She saw, in the distance, a green car approaching, closer and closer to the girl.

I'm coming, she told the child, not knowing if the girl could hear her. Not knowing what she could do. Only knowing that she had to try.

CHAPTER 51

The sound behind her was getting louder now. She didn't dare look over her shoulder. She knew what she would see.

Still, she tried to run, but after a few steps, her ankle gave way. She fell, got up, and tried again. She bit her lip to stop from crying with pain. A step was all she could manage. Step, half-hop. Step, half-hop. Step, half-hop. On each half step a blade of fire touching deep in her injured ankle.

The engine noise was closer. She had to look. Had to know. She twisted her head, got a quick glimpse, enough to see the flash of green and the silver lady flying directly at her.

"Ma," she cried. "Mama."

Pain stabbed her ankle and a new one knifed her ribs. She heard the car coming closer.

Then she smelled the scent of fall apples and new-mown hay. Same as she had smelled by the yard by Ruby's beehive just before she'd pushed it on top of Mr. Roubiam. She wondered if this meant she was going to die. And then, before she could think anymore, she felt the shock of the car hitting her.

She was conscious of being lifted—of floating in the air—and then of falling, landing, waiting for pain, but there was nothing. And then the sky, the sky that had moments before been so beautiful, was no longer blue and gold, but suddenly dark, as if night had come in one instant.

CHAPTER 52

She watched, helplessly, as the car smashed into the child. Watched the slender body flung into the air. For a long and terrifying moment the girl's arms and legs hung limp in midair, and then they crumpled and the body landed in the ditch by the road. No, she cried. She couldn't be too late. Not now.

The green car slowed, then reversed. She watched as the shadow man opened the door. The car idled like a waiting animal while he got out. He walked over to the ditch and stared at the child, stretched out a leg and nudged her body with his toe. Waited. Satisfied, safe, he returned to the car and sped off.

CHAPTER 53

Shoe was cold. It felt like something had broken in her stomach. She couldn't feel her legs. She wondered if she was dying.

Then she saw Thomas. He had come for her. Thomas had come back, had found her. Everything would be all right. She smiled. "Thomas," she said, but the word was muffled. She wondered if she was dreaming.

She tried to smile. "I'm so cold," she said. She tried to sit up.

"Don't," said Thomas. Except that now she saw it was not Thomas at all, but an angel. An angel—so beautiful, so beautiful—floating toward her. "Don't, child," said the angel who looked like Thomas. "Don't move."

Not dreaming. Then she must be dead. If an angel was holding her, she must be dead.

But it hurt too much. The pain made the bees in her ankle seem like a tickle. To hurt this much, she must be alive. She didn't think it would hurt this much in heaven.

The pain—red, searing—was hot now. Then it grew worse, turning white.

"Please," she whispered to her angel, the angel who looked like her brother, although she didn't know what she was asking for.

The angel held her tight. She looked like she was crying, but Shoe couldn't be sure. Shoe didn't know angels cried.

She heard another sound, like a puppy whimpering, and then knew she was making that noise. She didn't want to die like this. Didn't want the Lord Jesus to see her like this.

"Please," she whispered.

The angel bent her head close. "What is it?"

Shoe's eyes, once bright, grew dull. She felt the cold intensify, turn to ice.

"What? What do you want?"

"Please." She knew what it was. One thing. All she had wanted since the day the doctor had taken the bandages off. She wanted her face smooth again. She wanted the scar gone.

"Yes, I'm here. What do you want?"

Shoe looked up. "Can you . . ." she began, but it was hard because she felt so weak, like everything was leaking out of her body. "Can you make it go away?"

CHAPTER 54

The child was dying. Despair filled her. There was nothing she could do. There was no way she could heal her.

She heard the child try to speak. Heard her say again the name. Thomas. Shhhhh, she soothed.

She bent forward and kissed her, pressing her lips to the scar, tasted the saltiness of her own tears on the wound.

The cold place in her chest, the place where her heart belonged, the spot filled with black ice just like the ice that had swallowed Billy Bascombe, the darkness where her father had disappeared, began to ache.

CHAPTER 55

The angel held her, wept. The tears fell, hot against the icy chill that crept through her body.

"Don't cry," she told the angel.

Then she heard her pa whistling, just like he always did, two notes at once.

"Don't cry."

She heard her ma calling her, saying, "Oh, baby."

The angel's tears were hot. Shoe lifted her hand to wipe them away. Her fingers touched her cheek, felt the skin there, now as even and smooth as when she was five.

Then she saw her ma, waiting for her.

The darkness began to lift and the sky again turned gold and blue, like it had been that morning when she started walking down the road and saw fields bathed in the glorious rose and golden light. Lighter and lighter it grew, as if she were rising to meet the sun.

CHAPTER 56

Soleil woke. There was no transition and no confusion. No nausea or vertigo. Her chest ached. She was weeping.

And Andy was holding her.

"She's gone," he said, as if he understood everything.

She nodded. Somehow he had known.

"You okay?"

"I couldn't save her," she said.

He held her tighter.

"I tried."

"I know."

"I tried to save her. But I couldn't."

He held her and let her weep and was wise enough to keep still, knowing there was nothing he could say.

CHAPTER 57

As Andy had predicted, Soleil was hounded by reporters, cameramen. And again she had to go over everything with the police. He never left her side.

Louis Grunner, the man who'd attacked her and killed four other women, was on every newscast. Looking at his face on the screen, she remembered the feel of his hands on her neck. Shuddered.

"Want me to turn it off?" Andy asked.

She shook her head. Louis Grunner had lost the power to scare her.

Late in the afternoon they headed for the hospital.

"I wish . . ." she began, "I just wish that I could talk to her first. I've never told her that I love her. All she ever saw was my resentment, my withdrawal."

"She knew," Andy said.

She wanted to believe him, to console herself that those one loved somehow saw beneath the words and actions of anger and confusion, but she didn't know if this was true or only empty longing.

She tightened her grip on Andy's hand as she followed Dr. Allen to the three-walled cubicle.

"You okay?" Andy asked. She was pale, with dark circles under her eyes. The bruises on her neck were a startling yellow and purple. "Can you do this now?"

She nodded, afraid to trust her voice.

She made herself turn to the bed.

Her mother looked shrunken, a wasted puppet connected by tubes instead of strings. So many tubes.

I'm sorry, she said silently. Old pains, guilts surfaced and she let them go. Regrets are useless, she thought. Her mother was no longer here. Only a wasted body.

She nodded to the doctor. She could not repeat what they had discussed earlier. "You're sure?" he asked. Again she nodded.

Dr. Allen pulled the pole curtain around the bed, shutting out the rest of the unit. "Do you want to go in the waiting room? You don't have to stay."

"I want to be here with her," she said. Andy's hand was steady on her shoulder.

"It won't be long," he said.

She sat on the edge of the bed and held her mother's hand. The hands that had tended her, sewed and cleaned and cooked for her. Hands that had slapped her in anger, shaken her in fear. Hands that checked for fevers and cleaned up for and cared for the sick. Hands that had caressed a man in passion. Hands that had mothered her. At that moment, her mother's hands were as beautiful as anything she had ever seen.

She heard the doctor turn a knob on the machines. She felt Andy behind her, and allowed herself to lean into his strength.

"It's okay, Mamom," she said. "It's okay to go."

The cubicle was quieter. The machine had been turned off.

"I love you, Mamom," she said. "I've always loved you."

And she knew then that it was true.

EPILOGUE

It took the better part of a week to empty her mother's apartment, although there was actually very little to do beyond cleaning. She was amazed at the few possessions her mother owned.

The furniture was worn, nothing really that she could sell. She arranged for everything to go to Morgan Memorial. The clothes she dropped off at a thrift shop. She kept almost nothing for herself. A teacup and saucer with blue forget-me-nots painted on white china that, a long time ago, she had given to her mother for a birthday. A white cardigan she remembered her mother wearing.

In the back of the last closet she emptied, she found a cardboard carton. She pulled it out into the room and unfolded the top.

As she removed the contents, layer by layer, it seemed she was looking at her life: her first baby shoes; a thin piece of graph paper, folded in thirds, holding the precise record of her height and weight during the first four years of her life; a notation of the appearance of her first baby teeth, inoculation dates for polio, whooping cough, and measles boosters; a thick envelope of tissue paper wrapped around a blue, yoked dress with tiny red hearts she had worn her first day of nursery school; all her report cards and class pictures, from kindergarten through college; every card or letter she had ever sent her mother; the envelope holding the dress pattern for her senior prom gown, a swatch of pink material carefully pinned to the front. This evidence of her mother's devotion hurt too much. She folded the flaps as she had found them and set the carton aside to carry home with the teacup and sweater.

In her apartment, she put all her mother's things away, waiting until she felt stronger before again looking at the box her mother had saved.

That fall, she and Andy talked a lot about the dreams, trying to make sense of it somehow. She spent one week volunteering at the dream research clinic, but her REM sleep was entirely normal. Like a textbook, Andy said when he showed her the polysomnograph printout. She had known it would be.

He believed the dreams were a deep hypnotic state she had gone into, driven by subconscious needs provoked by her mother's final illness.

After the last dream and the death of the scarred child, she had never again dreamed of the girl or the town named Fortune Groves.

In late September, Andy accepted a slot as visiting lecturer at Harvard. He worked part-time at the U-Mass clinic in Worcester. Soleil returned to the museum library.

Fall progressed into winter.

Once, in January, when Andy came upon her staring into space, he asked her if she wanted to go to Ohio to see Fortune Groves, but she said no. Neither of them mentioned it again.

On Valentine's Day, Andy gave her an engagement ring, a square-cut emerald flanked by two diamonds. They decided to get married in the fall. She chose the date. It would be after she had observed a year of mourning for her mother, an old-fashioned custom that comforted her but about which she spoke to no one except Andy.

They both wanted a child. Neither wanted to wait. All talk of their future included this child, as if they had already conceived. This talk made Soleil happier than she ever remembered being. Her only sadness was that her mother hadn't lived to see her grandchild. They talked about names. Thomas, if it's a boy, Soleil thought.

In March, Andy and his *Dreamscape* collaborators finished work on a book about the exhibit.

Winter turned to spring, a spring that came to Boston much earlier than usual. After the gloom-shortened days of February and March, Soleil welcomed it. During her lunch hours she walked beside the Charles, smiling at the Harvard students who had also fled buildings to stroll in the promise of April. Sometimes she walked alone, and, often, with Andy when he came home from the clinic in Worcester in the evening.

One day in April she sat by her apartment window. It was open and a soft breeze floated in. Suddenly, as happened frequently over the past months, she thought of her mother. The sharpness of grief was muted now. The terrible heaviness and sorrow was lighter. Time, friends had told her. It just takes time.

This working of time frightened her a little. Along with relieving pain, it could take someone away. She closed her eyes, trying to conjure her mother's image, but all that would come was the vision of those last days, the shrunken body connected

to tubes. She needed a different picture. Not a mental one. One she could hold, set in a frame on her bureau.

She had no photographs of her mother. Helen hated to have her picture taken.

Then she remembered the cardboard carton. She hadn't emptied the box. Maybe somewhere hidden in the layers there would be one old snapshot of the way her mother used to look.

She pulled the box out from where she had stored it in the darkroom and pulled open the flaps. This time the things of hers that her mother had saved—all the mementoes of her childhood—now seemed comforting, familiar.

She was nearly at the bottom of the box when she saw the envelope. When she picked it up, it felt light, nearly empty. She recognized her mother's precise, squat penmanship on the outside.

"For Soleil," she read.

A burr of apprehension settled in her chest.

The flap was sealed. She had a wild, irrational urge to fling the envelope away. To burn it.

She slid her finger beneath the flap. There was a letter inside, written on thin paper, the type one used for airmail. She unfolded it. Saw again her mother's handwriting. A small black and white snapshot fell out, dropping on her lap.

The photo was of a man. He faced the camera, one fist on his hip; the other, wrapped in bandages to the wrist, hung at his side. He was smiling. She looked closely at the man's face. For an instant, he looked so familiar that she believed she knew him. He was handsome, with a grin that curved up a little more on the left side. He had a square jaw. A dimple. She could feel her blood pulsing in her throat, temples, wrists.

She turned back to the letter.

"Dear Soleil," she read. The ink was faded, blue. No date. No place. "This is the only photograph I ever had of him. He was traveling through our town and had injured his hand. My father was the only doctor. That's how I met him. He left at the end of the week. He never knew about you. Please find it in your heart to forgive me."

The letter could have been from a stranger. Not from her mother. Not the careful woman who had never dated a man, worn makeup, gone dancing. A woman other than her mother had known the man in the snapshot.

She picked up the photo again and, carrying it to the window, studied it in the light. Again saw the dimple in his chin. *"You. He looked like you,"* her mother had said that night so long ago when they sat on a porch glider and gazed at the stars. She turned it over and saw that her mother had written a name on the back in faded black ink. Thomas Arnett.

She ran her finger over the letters of his name. Said it softly. Felt it in her mouth. Thomas.

Thomas, she had wanted to name her first son.

Then, with a chill, she remembered the girl in her dreams. "Thomas," the child had cried before she died.

She flipped the photo over and again stared at the smiling man, saw the likeness, not only to herself, but to the blond-haired child of her dreams.

Thomas Arnett.

Her father.

She felt her heartbeat quicken and wondered if it was because her search had finally ended. Or if it was only beginning.